"Mr. Sutherland. What a coincidence." Her tone made it clear that she thought it was nothing of the sort. "I had a feeling we'd bump into each other again."

"And I rather hoped we would," I admitted, relieved to be able to speak something close to the truth.

"Why?"

She looked me straight in the eye when she asked the question.

"You interest me," I told her, which was honest enough.

"In what way?"

She quirked her brow again, such an odd thing to find alluring, but there it was, and there I was, despite my previous resolutions not to be distracted, struggling not to be distracted by my body's reaction. "That's a very personal question, from someone who has not even disclosed her name."

She narrowed her eyes at me, and I thought for a moment that I had crossed an invisible line with her, but what she said was not the reprimand I anticipated. "I have the distinct impression that you know it already."

UNCOVERING THE GOVERNESS'S SECRETS

MARGUERITE KAYE

Harlequin

HISTORICAL

Harlequin®
HISTORICAL

ISBN-13: 978-1-335-53964-9

Uncovering the Governess's Secrets

Recycling programs for this product may not exist in your area.

Harlequin Enterprises ULC
22 Adelaide St. West, 41st Floor
Toronto, Ontario M5H 4E3, Canada
www.Harlequin.com

Printed in U.S.A.

Marguerite Kaye has written almost sixty historical romances featuring feisty heroines and a strong sense of place and time. She is also coauthor with Sarah Ferguson, Duchess of York, of two *Sunday Times* bestsellers, *Her Heart for a Compass* and *A Most Intriguing Lady*. Marguerite lives in Argyll on the west coast of Scotland. When not writing, she loves to read, cook, garden, drink martinis and sew, though rarely at the same time.

Books by Marguerite Kaye

Harlequin Historical

A Forbidden Liaison with Miss Grant
"A Most Scandalous Christmas"
in *Regency Christmas Liaisons*
His Runaway Marchioness Returns

Revelations of the Carstairs Sisters

The Earl Who Sees Her Beauty
Lady Armstrong's Scandalous Awakening
"The Lady's Yuletide Wish"
in *Under the Mistletoe*

Penniless Brides of Convenience

The Earl's Countess of Convenience
A Wife Worth Investing In
The Truth Behind Their Practical Marriage
The Inconvenient Elmswood Marriage

Matches Made in Scandal

From Governess to Countess
From Courtesan to Convenient Wife
His Rags-to-Riches Contessa
A Scandalous Winter Wedding

Visit the Author Profile page
at Harlequin.com for more titles.

Chapter One

Edinburgh—
Thursday 2nd August 1877

The day began as it always did. I woke with a start, and the first thing I was aware of was the stench. Unmistakable, like nothing else, an acrid mixture of bleach, damp blankets and stale air, mingled with urine and over-boiled cabbage, resonating of fear and dread. There it was as usual, a tang on my tongue and in my nose, making my stomach roil, my breath come fast and shallow.

A cold sweat coated my body, making the thin cotton of my clammy nightshift cling to me. My fingers were like claws, pawing at the bedding, clutching it high up to my neck. And as usual I lay completely still, eyes scrunched shut, ears straining to catch whatever noise it was that woke me. The scratching and scuttling of vermin behind the skirting? Moaning? Howls of pain? Screams of fear and panic? Barked orders demanding silence?

Silence!

I listened intently, struggling to hear over the thudding

of my heart, but there was nothing. I forced myself to take a deep breath. Another. Yet another. All the time straining to hear. Still silence reigned.

It happened slowly as it always had since I arrived in Edinburgh, the fog of terror dispersing in my mind, the dawning awareness of my true surroundings. There were sheets on my bed as well as blankets. My pillow was soft, not scratchy with rough straw filling. I eased my glued-shut eyes open to see a watery grey light filtering in through the window, the curtains open to reveal the lack of bars. My heart slowed. My mouth was dry, but the vile taste was gone.

I breathed deeply again, easing the tension in my shoulders, and sat up in bed. *My* bed. In my own bedroom. I could see the reassuringly familiar outline of the chest of drawers, the stand with my ewer and bowl.

I shivered then, as I always did as the sweat cooled on my skin, and I placed my feet on the floorboards, easing stiffly upright like a woman much older than my thirty-three years, stumbling to the window to push up the sash. Cold air rushed in. There was a light misting of rain, the kind that soaks into your bones without you even noticing. They call it a smir here in Scotland. A soft word for soft rain.

'Smir...' I murmured under my breath. The word, in my English accent, sounded harsh.

The last echoes of the past that haunted me every morning retreated as I leaned out of the window as they did every morning. The memories would be locked away again until my guard was down, when sleep claimed me again. I had another day of freedom to look forward to, I reminded myself, as I did every day without fail. I would never, ever again take for granted the simple pleasure of opening a window, feeling the elements on my face, sucking in the fresh air. Not that the air in Edinburgh was fresh, not by any means. It's smoke-filled, sulphurous, and I knew the rain would leave smut on my skin if I continued to lean out of the window, but I didn't care.

The Old Town tenement that I called home was at the eastern end of the Grassmarket. The more respectable end, or perhaps the least disreputable would be a more accurate description. There was no trouble at night in the close, my neighbours locked their doors at nightfall, and if I met them during the day, they'd nod politely with their gazes averted. The close itself was clean, the roof in good repair, the rent dearer than the lodgings on the farther side of the square near the meat market and the West Bow, made notorious by Burke and Hare, the infamous resurrectionists. All in all, the Grassmarket was not the type of area you'd expect a woman of my upbringing to inhabit—which was, of course, one of the reasons I chose it.

It was a far cry from the large salubrious town houses of the New Town where I earned my living. My various employers would be appalled if they ever discovered where it was I lay my head at night, but when they asked—rarely, and only ever the wives—I would prevaricate. They never persisted, instinct or experience telling them that such questions were rarely rewarded with anything other than unpalatable answers. I could have told them some unpalatable truths myself, had I chosen. Not about my circumstances, but about their own, the injustices and betrayals which they unwittingly endured. I never volunteer my insights, not any more. I have suffered too much to risk the consequences.

Aware of my mind skittering back to the past, I focused

on the view. Across the Grassmarket, rising high above the cobbled square loomed the castle, grey, solid, imposing, perched on a huge crag of volcanic rock. In the shadow of that seemingly impenetrable fortress, the square below me was metamorphosing from night into morning. It was a ritual I loved to watch, for it was full of noise and bustle, a daily affirmation of life in all its various forms.

On the opposite side from my four-storey tenement, the dray carts were rumbling down the steep incline of the Bow, bringing in supplies from the railway and the canal and the docks at Leith for the many taverns and traders whose businesses were in the process of opening up for the day. Wooden casks of ale for the White Hart and the Black Bull, a multitude of goods for the other warehouses and carriers.

That morning there was the distinctive smell of tobacco leaves being delivered to the manufactory. I could smell the roasting beans too, wafting up from the coffee houses, as ever overlaid by the stench coming from the meat market known as the Shambles.

I kept well away from that end of the Grassmarket, even during daylight. The crowded, vermin-infested rooms of the cheap lodging houses down there doubtless continued to harbour other types of vermin, criminals and ne'er-do-wells of all types, but mostly they were home to the poor and displaced, those newest incomers to the city. Vagrants, they were commonly labelled, but they were simply desti-tute and desperate. They moved on quickly if they could, those people, away from the Grassmarket if not from the Old Town. I preferred to remain here, among the immi-grants and refugees, being one of them myself, though I kept myself apart.

On cue, regular as clockwork, the young woman with

her plaid shawl over her head appeared from the Cowgate and crossed the square to the Black Bull. I reminded myself that I was fortunate to be able to support myself doing work that I enjoyed, for I have always loved children. I named the woman Flora, for the plaid she wore made me think of Flora MacDonald. I watched her as she, a woman of habit as I had become, entered the tavern.

In my imagined version of her life, she ordered coffee and bread. It was more likely she drank strong spirits to help her sleep after the night she'd spent earning her living up near the castle. That part of the story I invented for her was unfortunately accurate, for I'd spotted her once, making her way there as I returned late from my own employment. She was not morning-tired as she was now, but evening-bright, her plaid draped to reveal the low cut of her gown, her eyes darting about in search of custom. I called her Flora because I would not call her harpy or slut. People, especially women, must do whatever it takes to keep the wolf from the door. It was dangerous work. Brave Flora.

Her arrival at the Black Bull was my signal each morning that it was time to prepare for the day. I shivered as the rain started to fall more heavily, and closed the window. My robe was faded blue wool. I wrapped it round me, pulling the sash tight. I had purchased it second-hand, like all my clothes, and made it good with my mending. I once loathed having to wield my needle, despite the fact that in that vile place there were times when my neat stitching saved me from more arduous tasks in the laundry or the kitchen. But every stitch I set reminded me, back then, that there would be no end to them. I was being stitched into the very fabric of the place.

The darns in my clothes were different. My stitches

made the garments mine. The smell of vinegar and carbolic soap and lavender water made these two rooms in the old, creaking tenement mine too. My sanctuary. I was safe here. Every morning, that was the final part of my waking ritual, to remind myself of this.

'I am safe here,' I told myself firmly.

As time passed, the odds were more and more in my favour that it was true. Three years had passed, after all. But I knew, that morning, as every morning before, as I dressed, as I made myself my cup of breakfast coffee, as I prepared to go out into the cold morning air, to cross from the Old Town to the New Town, I knew that my resolve would falter as night fell. In my bones, in my heart, I didn't believe I would ever be safe. I would always be waiting for that dreaded hand on my shoulder.

I locked my door and descended the close stairs, and made my usual final check of my surroundings, though after three years I wasn't sure who or what I was checking for. Then I set out for my current place of work. Today was another day like every other, I thought. I had no idea how wrong I would prove to be.

Chapter Two

Rory

Edinburgh—
Thursday 2nd August 1877

Standing in the doorway of the coffee shop, I wrapped my hands around the steaming tin mug of coffee. It was looking set to be another typical August day, with leaden skies and twenty different varieties of rain to look forward to. A pure minger, in other words. I'd forgotten what it could be like, the so-called Scottish summer. Seven years down south in England had clearly softened me up.

To be fair, those seven years had also kept me out of harm's way, and made me—comparatively, mind—a wealthy man. Being back here was the last thing I wanted or needed. The last thing anyone in this city wanted, I was willing to bet.

You can't say you weren't warned, Sutherland. I told you not to poke your nose in, but you didn't listen.

That old familiar voice resonating in my head made my hackles rise, for try as I might—and I'd tried, trust me, over the years—I still couldn't bring myself to believe I'd been wrong. The case stank to high heaven. It wasn't the first time I'd been warned off, nor the first time I'd been told that I was ruffling the wrong feathers. The thing was, I saw that as an essential part of my doing my job properly—without fear or favour. That's what sealed my fate in the end. The powerful person who felt threatened by investigation, whoever they were, knew I couldn't be bought, and they knew I wouldn't rest until I'd got to the bottom of whatever it was reeked.

I was warned, but I didn't see it coming all the same. Insubordination, I was accused of, as well as placing my fellow officers in danger, blackening the good name of the Edinburgh police and taking bribes—that was a belter! Trumped-up charges, all of them, full of innuendo and singularly lacking any evidence, but they were plastered over every newspaper in the city, the very same papers that had been happy to sing my praises over the years. I paid the price for my former success and the unwanted fame that accompanied it.

There's nothing like a dramatic fall from grace story to sell a newspaper. There was no need for the wheels to turn in any formal manner. I was found well and truly guilty by the press for crimes that didn't even exist, while the real crime I'd been trying to solve was swept firmly under the carpet. What's more, it was made very clear to me by my superior that there would be no road back.

You've made some very powerful enemies, Sutherland. So powerful that I can't guarantee your safety. My advice to you is to get out of this city, and if you value your life, you'll never show your face here again.

He reckoned he saved my skin, and he was probably right. He didn't need to either. He was a good man, but unlike me, he knew his place in the Edinburgh hierarchy. It pained him to stick the knife in, and it was bloody agony for me, but that wasn't even the worst of it. The worst part was the look on my da's face when I told him what had happened. He took my side without question, which was a small consolation, until he'd had time to think it over.

'You have to find a way to clear your name, Ruaraidh,' he'd said, in that soft Highland accent of his that decades in Glasgow hadn't rid him of. 'You can't let those vile things they said about you stand.'

'I can't, Da,' I'd told him, though I didn't tell him why.

'M'aither,' he'd corrected me, as he always did when I called him Da. Aside from the curses and the way he pronounced my name, it's the only Gaelic I have. No one pronounces my name the way he did. Ruaraidh. Rory. It's a subtle distinction, too subtle to bother with now that he's gone.

I stuck to my guns and I never promised to do as my da bid me, not even at the end, when he was dying. It's a salve to my conscience, though not much of one, that I never lied to him. I did what I had to do to save my skin, and I kept well away from Edinburgh. Until now.

Not that I was back, risking life and limb, to stir all that up again. No, I'd have to put up and shut up on that one, as I'd been doing for the last seven years. I was here to get the job I'd been employed to do done, and that was all. I planned to keep a very low profile and get the hell out of the city for the second time and for good as soon as I could, with my hide intact. Edinburgh was a big city. I, of all people, should know how to keep myself hidden in its shadows.

It stuck in my craw, I'll admit that, but what choice did I have, save to let sleeping dogs lie? I wasn't going to rake over old ground, and I definitely wasn't going to set about rattling the skeletons in the closet that likely still lurked here. I'd moved on, made a new life for myself, and it was one that I enjoyed, where I was my own man. The fact that it had brought me to Edinburgh, where my old life had begun and ended in disgrace was just a very unfortunate coincidence. That's what I told myself, and it was the truth, though not all of it.

It was the mystery of my current case that piqued my interest at first. Solving mysteries was my bread and butter, I was good at it, and this had smacked of something I could really get my teeth into. Then there was the fact that the outcome would prove life-changing for the woman concerned, if I found her. Life-changing in every way, mind. Some of what I knew was going to come as a hell of a shock to her. Mind you, what I'd learned myself about her in the last few weeks had shocked *me* to the core. She'd been to hell and back. It made my blood boil, every time I thought of it.

All the same, when it became clear that she was most likely here in Edinburgh, well of course I thought twice about it—though no more than twice. Maybe I should have, but I'm not superstitious like my da. *M'aither!* I'm practical, like my ma. A real Weegie, my ma was, a salt of the earth, Glaswegian to her bones. My da never really got over losing her.

Any road! There I was in Edinburgh, finishing my coffee, and there she was, the subject of my current case, right on the stroke of eight, coming out of the tenement close. She was tentative, always so wary. Standing in the open doorway peering out carefully, as nervous as a deer emerging into a forest clearing, her nose tilted in the air as if sniffing for danger. And on cue, there it was again, the minute

I set eyes on her, that odd lurching in my belly. My gut was telling my brain that she needed protecting, and bits of me that I didn't care to acknowledge were sending another message entirely to another part of my body, a part that shouldn't have had any interest in this case whatsoever. I was the hunter, she was the prey, I reminded myself, but that word didn't sit right with me. Quarry? More accurate, but I still wasn't happy with it. Quest? I liked that word better.

She stepped into the street and set off, passing within a couple of feet of me. I didn't need to stay too close though, I knew where she was headed, up the steep incline of Victoria Street, past St Giles and on to the Mound, before crossing down into the New Town past the National Gallery and on to Princes Street.

I scanned the broad cobbled street to make sure the Grassmarket was clear of former acquaintances, though I wasn't really expecting to see any. There had been a good few of them down at the West Bow end of the street, men I'd put away, men who'd helped me put others away, but seven years was a long time. They'd have moved on, one way or another. Then I pulled my hat further down over my brow and set out in pursuit.

I strode out, a man with every right to go about his business, neither furtive nor swaggering, hiding in plain sight. I was good at that, I always had been. I'd changed my appearance too, since those Edinburgh days, my hair cropped much shorter, my face clean shaven, my clothes the sombre, well-cut attire of a gentleman of means. Stay alert, but don't keep looking over your shoulder, that was the key to invisibility, and I needed to remain invisible, because though I might be perceived as the hunter, I was very much aware that I could easily become the hunted if my presence in Edinburgh was discovered. My quest was ahead of me, but if I was discovered, I'd be the quarry, unwittingly being stalked by someone else. And unlike me, their motives would be malign.

It might sound difficult, following one person while keeping an eye out for anyone who may be interested in me, but it was second nature. Only when I got close enough to *her* did I become more focused on what was ahead rather than behind me or off to the side. There was a supple sway to her body, a natural grace that would have drawn more eyes than mine were it not for her pace, which was fast, covering a lot of ground very quickly, though she never gave the impression that she was in a hurry. It was an easy, confident pace, completely at odds with the nervous way she peered out into the street every morning and one of the many contradictions about her that I found intriguing. Mind, if she really was the woman I was looking for, the way she walked was hardly relevant.

'You know fine and well she's the one,' I muttered to myself as I waited for her to cross over Princes Street before continuing, for the traffic this morning was surprisingly light. I was procrastinating, which wasn't like me, delaying concluding the matter because I was drawn to her, and I wanted to know more about her. I told myself I needed tangible proof, but I *knew* it was her. The last photograph I had might be nearly five years old, but the haggard woman with the dark circles under her big eyes staring at the camera in what I had learned was a classic institutional pose, was definitely the same woman in the faded blue cloak who was now walking up Hanover Street.

Then there was the name she'd assumed—too much of a coincidence, that. And there was also the address of her rooms. I knew she was in demand, I knew roughly what she must earn, and I knew she could afford better, a respectable area where everyone knew their neighbours and their business. In the Grassmarket, people didn't ask questions, they made a point of not being curious, and I reckoned that's why she chose to live there.

Marianne Little, who was now Marianne Crawford, was also entitled to yet another name. And to another life too, very different from the one she now led, as an agency nanny or governess, currently employed to look after a prominent businessman's nursery while his wife awaited delivery of their fifth child. She hadn't a clue what fate had in store for her and that was starting to bother me. That she'd endured and survived the last few years and come out of it in her right mind was nothing short of a miracle. I'm not sure I'd have fared as well in her shoes.

And now, just when she must be thinking herself settled, I was going to unsettle her. I would be the bearer of extraordinary good news, true enough, but it was going to turn her world upside down, and it was complicated. I had no clear notion of how I was going to go about telling her and no idea at all how she'd take it. I was a complete stranger, I couldn't exactly go walking up to her without a by your leave and launch straight in. Thankfully, I was under orders to say nothing yet. For once, I was glad to be obeying those orders.

I ducked behind a brewer's cart piled high with wooden beer kegs and set off again on her tail. The New Town was problematic for me. It's where the great and the good of Edinburgh reside, and some of those men were high on my list of people I wanted to avoid. I was prepared to bet that whoever had had me silenced was among them. I couldn't get over how far the area had expanded in the years since I was last here, new crescents and circuses with private gardens, imposing town houses and terraces stretching all the way towards Coates in one direction, and Stockbridge in the other. Who was buying all those grand houses, on land where no one of note would have dreamed of residing only a few years ago? I couldn't be sure any more, of who lived where, so my heart thumped a bit harder every time I went near those big, wide cobbled streets. During the daylight hours, most of them would be at their place of work, but not all of them. I looked different. I acted confident. It was enough, I told myself, trying to put it to the back of my mind.

I got to the corner of Queen Street just as she mounted the steps of the town-house door. She used the front door, not the servants' entrance at the back in the mews, and there was a few moments' delay today, in answering her knock. It gave me a chance to study her. It wasn't a hardship to look at her, not in the slightest. She was tall, likely she'd be able to look me straight in the eye, which wasn't something I was used to, being over six foot in my stockings.

She was too thin, in my humble opinion, lack of appetite rather than lack of funds, I surmised, and she *had* put on some very necessary weight since that last photograph I had in my keeping had been taken. Her hair was a deep chestnut colour with a natural curl. High cheekbones. A nose that wasn't in the least bit pert and that some might even call assertive. A determined chin. Big wide-set eyes. Hazel in some lights, green in others. Cat-like, was how one of her self-styled carers had described them. That particular man had been very insistent about her eyes being her most striking feature other than her height.

'Ordinary otherwise, you'll struggle to pick her out in a crowd,' was what he'd said dismissively to me as he handed the photograph from their official records over, but even in that image, the first I'd seen, with her face set, part-defiant, part-fearful, I was struck by her. In the later images, the defiance was harder to detect. Doubtless, they'd tried to grind it out of her. They hadn't succeeded though. Despite everything she'd been through, despite all they'd inflicted on her and all the cruel names they'd labelled her with, she'd escaped, and here she was, making her own way.

Just like me? I'd been wrongly tagged too. I'd been called names that could have destroyed me, and my ability to make a living, just as she had. We were both survivors. I knew I shouldn't be drawing parallels. It was one thing to admire her, to feel sympathy, even to acknowledge the attraction I felt, but quite another to be finding connections between us.

Detachment, not becoming involved, not taking sides, were the watchwords of my profession. True, I rely on my instincts, that goes without saying, but I back everything up with facts, logic, hard evidence. Generally, I don't allow myself to feel anything save sympathy or pity or most likely suspicion. But this woman—ach, I keep coming back to it, she *drew* me. I felt that we were alike in a profound way, that there was an affinity between us. That was a very dangerous road to go down, for it affects your judgement, so I decided the best thing to do was to ignore it.

The door to the town house was opened by a male servant. She stepped inside without looking over her shoulder. Above me, the grey skies were very reluctantly parting to reveal the odd patch of blue, just about enough to make a pair of sailor's breeches, as the saying went. I'd been keeping her under surveillance for almost a week now, and without fail, she brought the weans into the communal Queen Street Gardens to play, often remaining there for much of the day. I usually stayed outside and out of sight, but on impulse I decided to use the key I'd managed to obtain, at no small cost, to gain entry. I took up position on a bench in the furthest corner, opened my newspaper up, and waited.

Chapter Three

Marianne

Edinburgh—
Thursday 2nd August 1877

I noticed him the moment I entered the gardens with my current charges. Queen Street Gardens are private, for residents only, but they don't belong exclusively to the Oliphants, the family who then employed me. We regularly had them to ourselves however, we children's nurses, nannies and governesses, and when the weather was what they call driech here, I was often the only one to venture out. My four charges had protested the first day I insisted they come outside with rain threatening, but they quickly came to enjoy playing outdoors when they learned they could shout and squeal and run about as much as they liked, without having to keep quiet for fear of disturbing their mamma, who was close to her due date.

It's only a man in search of some peace and quiet to read his newspaper, that's what I told myself, for I sensed no threat from him. Quite the opposite. Oddly, my first instinct was that he was a man to be trusted, and that's what piqued my interest, for it's such a rare feeling—in fact I'd go so far as to say unique in my experience, when it comes to the opposite sex. No, not entirely unique. I trusted once. Never again.

I kept an eye on him as we set about playing our game, myself and the children, and though he was very good at covering it up, I was aware that he was watching me. I have always been sensitive to other people, to their moods, their thoughts. I don't mean in the common way, it goes beyond that, my talent, or gift, or whatever you care to call it. I think of it like the valve on a gas light or an oil lamp. It's always on at a peep, a low glow, just sufficient for me to see by, and provided there's nothing of interest it stays like that.

But if there's something needing more light shed on it, or if a person was suffering an extreme emotion, it's turned up, allowing me to—to sort of focus. Like the microscope in the playroom, that's a better analogy. The microscope was a gift to Mr Oliphant from the famous Dr Simpson who lived next door at Number Fifty-Two. Mr Oliphant, having no interest in matters scientific, gave it to Ronnie, his eldest boy, who wasn't in the least bit interested either, but his sister Lizzie was—it was she who showed me how to peer through it. The object on the glass slide was a blur at first, then you turn the dial and it becomes clearer, and the more you turn the dial, the more detail you see.

Only I don't have any control over my personal dial, it adjusts itself. There have been many times when I have wished that I had the ability to switch the blasted thing off, for it has led me to understand things I didn't wish to understand, provided insights into others that cannot be 'unseen'. I have learned to live with my skill, but I have also learned to keep it to myself. A lesson I will never forget.

Not long after we arrived in the gardens, we were joined by Mrs Aitken, the governess from Number Forty-Two, and I concentrated most of my attention on the children for a while. Mrs Aitken was always more than happy to leave the management of her charges to me while she sits on a bench and imagines herself by a fire in a cottage in the country with a cat on her lap and a companion seated in a chair opposite. She takes such enormous pleasure in it that I don't mind looking after all the children, and in any event they play happily together.

Ronnie it was, who threw the ball far too forcefully over the head of its target, his sister Maureen, making it bounce across the grass towards the man on the bench. Maureen protested loudly, while Lizzie went running after the ball and I followed her. The man caught it before it went into the bushes, clutching it close to his chest.

'I beg your pardon,' I said, 'I'm afraid we interrupted you.'

He blinked at me, staring, and I had the oddest feeling that he didn't want to talk to me, but at the same time, he was most eager to do just that. When he did, his words were mundane enough.

'Here you go, wee one,' he said, handing the ball to Lizzie and smiling down at her. She smiled back, and ran off to re-join the game.

'Thank you,' I said, knowing I should follow her but finding myself reluctant to move.

'No problem. My name is Sutherland. Rory Sutherland.'

My hand reached for his outstretched one of its own accord, though it was my wont to avoid the touch of men. I don't wear gloves when I'm with the children. His were tan, good quality, and obviously custom made, for they fitted very well over his big hands. The contact sent a shiver, of the warm kind, if there was such a thing, through my body. Instead of snatching my hand away, I wanted to curl my fingers around his, which reaction so distracted me I just stood there, my hand in his, looking like goodness knows what.

It was he who broke the contact, and now it was my turn to look confused. I didn't offer my name. I said nothing, yet I could not make my feet turn around to walk away. I tried to make sense of my reaction, for I had to concentrate on breathing, yet I was not afraid.

'It's good to see the wee ones out enjoying the fresh air,' the man said, after what seemed like an age. 'Though it's fresher than it should be, for August, even for here.' It seemed that he too wanted to prolong the conversation.

I clasped my hands together, keeping them safely away from the draw of his. I was belatedly wary, though still I sensed no danger, only—I don't know, curiosity? No, it was stronger than that. 'You're from Edinburgh, then?' I said.

'Glasgow originally, though I'm told I have too much of the Highlander in me to sound like a proper Weegie.'

'Weegie?' I queried, for it was a word I'd never heard before. *'Weegie?'*

'Weegie,' he repeated. 'It's a nickname for Glaswegians. Not always intended as a compliment either.' There was a smile lurking in his eyes, which were brown, fringed with long lashes that were much darker than his fair hair.

I raised my eyebrow, allowing a smidgin of my curiosity to show. 'Would that make a native of Edinburgh a— an Edinburghian?'

He laughed. 'Truth is,' he replied, 'there's no name for a native of Edinburgh. They've not the unique identity of we Weegies, you see. In fact,' Mr Sutherland added, affecting a stage whisper, 'they're an inferior tribe, though they cover it up well with their superior airs and graces.'

His smile was infectious, though I'm usually immune to such things. Combined with the soft brogue of his accent, it had a most unsettling effect on me. Drawing me in, was the only way I can think to describe it, a physical pull or lurch or—oh, it was obvious what I was feeling, even if I didn't recognise it at the time. 'I have not noticed that,' I said to him, inanely. My mind was distracted by my body, which made my voice sound very unlike my own. 'I find everyone very friendly in this city.'

'Aye,' he agreed, his accent and his smile broadening in an extremely appealing way, 'but that's because you've never been to Glasgow, have you? You don't know what you're missing,' he added, when I shook my head. 'How did you end up here, may I ask? Judging from that accent, I'd say you hail from well south of here. Do I detect a trace of Yorkshire, maybe?'

'You are a linguist, Mr Sutherland?'

'So I'm right, then?'

It has become such a habit of mine, to refuse to answer a question or to prevaricate, I had done so automatically. I couldn't see what possible harm it would do, to answer him, yet I still chose to prevaricate. 'To everyone here, I'm a Southerner, they make no distinction.'

'It matters all the same though, doesn't it? A Glaswegian like myself doesn't like to be labelled an East Coaster. A Yorkshire woman such as yourself would take umbrage if I thought you a Brummie?' He waited, but when I volunteered only a shrug, he smiled again. 'Either way, you're a long way from home. What brought you here?'

'I am employed as a governess,' I said, unwilling to end

the conversation, but not willing to volunteer more than necessary. Should I be concerned by his interest or was he simply making conversation? It was odd, but the more I tried to read him, the more opaque he became to me. I was conscious only of the persistent feeling that I could trust him, and the equally persistent tug of attraction.

'Those weans look like a handful,' he said. 'Have you looked after them for long?'

'Only four of them are in my charge, and my position is temporary.'

'It looks to me like they're pretty fond of you.'

'And I of them, most of the time.'

'Then may I ask why...?'

'Their nanny has taken leave for six months to nurse her mother. I am covering for her, but as a matter of fact, I prefer not to stay too long in one household. I like the variety,' I added, before he could ask. 'And I do not like to risk becoming overly fond of my charges.'

'Is it easy to get work in your line? Are the recommendations by word of mouth, or is there an agency? I know nothing of it.'

'Why do you ask? Are you married yourself, Mr Sutherland? Do you have children?'

'No, and no.'

'Then I fail to see why you could possibly be interested in how to acquire a nanny or a governess.'

'Very true, I...' His voice trailed away. While we had been talking, he had been fully engaged in our conversation. Now, he was distracted, looking over to Queen Street, adjusting his stance marginally to put his back to the iron railings. 'I was merely curious, as I said.'

His attention was still on Queen Street. Mr Sutherland

was a rugged, rough-hewn man, broad and solidly built, but his features were handsome. I reckoned he must be about forty. Tanned skin. Clean shaven. Good clothes, but unobtrusive. A man who didn't dress to impress or be noticed. A man who was now most determined not to be noticed by the policeman who had stopped to talk to a manservant on the steps of the house next to my employer's home. Distracted as he was, he relaxed his guard on his feelings, and the wariness in him was unmistakable to me. 'What's the matter?' I asked, before I could stop myself.

He gave himself a shake. 'Nothing at all.'

A lie, and now I could not contain my curiosity, which was odd, for I do not court interest, and simply by remaining with him, continuing the conversation, that was what I was doing. It felt like the right thing to do. I had no idea why, only that it was. 'That policeman you were looking at comes along Queen Street every morning, around this time,' I told him.

'Good to know that some things don't change.'

'I don't know what crimes he thinks will be committed in broad daylight.'

Though he was obviously itching to turn around to get a better view, Mr Sutherland maintained his stance and his pretence of indifference. 'Just as well I didn't steal the children's ball and run away, then.'

'You don't seem the criminal sort.'

He gave a bark of laughter. 'You'd be surprised, they come in many guises.'

The truth of that statement sent a shudder down my spine. So many crimes I had witnessed and experienced, though none of them were against the law of the land.

He sensed my change of mood immediately. 'What is

it? Someone walk over your grave? It's a saying,' he added. 'It means…'

'I know what it means. Your policeman is on his way again.'

He allowed himself a quick glance and on seeing the policeman halfway along the street, I sensed his relief. But his guard was then immediately up again as he turned his attention back to me. 'I've enjoyed talking to you. Do you think—?'

'I must get back to the children.' I interrupted him before he could propose another meeting, because I was worried I'd say yes. I was then contrarily disappointed when he nodded in agreement.

'I've taken up enough of your time, I'll take myself off.'

'The gate is locked.'

'I have a key,' he said, producing the item from his coat pocket. 'How do you think I got in, by vaulting over the railings?'

I meant to bid him good day and walk away, but my feet continued to refuse to co-operate. 'A man your size would find that easy enough to do.'

My quip amused him, though my own tone, light and almost teasing, took me aback. 'Aye well,' he said, with another of those beguiling smiles, 'I'll admit I've vaulted a good few in my time.'

'While on the run from the long arm of the law?'

'Quite the opposite, in fact.'

'Quite the opposite? What do you mean by that?'

He studied me for a moment, his lips pursed, and I had the strangest feeling that beneath his heavy lids, those brown eyes of his could read my thoughts. 'It's a bit of a long story, but I could tell you, if you're interested. Maybe I could walk you home after work?'

'No.' He couldn't possibly read my thoughts, but all the same, I felt—wary. Not threatened, definitely not threatened. It was so very odd. 'No,' I said again, because I wanted very much to say yes. 'I really must get back to my charges.'

I was already backing away. He sketched a bow, and made no attempt to stop me. I joined my happy little band of children, throwing myself into the game. Out of the corner of my eye I watched him fold up his newspaper, unlock the gate, and quit the gardens. I would have willingly bet he walked in the opposite direction of the policeman, though I couldn't see him.

The strange encounter gave me much pause for thought as I resumed my duties, with only half my attention on the children. To say that my encouraging Mr Sutherland's attention was unusual would be an understatement of the greatest order, yet that was what I had done. I couldn't understand why. He was interested in me, which ought to have put me on my guard—and it had to a degree, but I had never at any point felt endangered. I was horribly accustomed to being questioned, interrogated, *investigated.* I once was foolish enough to believe that if I answered questions honestly, earnestly, it would make a difference.

I eventually realised that what was required of me was to echo my inquisitors' opinions, not to offer up my own. I couldn't bring myself do that, despite everything that I suffered as a consequence, so I developed the habit of silence. A habit that I had willingly broken with Mr Sutherland, who had been questioning me but who had been *interested* in what I had to say. Then there was the fact that I found him difficult to read. He was a challenge. And he was also a conundrum, a man who was not a criminal, but who was afraid—no, wary—of the law.

I tried to dismiss Mr Rory Sutherland from my mind, but my inner dial was already turned up too high for me to do that. Ought I to have agreed to another meeting? Funnily enough, and I had no idea why or how, I was sure our paths would cross again regardless. That certainty gave me another of those odd shivers. Not cold but anticipation—excitement.

The children's ball hit me square in the middle, brought me back down to earth. 'It's time for our luncheon,' Lizzie informed me. 'Did you not hear the one o'clock gun?'

'Mrs Crawford was away with the fairies,' Ronnie said gleefully, a phrase that always made me shudder, however innocently intended. 'And Mrs Aitken has been snoring her head off for the last half-hour.'

Hearing her name awoke the governess who, to give her credit, was on her feet and quite herself in an instant. 'Gentlewomen do not snore, Ronald, and even if they did, you ought to know that a young gentleman would never mention such a thing. What's more, if I had been asleep, how is it that I know you took two of the boiled sweets that Maureen offered you instead of one? Now what do you say to that?'

Ronnie's answer was a blush and a muttered apology. 'How did you know…?' I asked Mrs Aitken.

'Since I was asleep?' she asked sheepishly. 'An educated guess. He's a greedy little boy. I must thank you, Mrs Crawford, for keeping an eye on my charges.'

'There's no need. You have been having trouble sleeping.'

'Why yes, I have. How did you—?'

'A guess, that is all,' I interrupted her.

'It is true what is said of you, you are a most perceptive woman, Mrs Crawford. Mrs White at the employment agency considers it a very happy day, when you arrived in Edinburgh and chose to register with her.'

A very happy day it was indeed. The first day of the new life I had almost despaired of living. I will never forget it.

Chapter Four

Marianne

Three years previously

The Trustees of the institution located in the Scottish borders where I had been confined for almost four years were extremely proud of their forward-thinking reputation. In addition to gardening, the inmates here could contribute to the monthly magazine, read in the library, and even on occasion attend theatrical performances. The Physician Superintendent was a pioneer in his field, a revered and respected man in the community with a genuine vocation—or so he believed. He was much admired by the other staff, and held in great awe by many of the other inmates. Though not by me.

In the first institution where I had been held, I defied them and tried to escape. I was moved here after that, and kept confined. I experimented with compliance in the hope of release, but they kept setting the bar higher, so I resumed my former tactics, and returned to my former defiance. I was intent on one thing only, and that was freedom.

The price I paid form my lack of co-operation became

increasingly high, for they don't like to fail in these places. They ensure that all dissenting voices are kept from their precious trustees and benefactors, so I was forbidden access to the privileges of the library, the theatrical performances, the garden. After my first attempt at escape, I was placed in isolation. But they did not break me. The punishments they inflicted fed my burning sense of injustice. I would not give in. I would not even pretend to be the woman they proclaimed me to be. I would be myself.

It was a beautiful spring morning, that momentous day. I could see the cloudless pale blue sky from my tiny window. Those fortunate inmates considered to be low risk were working outside in the fresh air. I was inside, in one of the locked cells at the rear of the building, the wing to which none of the trustees or benefactors were given access. Perhaps they didn't even know it existed. More likely they did not ask, content to tell themselves that carpeted, panelled rooms and corniced ceilings, the wide staircase that swept upwards from the light-filled atrium, reflected the full extent of the building. It did not.

In this particular wing the institution was laid bare to the bones, making no pretence of being other than what it was. We were isolated, but we were never alone, we, the most problematic and troublesome of the inmates. Screams and moans seeped through the walls of the cells. Smells oozed under the doors. Footsteps echoed in the corridors. At night, shadows danced menacingly and ghosts haunted the halls.

When the bell began to sound, I thought I had confused the day, and that it was the call to Sunday service, but the jangling, clanging peels were too frantic and irregular for church bells. The rush of staff outside my door made it clear what was happening. An escape! I closed my eyes, focusing my entire being on that other person fleeing, wishing them well, urging them on, even though I knew that this was well beyond my powers. I can sense things, but I cannot change them. When my cell door was flung open I was deep in my thoughts, so that the hand roughly shaking my shoulder made me cry out, jump up, arms raised in defence.

'Marianne! Marianne! You must hurry.' The woman grabbed at the rough cotton shift that was my only permitted clothing. 'Take this off. Quickly.'

My troubled mind could make no sense of this demand, for the woman was one of my few allies. Was a new form of treatment about to be inflicted on me? Cold water dousing, which they called hydrotherapy, presumably to make it sound less barbaric, was the latest innovation here. I clutched at my shift, retreating from her.

'Marianne! There's been an escape. They are all rushing after him, do you understand? There's a little time, only a little, if you want to risk it.'

'Risk it?' Understanding came fast, and with it I acted, grabbing the bundle she was holding out. Not towels and a robe, but a uniform, like hers. Fumbling, heart thumping, my breathing shallow and rapid, as was hers, between us we got me into the clothes and boots. Outside, the corridor was deserted but not silent, the cries of the others locked behind those doors making an unearthly din.

I turned to bid my saviour farewell, but she grabbed my hand. 'This way.'

'You cannot risk…'

She pulled me forward. 'Keep your head down and follow me. If anyone stops us, let me do the talking.'

Her livelihood was at stake, I knew how much she needed the work that the institution provided her with, but there was already no going back for me, so I did as she asked me, hurrying after her along the corridor, through locked door after locked door, down unfamiliar passage-ways and staircases smelling of urine and cabbage and bleach and fear, until we emerged suddenly into the bright sunlight at the rear of the building. The alarm bell was still peeling insistently.

'He was in the market garden. He'll have gone over the wall to the east—or tried to,' my saviour said. 'I doubt he'll make it. Come on. Don't run, just walk purposefully, as if you are one of the staff like me, as if you have a right to be here, do you understand?'

Without waiting, she set off. I followed, my heart thump-ing so hard I thought I was going to be sick. My feet were not used to wearing boots. The heels rubbed, they felt heavy, awkward, as I made my way along the gravel paths, past stables and outhouses, past the macabre carriage we all dreaded seeing, the one they used to cart us on the final journey from the institution to the church crypt, an open coffin on four wheels. I shuddered, thinking of the man who was even now perhaps over the wall, fleeing in a bid for freedom.

On we went, on a seemingly endless, roundabout jour-ney towards another gate in the high stone wall.

Make haste. Freedom. Make haste. Freedom.

I repeated the words like a litany, a prayer, with every painful step, struggling to keep pace, struggling not to break into a run.

At the gate, she fumbled for the key, struggling to turn it, cursing under her breath. Her cheeks were bright red. I felt my own face, pale, damp, with shaking hands. At last the lock turned. She pushed me through. 'Good luck, Marianne.'

I paused for a moment to take her hands. 'What if they find out you helped me?'

'They won't. I'll join the search party as soon as I've locked the gate.'

'Thank you,' I said fervently. 'Truly, I cannot thank you enough.'

'I owe you, Marianne. You literally saved my life. One good turn, and all that.' She pulled a scrap of paper and a bundle of coins from her apron pocket. 'Go there, as quickly as you can.' She pushed me forcefully through the gate. I heard the lock turning. I fled.

I don't recall much of the journey to Scotland's capital city from the Borders, which I made by stealth, not daring to travel to the nearest town and the nearest railway, but walking for days, sleeping in barns, sending heartfelt gratitude to my saviour, though I knew she would not sense it. *I owe you,* she had said. I had saved her life. The one time since my incarceration when I had revealed what my instincts were screaming at me. It had been a huge risk, given her position of authority, but now it seemed it had paid off.

I walked and I walked, until I deemed myself far away enough to risk a train to Edinburgh. There, hungry and bedraggled, I sought out the address my saviour had given me. An employment agency. It took the last reserves of my courage to make myself cross the threshold. I was braced for immediate rejection given my appearance. Mrs White studied me for a long moment before she ushered me into a back room and gave me tea. I had no references, but Mrs White didn't ask for any, nor did she question where I had come from, what or who I was running from, who I was. She asked me what I could do to earn my keep and I answered honestly. My love of children and the pleasure I took in looking after them was genuine.

Mrs White took me at my word. Later, when I was settled in lodgings, and had taken up my first assignment, I asked her why had she taken such a chance on me, a complete stranger.

'Because once, a long time ago, when I was seeking refuge and a fresh start, another woman helped me. We need to stick together, we refugees from the injustice the world heaps upon our sex, Mrs Crawford,' she said, using the name I had taken in tribute to my saviour.

'I promise you,' I told her most earnestly, 'that I will never give you cause to regret it.'

Chapter Five

Rory

Edinburgh—
Friday 3rd August 1877

What an eejit I'd been, sitting there on that bench skulking behind my newspaper without a plan. Back at my digs, once I'd calmed down a bit, I saw that the time had come to stop messing about and act. *Mrs* Crawford, she called herself when she registered with the employment agency here, three years ago. If she *was* married, it made things a hell of a lot simpler in one sense, but if Mrs Crawford was Marianne Little, she couldn't possibly be married. Crawford also happened to be the surname of the woman who had helped her gain her freedom. Having spoken to her now and re-examined the various photographs, I knew I'd found her, and I sent my employer a telegram telling him so.

The conversation that morning had added fuel to the fire of my wanting to know the woman better. It wasn't only the strength of character she must have to survive, I wanted to know what made her tick. She fascinated me. Aye, that was it, fascination, a good word, for it was more than physical attraction. *That* I could have ignored easily enough, until the case was done and dusted, and I could return to London. I'm not a saint, I enjoy the company of women, when I have the time and inclination for it. That sounds callous. It's not. I know my limitations, they were brought home to me by a woman in this very city. I'm a man who enjoys physical intimacy, but I'm not the domestic kind. I made the mistake of thinking I was, once. I make no promises these days, I keep company with women who don't require promises. Was that callous? I prefer to think it's being honest.

Any road, what I was feeling for Mrs Crawford wasn't like that. It was more a—I don't know, something more basic and at the same time, something more—more like a pull. I'm not going to say anything daft, like she was meant for me, because that would be bloody stupid, but I was right taken with her. She wasn't what I'd expected. Her wry sense of humour, for a start. After what she'd been through, I expected—well, someone more bleak, I suppose. Her experiences must have scarred her, but she hid the scars very well.

I knew some of what she'd been through, from the real Mrs Crawford, the woman that Marianne Little took her name from. It had taken me a couple of weeks to get to that point in my search. As usual when you're looking for someone or something, it's about knowing who to ask and what to look for. Was she dead, was she married, the woman I had been tasked with finding? Parish records are a slog to wade through, and back in the day, when I worked here in Edinburgh, it was a task that was always delegated to the newest and most junior member of the team—provided they could read, of course.

I never delegated. You can tell someone to check this

name and see if they're on the burial list, or see if they're married, but that's all they'll do, and in my experience, it's just as often what you find that you're not looking for that's important.

In a way, that's what happened with Marianne Little. I was in the right parish, and I was looking at the right registers, but there wasn't a trace of her, alive or dead. My next call was the parish priest, a new appointment, but he put me on to his predecessor, and there was a man who liked to talk, especially if you had the foresight to bring a bottle of his preferred tipple. Which I did. It was he who remembered the scandal of the woman some branded a witch. It was he who pointed me in the direction of the York institution.

Dealing with the men in charge of those places requires a different approach. You can't come out and tell them what it was you want or they'll start harping on about confidentiality and patient privacy. Places like that, what they're always in need of was money. New inmates or new funding, and if you offer the possibility of both it gets you through the door. I can put on a posh accent. I can play the gentleman if required. And I'm very, very good at leading a conversation down a certain path.

That's the other thing about those professional men. They like the sound of their own voices. They like to expound their theories. And in doing that, they tell you about their cases. Marianne Little was one of their failures, though the man I spoke to didn't put it that way, needless to say. Incurable, he said of her, and not suited to their trusting environment. What he meant was, she'd escaped, and the man who paid to keep her locked up had caused a stooshie. That's when I got the proof I'd been looking for. The signature on the papers of the man who paid her bills was the man I'd suspected from the first. It was no surprise to discover that it was all about the money, but I can't tell you the blind fury that took hold of me, seeing that name.

I nearly gave myself away, but when I'd calmed down and rid myself of the very pleasant image I had of throttling him, I got things back in perspective. He was oblivious of the fact we were on to him, and like to remain so. Once I'd found his victim and got her safe, assuming she was still alive, then I'd find out how he managed to get her locked up. Then I'd have all I needed to get him locked up in return. But for now, that could wait.

Marianne Little had been transferred to somewhere distant and secure. That was my next port of call, and it was there that I discovered she'd managed to free herself. My heart soared at that news. I wanted to cheer. I struggled to keep the smile off my face as I listened to the man in charge of that much larger institution, who clearly bore a grudge against her. He had been hoping to publish a ground-breaking paper. He had been planning on making his name by curing her. She'd let him down badly by escaping. I could tell he knew nothing about how, and it was clear he didn't care what had happened to her either. I had to sit there for another half-hour listening to him going on about his next pet project, and fervently hoped that he or she would blight his ambition by escaping too.

I'd seen enough of the place by then to work out it would take some doing to get out of it, which meant the woman I was looking for must have had help. It was by trawling through the local press that set me on the right track this time. Another escape around about the time I reckoned Marianne Little disappeared.

A man, poor soul, he was once Queen Victoria's piper,

and had convinced himself he was her husband. He was last seen on the banks of the River Nith and it was assumed he had been swallowed up by the quicksands. The search for him had involved nearly every member of staff at the institution, so it would have been the perfect diversion. I tracked down Mrs Crawford easily enough since she was in charge of the most secure female ward, but persuading her to talk was more difficult.

I knew better than to offer *her* money. If she'd risked her position to help an inmate escape, she must have had a very strong motive for doing so. She was prickly when I mentioned Marianne Little, and by that time I was prickly enough myself about what had happened to the poor woman and what she'd been put through. It was gie easy for me to let fall enough sense of the disgust I felt to set her off on the injustices of the case. Mrs Crawford was adamant that Marianne Little had been held unfairly and unnecessarily, and I counted her opinion considerably higher than any of those in charge of the institution, who were happy to bend the truth to fit their desire to keep banking the fees and donations. Besides, I knew what Mrs Crawford did not, the real reason *why* Marianne Little was being locked up.

Knowing when to take a risk with someone, when to trust them, was vital in my job. So I told Mrs Crawford the bare bones of why I wanted to find the woman she'd helped escape, and I let her see enough of the proof to assure her that Marianne Little's fortunes were going to change radically, if only I could find her. Thanks to Mrs Crawford, I then had a city, an employment agency, and a fairly accurate date. It wasn't long before I found the woman herself. Alive and looking very well indeed, to my immense relief and delight.

So there I sat, having my coffee that morning in Edinburgh's Grassmarket, mulling over what to do next. Against the odds, I'd found the woman I had been paid to find. Marianne Little had been judged and condemned without a trial, just like me. I hadn't suffered anything like what she had, but the fact we had that in common added to her appeal—I could see that. It was also a very big part of my determination to see justice done for her, make sure the bastard responsible for what he'd put her through paid the price for what he'd done.

Four years of suffering he'd inflicted on her. Four years of being held unjustly, treated in ways that would make your blood run cold. Once I'd done collecting the evidence against him, he'd be locked up for the rest of his wretched life. Meantime, he was carrying on oblivious of the clock counting down his remaining days of freedom, and what I had been instructed to do was think about what might be the best way of going about informing Marianne Little of her change in circumstances and pending good fortune.

Think about it, but don't do it, thank the stars. I wasn't much more than a complete stranger to her, and it was all going to be a huge shock. Did she know anything of her heritage? Very little, would be my guess, so what she was going to hear would pull the rug from under her. I had the proof of it, it wasn't a case of her not believing me, but would she listen? And if she did, what would it do to her? She seemed strong-willed, but it was clear to me, from the way she hid herself away from the world, from her wariness every time she left the sanctuary of her rooms in the Grassmarket, that she was still looking over her shoulder. She'd escaped, but she wasn't free. She was much more vulnerable and fragile than she appeared.

What's more, if she was going to lay claim to her real heritage, the press would be all over it, for it's not often a lost peeress was rediscovered. The sorry tale of her recent past was bound to come out too, especially if she was to give evidence against the man who had locked her up. I knew what it was like to find your name all over the press. Just thinking about how she might react to that gave me the heebie-jeebies, because all my instincts told me she'd run for the hills, and then I'd be back to where I started from.

It would need to be done sensitively, in a way that didn't make her take fright and bolt. I'd need to get her to talk to me, find out what she knew, what she didn't and fill in some of the gaps. And how was I going to do that, when she'd already turned down my suggestion of meeting up again? Though on reflection it seemed to me, she hadn't done so very convincingly, and that gave me hope. The obvious thing would be to sit in Queen Street Gardens again, but there were several reasons for not doing the obvious thing. I needed to speak to her on her own, without the children to distract her, and without putting her on her guard.

Then there was my most ardent desire to avoid becoming an object of interest to the locale's regular policeman. I doubted very much that any of the constables on their beats would know me, they'd all have retired, moved on or moved up, but if the man was worth his salt, he'd notice me. It was what a good policeman did, took note of strangers, kept an eye out for anything unusual, and the more conscientious among them—which was most, in my experience—took notes. Last, but certainly not least, was my desire to avoid the New Town when possible. Despite the passing years, the risk of sticking my head above the parapet was real, the potential consequences genuinely fatal.

And then there was the woman herself. She seemed to be quite content with the life she had made in this city. Just as I had done myself, she'd forged it from the ashes of another life, out of necessity. It was nothing short of a miracle that she'd done so. If any of the families who had entrusted her with their children's well-being got so much as a sniff of her recent past, there would be hell to pay— and she'd already been to hell and back. Mind you, if any of them discovered that they'd been employing a peeress as their governess, that would be a whole other story in the newspapers.

The more I thought about the situation, the more complicated it seemed to me. She'd escaped, she hadn't been released. Once the full story came to light and the wheels of justice were set in motion, there was no chance that the private institution she'd escaped from would want her back, but she'd be branded as an ex-inmate for ever. The press would have a field day with that one, and she—I swear, when I thought of what she would have to go through in front of a judge and jury, it made me sick to my stomach.

Was I making too much of it? At the end of the day, what she would hear from whoever told her in the end was life-changing—and I mean seriously life-changing. Provided the legalities could be ironed out, that was. I sighed, not for the first time wishing that at least one bit of the situation was simpler. Baby steps, I said to myself. That's what I'd take with her. Edge forward, but slowly. That was the only sensible approach.

I threw some coins down on the table and headed out into the Grassmarket, scanning the crowd first. Better safe than sorry. I'd stretch my legs and clear my head. There were so many parts of the city I'd be wise to avoid, but up on Salisbury Crags, I'd be unlikely to meet anyone I knew. And the view from Arthur's Seat over the city spread out below me in all its glory had always been one that did my heart good.

My walk blew away the cobwebs, and gave me an appetite, but the only plan I came up with was to try to bump into Marianne Crawford on her way home from work. For this, I chose the Lawnmarket. In the years I'd been away from Edinburgh, they'd finished the work on the High Kirk. St Giles certainly had a new majesty, along with a whole new look, though the famous crown steeple that was a landmark of the Old Town had been left untouched. The new stone was already blackening, and the kirk brooded over the square now that all the old buildings had been demolished, like a big black crow.

I positioned myself in the shadows of the main entrance in the early evening, eyeing the carved gargoyles that guarded the portico. Malevolent creatures, with their tongues sticking out, they were presumably intended to prevent evil spirits from entering the sacred edifice. The evil spirits, in my humble opinion, were those flapping about in their legal robes over at Parliament Square, but I'm willing to admit to a bit of bias there.

I was beginning to get concerned that somehow I had missed her, when I spotted her—at precisely the same time as she spotted me, and made her way across the Lawnmarket to join me.

'Mr Sutherland. What a coincidence.' Her tone made it clear that she thought it was nothing of the sort. 'What are you doing here, lurking in the shadow of St Giles?' she asked.

'I like to take a walk before dinner, and this is a good place to watch the world go by.'

'While keeping yourself out of sight?'

'Evidently not, since you spotted me.'

'I had a feeling we'd bump into each other again.'

'And I rather hoped we would,' I admitted, relieved to be able to speak something close to the truth.

'Why?'

She looked me straight in the eye when she asked the question.

'You interest me,' I told her, which was honest enough.

'In what way?'

She quirked her brow again, such an odd thing to find alluring, but there it was, and there I was, despite my previous resolutions not to be distracted, struggling not to be distracted by my body's reaction. 'That's a very personal question, from someone who has not even disclosed her name.'

'I am not one for small talk.'

'Yet you made an effort yesterday, in Queen Street Gardens, when we met,' I retorted.

'I felt obliged to fill the silence while you were watching the policeman.'

'In fact, what you did was interrogate me about my interest in him. That was not small talk.'

'And you did not answer my questions, Mr Sutherland.'

'I've answered more of your questions than you have of mine. You have still not put me in possession of your name.'

She narrowed her eyes at me, and I thought for a moment that I had crossed an invisible line with her, but what she said was not the reprimand I anticipated. 'I have the distinct impression that you know it already.'

What to say to this? The woman was a most astute observer, and I didn't want to lie, never mind have her catch me out. Truth was, I knew all three of her names, which was one more than she did herself. 'Mrs Crawford,' I conceded. 'That's what I heard the other nanny call you, though she did not mention a first name.'

'It is Marianne, and she's a governess, not a nanny.'

'I am never sure of the difference.'

'They have much in common, for both are usually underpaid, over-used and under-valued. Oh, and always of the so-called weaker sex, of course.'

'And which are you, Mrs Crawford, nanny or governess?'

'Either or both, depending upon what is required. I am fortunately in sufficient demand to be able to quit any establishment which under-values, under-pays or over-uses me.'

'You are good at your job?'

She gave me a crooked smile, taking her time, as I was now realising was her wont, before answering. 'The women I work for know that they can trust me.'

'And they can pay you well too. Queen Street is a very prestigious address.'

'Edinburgh has a great many wealthy families, and the New Town is full of prestigious addresses.'

'You must have come to Edinburgh armed with excellent references.'

'Must I? You make a great deal of assumptions about me.'

'And you deny none of them, so I reckon I've been pretty close to the mark.'

For the first time, she looked uncomfortable and failed to meet my eyes. She was difficult to pin down, this conversation was like a game of chess, but she wasn't a liar.

I decided not to push her for the moment. The clouds had finally decided to drop some of their rain, and it fell lightly but persistently. 'You'll catch a cold if you stand here in this,' I said to her. 'May I escort you to wherever you were headed?'

'No,' she replied, immediately on her guard. She had taken a small step back, but she had not turned to leave. 'Why are you here, Mr Sutherland? In Edinburgh, I mean. It's a bit of a long story, you said, yesterday. I'd like to hear it.'

She had surprised me, and I surprised myself at how pleased I was. 'Shall we go inside, out of the rain?'

'Inside?' She glanced around at our surroundings, and then over at the church. 'Do you mean the church?'

'It will give us some shelter from the weather, and though it's Presbyterian now, it was originally built for the faith in which I was raised. I am fairly certain I'll not be smited for crossing the threshold.'

'What about me? I have no faith, will I be safe inside, do you think?'

I glanced about me at the Lawnmarket and the High Street, where those who lived in the shadows of the Old Town were emerging as night fell, and the lights from the taverns in the wynds were beginning to flicker. 'Safer inside than out here.'

'On the lookout for the police again, Mr Sutherland?' She didn't wait for me to reply, but turned towards the church. 'Come then, let us converse inside.'

Chapter Six

Marianne

Edinburgh—
Friday 3rd August 1877

The interior of St Giles brought me up short as I crossed the threshold, for though I had never been inside, it felt familiar. The cathedral was a vast echoing structure, the vaulted ceiling of the nave soaring so high above us that it could barely be made out in the gloom, intimidating, and much bigger than any church I had ever entered. There was so much space, so few places to hide, and the glimmer from the various stained-glass windows I found oppressive rather than impressive.

Aware of Mr Sutherland behind me trying to close the door softly, I forced myself to take a few steps further in. The church had undergone extensive renovations in the last few years, I knew, and my sensitive nose twitched at the smell of newly sculpted stone that mingled with the musty smell and a depressing sense of the urge to repent that I associate with all places of worship. Which explained the feeling I'd had, that I'd been here before. Religion, in the institution from which I had escaped, was deemed to be soothing to troubled souls. I had never found it so, but perhaps that was because it was not my soul that troubled me.

There were a few figures scattered about in the open pews beyond the transept, closer to the altar, but one of the aisles on the left was empty and slightly less exposed. Mr Sutherland followed my lead, his tread light for such a big man.

'I promise that I intend you no harm, Mrs Crawford,' were his first words to me, spoken softly and with a mind to the acoustics of the place.

'I would not be here with you if I thought so,' I replied. And yet, what on earth was I doing here at all, with a man who was always looking over his shoulder, and who looked too closely at me? I should be avoiding him at all costs, yet here I was, conniving with his desire for my company. 'What is it you want from me?' I asked, thinking it might help me to understand what it was I wanted from him.

'I thought it was a case of what *you* want from *me*? Why I'm here in Edinburgh, wasn't that what you wanted to know?'

I took my time answering, concentrating all my attention on him. He baffled me. I was here because I was convinced, though I had no idea why, that I ought to be here with him. What I got from him was the same, a strong sense of his *wanting* to be with me, but nothing more, save that I felt—no, safe isn't the right word, I felt anything but safe. I felt jumpy, as if I was expecting something exciting to happen. Jittery was the word Mrs Oliphant would use. My blood was tingling with anticipation. I wanted more—more of this man's company, I mean, and that was such an unusual feeling—these days, unique.

I had been silent too long. He had been studying me, just as I'd been studying him. It didn't make me uncomfortable, it wasn't as if he was analysing my features for signs of my condition! It made me blush. It made me acutely aware of myself. And of him.

'Would it help,' he asked me, 'if I told you that my intentions are not in the least improper?'

No, I imagined replying, for my own thoughts are extremely improper. As if I would say such a thing, but the idea of it made me smile. Then he raised his brows, wanting to know what had made me smile, and I felt my cheeks getting hotter. 'Not that it is at all relevant, but you have already told me you are not married. And neither, as it happens, am I.'

'Really, *Mrs* Crawford?'

'An employer's wife can confide in a widow, Mr Sutherland. I would not be so popular if I was *Miss* Crawford.'

'Do wives commonly confide in their governesses?'

'The role of wife and mother can be very lonely. I am a very good listener.'

'And wise counsellor?'

'What do you mean?' The question startled me out of the conversation.

He spread his hands, shaking his head. 'I am interested, that's all. I have never been married, but I'd always assumed that a wife would confide in her husband. The idea that she'd be lonely...'

'When a man comes home from whatever business takes him out all day, he wants to see his wife in a pretty gown smiling across the dinner table, listening to his tales of the outside world. He isn't interested in the mundane domestic world she inhabits, the exhausting task of raising his children, and the painful task of bearing them. I listen, Mr Sutherland, but that is all. My days of providing counsel of any sort are over.'

Too late, I realised my mistake. Had he missed the implication? I couldn't understand my outburst. I couldn't understand why I had even answered his questions. I was so intent on trying to find a way to change the subject, his next one caught me off guard once more.

'I'm lost now,' he said, looking anything but. 'Are you saying you have been married, or what?'

'No, I have never been married, and I never want to be!' I had spoken too loudly. I clasped my hands tightly together, taken aback by my own vehemence. I ought to walk away from this conversation and this man, but once again my feet refused to co-operate.

'I didn't mean to upset you,' he said softly. 'I beg your pardon.'

'I am not upset.' I spoke through gritted teeth.

'I'm sorry all the same,' he said.

He was, I could tell that he meant it. I wondered if he'd leave now, but he made no move, looking at that moment just as baffled as I felt. I found that reassuring. I tried to assess his thoughts but with little success, and so instead I tried to understand my own motives. I don't believe in fate, but my instincts were telling me that I was meant to know this man. Why?

Was it a simple case of finding him attractive? I thought myself immune to such feelings, my body numbed for ever by the betrayal and scars that had been the result of my first and only experience of love. What I mistook for love. Was my body finally healed enough to make its own demands, even if my mind was damaged for ever? I did not wish to recall that other man, nor to compare him with Mr Sutherland. This was different. Not love, that I would never risk, but allure? Magnetism? Was it that which made me seek him out, and which kept me in his company even when I knew it was unwise?

It was not Mr Sutherland who made me feel unsafe, it was his effect on me. I liked the way he looked. He was a tall man, and well built, but he was not one of those men who use their size to intimidate. I shivered, the pleasant kind of shiver, recalling the heat of his hand through his gloves, and wondered, what would it have been like had he removed his glove? What would his touch be like? His lips?

Once again, I realised I'd been silent, and that I was being silently studied. Could *he* read *my* thoughts? At that moment, as our eyes met, I felt it, a tug, like a rope tightening between us, the absolute certainty that he too felt this—this compulsion. That we were two haunted, hunted souls destined to meet.

It was a ridiculous and fanciful thing to think, especially in a church, but the conviction took root, and allowed me at last to focus on what mattered—not what I felt for the man, but why I gravitated towards him. 'We have strayed far from the point of this conversation,' I said. 'Which was not for you to question me, but for me to question you. Were you in the gardens yesterday, by accident or design?'

'I didn't arrive with the intention of speaking to you,' he answered, taking his time, choosing his words carefully, which was something of a habit with him. 'If the ball hadn't been thrown in my direction I wouldn't have spoken. But it did and I'll confess I was glad it did, for I wanted to speak to you, and once I had spoken to you, I wanted to speak to you again. I was curious about you and if you don't mind my saying, I got the strong impression you were curious about me. Even if you did turn down my invitation to meet again,' he added with a faint smile, 'here we are, after all.'

I had regained control of myself, and saw no harm in admitting that much. 'A man who is afraid of the law, but who is not a criminal, is interesting.'

'I'm not afraid of the law.'

'You didn't want that policeman to see you.'

'I didn't think he'd recognise me. I just didn't want to stand out. Look, I'm not trying to lead you a merry dance, I promise you. I'll be blunt, shall I?'

'I would appreciate it.'

'I'm here in Edinburgh on a job of work, the nature of which is confidential. I have no intentions, honest or wicked, save what I've already confessed, to get to know you a bit better. I am—I am drawn to you. That's the description that I keep coming back to, whatever that may mean.' He shrugged, looking sheepish. 'There you have it.'

Drawn. The very word I had used myself to describe my reaction to him. It was reassuring and yes, it was slightly thrilling, to hear him articulate something akin to what I was experiencing. That he did so, I think against his better judgement, persuaded me that my instinct to trust him was sound, and that I could therefore indulge my wish to further our acquaintance. That sounds calculated, but it was rather caution born from experience. I cannot emphasise strongly enough how unusual this conversation was for me.

'What is the nature of your work?' I asked him.

'I'm a detective.'

'A detective! So you are a policeman after all!'

'Not exactly. I'm a private investigator.'

'Good grief!' I had not even considered such a thing and

was once again on my guard. 'What are you investigating? Not me, I presume, though it would explain the number of questions you have thrown at me.'

'I told you, I'm interested in you, it's just my way. As to why I'm here—it wouldn't be right to tell you that, not at the moment. My clients rely on my complete discretion.'

I could barely see his face in the flickering candlelight of the church, but my inner senses were on full alert. He was wary, but he was not lying. Despite what I have been accused of in the past, I am not a mind reader. I certainly cannot read people's thoughts precisely, but I am acutely sensitive, far more than most, to feelings, and at times, this gives me insights that have been seen as malign, even sorcery, when they most definitely are not.

My skill was more adept when a person was unaware of my interest. Rory Sutherland was very much aware that I was studying him, and his feelings were complex and confusing, as my own were becoming. Caution warring with heightened interest, mainly. 'If you are a detective,' I said, trying to focus on what he had told me rather than what I was experiencing, 'then why did you want to avoid that policeman? Don't the police and private investigators work together to solve crimes?'

He laughed at that, a snarling, vicious sound that was loud enough to echo, reminding us both of our surroundings. 'Solving crimes is something the police do selectively, in this city.'

The bitterness in his voice startled me. The black wave of anger and regret that enveloped him took me utterly aback and took me right back too, to the countless nights when my own anger at the injustice of my treatment was my only defence against despair. Before I knew what I was doing I stepped closer, putting my hand on his arm. 'Mr Sutherland, whatever it is that ails you, you can conquer it.'

His gloved hand covered mine. He looked at me with such bleakness that my heart contracted. 'The case I'm investigating now is of no interest to the police. What ails me is unfinished business that must remain unresolved for ever.'

We were close enough for me to feel the warmth of his breath, to smell the faint trace of soap on his skin. My gloved hand was enveloped in his, held but not constrained. I didn't feel trapped, and again I cannot say just how important and unusual that was. On the contrary, I wanted to close the gap further between us, to ease the pain that brought back so many memories of my own. 'The past, if that is what it is, is best left behind, Mr Sutherland.'

'Aye, I know that, it's why I shouldn't be in Edinburgh.'

'But you said your case…'

'Brought me here.' He gave me a strange look then turned away, making a pretence of studying the ancient stonework. 'It's the last place I should be, all the same. I love this city—sacrilege for a Weegie to say, but there it is. It's where I made my name, and it's where my name was blackened. If they find out I'm back…' His voice cracked. 'Well, I'll just have to make damn—blooming sure that they don't find out.'

'They? I don't understand, do you mean the police have forbidden—is your presence here illegal?'

'No. It's complicated. It's not the police, so much as— no, I'm sorry, I truly am, but there's no point in my saying any more.'

'But—but surely—you have told me almost nothing. Is your life in danger?'

'Ach no, it's not that serious.' Mr Sutherland turned towards me, trying and failing to summon a semblance of a smile. 'I'm sorry, I didn't mean to tell you any of this.' He was gathering himself together again, tucking away the dark emotions that had escaped his restraint, and my goodness that felt so horribly familiar. 'I have no idea why I just blurted that out. As you pointed out, it's all in the past now.'

But it clearly wasn't. Haunted. Hunted. No wonder I felt such an affinity with him. 'Who are these people?' I asked, with difficulty refraining from tugging at his sleeve. 'The ones who blackened your name? And why—how—if you did not commit a crime? I don't understand.'

He sighed heavily. 'My crime was not to listen to the advice I'd been given. To interfere when I'd been told not to. In short, I ruffled the wrong feathers, and the chickens came home to roost, so to speak.'

In short, I ruffled the wrong feathers.

Precisely what I had done, and with the same result. I very much wanted to know more, but I could tell from the way he set his mouth firmly that persistence would lead to resistance. 'I know what that's like,' I said, willing him to understand just how sincerely I empathised. 'It's clearly a painful subject, but if you wish to confide in me, I assure you, you can trust me.'

'Aye, I know, I can trust you. Intuition,' he added, before I could ask, 'I've good instincts in that department. But I've already told you more than I should have, and it's getting late. You shouldn't be out and about in this area, it's not safe. I think I'd best see you home.'

I remained rooted to the spot. 'But—but if you have been threatened—if it's true that you could be in danger—then this case that has brought you here to Edinburgh, it must be very important to you?'

'Oh, it is,' he said, giving me a look I could not interpret. 'Much more important than I thought when I took it on.'

I allowed him to accompany me to the Grassmarket, because he seemed determined that I needed chaperoning, and it was easier to accept that than to argue with him. We passed Flora flitting up Victoria Street on her way to earn her keep. I smiled, a friendly smile I thought it was, but it startled both her and Mr Sutherland, who asked if we were acquainted. I answered honestly enough that we were not. He saw me to the entrance of my close, and would have escorted me up the stairs to my rooms had I permitted him to do so. I bid him goodnight.

Once inside I opened my window without lighting the lamp, and spotted him immediately, on the other side of the Grassmarket gazing up at my tenement. He nodded, though I did not acknowledge seeing him, and then took himself off towards the Cowgate. Where was he lodging? What on earth had he done all those years ago, to result in his exile from Edinburgh? And what was this case of his that was important enough to make him risk returning? We had made no arrangements to meet again, but I retired to bed that night certain that we would.

Chapter Seven

Rory

Six weeks previously

I met Lord Westville in a hotel in central London. He was younger than I had imagined, in his late twenties, I estimated, tall, slim and very fair. Though it was a pleasant summer's day, his handshake was icy, and throughout our conversation he would every now and then give a violent shiver and complain about the room being cold. His eyes were the strangest colour, a blue so pale it was almost translucent, what diamonds would look like if they were blue, hard chips of precious stone glinting under his thin, arched brows. The Marquess was what passes for handsome in a man of his class, especially when what they call good breeding was accompanied by wealth. I found him as distasteful as all of his entitled ilk.

'I have spent a great deal of my life in sunnier climes,' he said to me, examining the contents of the teacup he had graciously allowed the maidservant to pour. 'If I am to settle in this country, I shall have to acquire a more suitable wardrobe.' He took a sip of his tea, shuddered and pushed it aside. 'That is one English habit I doubt I will acquire. You come highly recommended, Mr Sutherland.'

'Do I, now?'

'You are wondering by whom, and how I, who am almost a stranger to these shores, can have known how to set about finding you,' Lord Westville said, forcing me to reappraise the man. He smiled thinly. 'I am not the dilettante you imagine me to be, Mr Sutherland. My father was an extremely rich self-made man of independent means long before he inherited the Westville estates, and while it is true that I have been raised in what you might call the lap of luxury, I am not the idle type. My father instilled a strong work ethic in me. Diplomacy has been my calling, and it is one that has provided me with a great many contacts. I am told that discretion is your watchword, and discretion in this case is paramount.'

He had surprised me again. 'And what is this case, Lord Westville?' I asked him, pushing my own cup of tea aside, it being of the fragrant variety that tasted like perfume.

He steepled his fingers, studying me with those strange eyes from under deceptively languid lids. 'Tell me first what you have uncovered, Mr Sutherland, of my own circumstances? I give you credit, you see, for having carried out due diligence before this meeting.'

That was true enough, and I gave *him* the credit for that. 'Not very much,' I admitted reluctantly. 'Your father inherited the title and the estates from his distant cousin about seven years ago, but he remained abroad and has shown no interest in either. I understand the lands and estates are managed by a family lawyer.'

'His name is Eliot.'

His tone gave me pause. 'The way you said that implies you have some reservations about Mr Eliot.'

'You are on the right track, Mr Sutherland, but it is not the estate itself that causes me most concern. It is the...'

'Money,' I finished for him, since it was always at the root of everything.

'The crux of the matter, indeed. Filthy lucre, Mr Sutherland, and a great deal of it, which is why I must entreat you to tread very lightly with Mr Eliot. He must not know that I suspect him.'

'Misappropriation of funds, is it? That is not really my field of expertise, Lord Westville.'

'What I'm rather more concerned about is the misappropriation of a person. Or, more accurately, the absence of a person. That, I believe, *is* your field?'

'It depends upon the circumstances,' I said warily, but I have to admit I was instantly intrigued.

'Then let me enlighten you, Mr Sutherland, but first...'

'You have my assurances, Lord Westville, that whether I take the case or not, the content of this conversation will go no further.'

He smiled his thin smile. 'That I took for granted. What I was about to say was, first let us have something more refreshing to drink than tea.'

It was the kind of tale I'd have found difficult to believe, had Lord Westville not produced the evidence for me to read—including the will written by the cousin from whom his father had inherited the title. That previous Lord Westville had lived as a bachelor, but it transpired that he was a widower and moreover the father of a daughter.

'He secretly married a woman named Anne Little,' the

current Lord Westville informed me. 'And she, rather inconveniently for the infant, expired in the process of giving birth to her. The child was handed into the care of a couple, and a stipend was paid to them every month for the raising and education of her. When she was twenty-one, arrangements were made to pay the stipend directly to her.'

'Arrangements were made? Was she aware of who her father was?'

'Though she was baptised, and undoubtedly legitimate, I am afraid we must conclude that her father did not wish to know her,' Lord Westville said, a slight frown marring his pale brow. 'She was raised under the name Marianne Little, and if she ever enquired as to the identity of her benefactor, the arrangements ensured that she would receive no answer. Which makes her father's will very odd indeed. Lord Westville—my father's cousin, that is—really, there are too many Lords Westville in this tale—was extremely rich.'

'Railways, I believe, and canals.'

'Very good, Mr Sutherland, that is it exactly. Railways and canals and also coal. The lands, the estate and the title were inherited by my own father, but the money—and there is a vast amount of it—the money was left to the daughter.'

'Making her a considerable heiress, I take it?'

'Well now, here we reach the crux of the matter. It would make her husband a considerably wealthy man, but until she married, then she was to continue to receive her stipend, but nothing more.'

'And what was to happen if she didn't marry?'

'As I said, matters were to continue as before.' Lord Westville poured himself another glass of Madeira, shrugging at my refusal to join him. 'My own father did not, I'm afraid, cover himself in glory in this matter. He was not interested in the estates, though he was happy enough to assume the title. I fear we must conclude that Anne Little, the mother of our heiress, was of humble origins, and therefore not a connection my father would have wished to acknowledge.

'The will nominated Eliot, the lawyer, as both Executor and Trustee, which as far as the law is concerned, made him effectively legally responsible for the woman. She would of course have been oblivious to this, just as she had been oblivious of the fact that her father—our first Lord Westville—was previously, legally her guardian. And my own father—the second Lord Westville in this little drama—was happy to let matters be.'

At this point in the tale I was tempted to take a glass of the Madeira, even though it's not my kind of drink. However, I made do with a cup of coffee. 'Just to be clear then, as matters stand with you—the third Lord Westville—the woman in the case is still legally under the guardianship of Eliot, who is also her Trustee?'

'In the matter of her inheritance, that is correct.'

'Was she contacted, then? Made aware of her inheritance when her father died?'

Lord Westville shrugged, looking distinctly uncomfortable. 'You need to understand that these events are almost as new to me as they are to you. My father never mentioned her existence to me. The first I knew of her was when I met with Eliot last week. I've decided to move back to England for a while, at least, and intend to do what my father did not, get to grips with my inheritance. I am told that my cousin—for she must be some sort of cousin—has disappeared.'

'Disappeared! What do you mean by that—exactly?'

'Alas, I cannot be precise,' he replied, looking pained. 'I am reliant entirely on the testimony of Mr Eliot. He tells me that he attempted to contact her when her father died, in order to make arrangements to continue the stipend or to pass on her inheritance to her husband, were she married. Apparently she could not be found.'

'So he's not had any contact with her for—how long?'

'He was rather vague on the subject. It is about seven years since her father died and the trust was set up, delegating power to Eliot.'

'What age would the woman be now?'

'She was twenty-five or six when her father died, so that would make her thirty-three, I think.' He consulted a piece of paper, on which a number of dates were written. 'Yes, she was born in June forty-four, so just turned thirty-three.'

'She's most likely married years ago with a clutch of weans—children. And what has this lawyer been doing? Sitting on his backside twiddling his thumbs and making no effort to find her? There's more holes in his tale than a fisherman's net.'

'You express yourself more colourfully than I, but we are of one mind, Mr Sutherland.'

'Your own father, he wasn't exactly an old man when he died, was he?'

'He was fifty-two, in robust health until typhus claimed him, and importantly, persistently uninterested in Mr Eliot's management of his affairs. The circumstances are most— conducive—to exploitation, alas.'

'And has there been exploitation? Have you looked at the accounts?'

'It is a delicate situation. The money in question is not part of my inheritance, and I did not wish to make Mr Eliot suspicious. I have therefore feigned my father's indifference to the matter.'

'You did the right thing there, but we'll need to find a way to take a look at what he's been up to.'

'Thank you, Mr Sutherland. I am not an idiot.'

Clearly he wasn't. 'So you'll make arrangements, will you, to authorise me to do a bit of digging with the bank?'

'As soon as you agree to take the case and provided you can do so without alerting him.'

'I've a few contacts myself, obviously, that will help me find out if he has money problems. Or too much money. Talking of which, what happens if the woman isn't found?'

'Nothing at all. The money continues to be held in trust, unless she is dead, or declared dead.'

'She's been missing nearly seven years, after which, if no trace can be found of her, you can have the law declare her dead. And if she is already dead, then the money…'

'Unless she has legal progeny, then it will default to me,' Lord Westville said. 'Am I then also under suspicion?'

'Suspicion of what?' I countered. 'If you were in cahoots with the lawyer, then the last thing you'd want to do was find the woman. And if you wanted to pay lip service to trying to find her, you wouldn't have come to me.'

He laughed at that, a surprisingly hearty sound. 'Because you will succeed where others might fail, you mean? That was your forte, was it not, back in your days as a policeman north of the border? To go boldly where other men feared to tread? Until you fell on your sword.'

His words made my blood run cold. There had been a couple of times, when I first settled in the south, when my infamy lost me work, but few people in the south were much concerned with what happened *north of the border.*

I had made my name afresh, and put it behind me. Or so I had thought.

'You are surprisingly reticent, Mr Sutherland. You don't leap to your own defence?'

'If you believed the accusations, you would not be here, Lord Westville.'

'You were held in such high esteem, and your fall from grace was so very—so very complete—that it struck me as simply too dramatic to believe. A contrivance, in other words, Mr Sutherland. Am I correct?'

Aside from my da, he was the first person to give me the benefit of the doubt. Guilt made me cringe inside, for I'd judged him in a way he had not judged me. 'I thank you for your faith in me,' I said, swallowing the embarrassing lump in my throat.

'I hope it is not misplaced.'

'You do want her found, then?'

'Dead or alive. Married or unwed. One way or another, I wish the matter resolved for her sake as well as my own.'

His tone was cool, utterly lacking in emotion. Dead or alive, he said, seemingly quite indifferent to which. If this had been simply a matter of fraud, of a lawyer giving in to temptation and dipping into funds, I wouldn't have been interested. But the funds in question were huge and besides, it was really about a missing woman and her missing heritage.

I couldn't help but think of that other missing woman I had let down seven years before. My one failure. It was daft, there was no logic behind it, but from that minute, I linked the two cases in my head. I would find this heiress and remedy my failure in the other case. Bloody stupid thinking, completely illogical, but that's what I thought all the same.

Decision made, it was down to business. 'You're sure the

lawyer doesn't know you're set on this course?' I asked the man who was now my client. 'No,' I added hastily, 'forget I asked you that, you're not daft.'

'I am positive. If that changes, rest assured that I shall let you know. For now, I have him focused on my own concerns—the lands and the estates, I mean. Those, he has in fact managed competently. I plan to keep him busy while you investigate the other matter.'

'Good, make sure you do. Of course, it might be he's guilty of nothing other than a lack of care in trying to find the heiress himself.' I said it, because it needed said, though I didn't believe it.

Nor did Lord Westville. 'That may be the case, but there is, as we have both remarked, a great deal of money at stake.' He drained his glass. 'It sounds to me as if you have decided to take the case, Mr Sutherland. Or am I mistaken?'

I ought to have taken the time to consider, but I did not. The stakes were extremely high. It was, besides, a puzzle that might be tricky to resolve, something that might stretch me a bit. That's how I explained it to myself later, mind. At the time, all I could think about was, if I get this right, it will balance out that other one, at last. 'I'll need you to give me what little information you have on her.'

'I came prepared.' The Marquess pulled a paper from his pocket and handed it over. 'Here are the details of where the stipend was last paid to, and the address of the people who raised her. She was known as Marianne Little, but she was baptised Lady Mary Anne Westville. I have no desire for regular updates nor any interest in your methods. When you have significant progress to report, let me know.'

This suited me very well. 'And when I have an answer for you,' I asked him, 'what then?'

'Then your work will be done. I'll take care of the matter from there.'

With that, I was less happy. 'If I find her alive, what should I tell her? I need to tell her something.'

'Do you know, I haven't thought of that?' Lord Westville frowned down at his long-fingered hands. 'I suppose you must tell her the truth. I will provide you with copies of the will, her birth certificate.'

'It's going to come as a hell of a shock. Not only the money, but presumably all she thinks she knows about herself is wrong. She doesn't even know her own name.'

'Dear me, when you put it like that.' He shuddered dramatically. 'I detest emotional scenes. I suppose, as her only known relative, I should be the bearer of good news, but the problem is, the news as matters stand is not necessarily good.'

'You mean the money may not be hers, if she is alive but unmarried?'

'That is precisely what I mean. Contrary to what you may think, Mr Sutherland,' the Marquess said, looking pained, 'I have no desire to benefit from my predecessor's lack of foresight—I mean the first of the Lord Westvilles. Why he did not make provision for the possibility of his daughter eschewing the marital state, I do not know. *If* you find her, *if* she is alive, *if* she is a spinster, then she deserves her legacy. I do not know how I shall go about it, but I am sure the terms of the will can be altered. Until I have confirmation that this can be done, it seems to me that we should tread lightly. Say nothing, in other words, without consulting me.'

It pained me to be told what to do, but I knew he was right. Besides, it was quite a turnup for the book, hearing that he was promising to do himself out of a fortune, admittedly under highly unlikely circumstances. 'That seems sensible.'

He laughed lightly. 'Quoth he, through gritted teeth. I shall take account of your advice on the matter as we proceed, rest assured.'

I believed him, and so was satisfied. I had no idea where the quest would take me, what horrors I might uncover. Marianne Little was a name on a piece of paper, a lost woman I was set on finding. It was all about the money, I thought, and it was, in a sense. Lies and deception were at the heart of it, as they had likely been central to that other case of mine. And in both cases, it was the woman who had suffered. This time, I was determined to serve up justice. As subsequent events would prove, it would turn out to be far from straightforward.

Chapter Eight

Edinburgh—
Sunday 5th August 1877

The view from Dean Bridge was the closest I had been
to the industrial village which lay beneath, the mills and
leather works which clung precariously to the banks of the
Water of Leith. The works were Sabbath-silent today, but
the peculiar odour which hung over the place like a miasma
was still strong enough to make my nose itch.

'Can you smell it?' His voice made me jump as I hadn't
seen him approach. 'Sulphur and lime,' Mr Sutherland said,
'it's what they use to cure the hides. Sheep fleeces, mostly.
Sorry, did I startle you?'

'You did.' My heart was fluttering, though it wasn't so
much with fright. He was standing close, but not too close,
dressed in the same sombre clothes that were obviously a
kind of uniform for him, his shirt very white, the collar
very stiffly starched. In the unusually bright sunlight, his
skin had a healthy glow. His eyelashes were very long, for
a man. He had a most appealing smile. I returned it.

'We choose the strangest places to meet, Mr Sutherland,' I said, though the choice had been his. He had been waiting for me yesterday morning when I set out for work, drinking coffee in the tavern where Flora breakfasted each day. He had not pretended it was a chance encounter, nor had he wasted his time on niceties. I had been not a whit disconcerted to find him waiting for me, something that didn't strike me as strange until much later.

He wanted to see me again, he had said, because he wanted to continue our conversation, and he wondered if I would take the air with him on Sunday, assuming it was my day off. Which was why I found myself on Dean Bridge, dressed in my one summer gown, of pale green, with a matching bow in my straw hat, and a shawl. I had dressed for the weather, certainly not for the man, though he looked both relieved and pleased to see me.

'I wasn't sure you would turn up,' he admitted. 'I thought you might have changed your mind.'

I hadn't even considered it, though I knew I should have. For as long as I felt safe with him, I had decided to indulge my compulsion for his company. Today's arrangement had given me something to look forward to. Something pleasant. That was unusual in itself. 'I had no way of letting you know if I had,' I said to him. 'I wouldn't have known where to send a note.'

'I'm here. You're here. And the sun has joined us. We should make the most of it.'

'Having the sun on my face is something I never take for granted, Mr Sutherland,' I said, lifting my face to the warmth and closing my eyes for a moment. It was a mistake, for in that moment a memory pushed its way in, of an open window, myself leaning out, craning my face to the sunshine, drinking in the smell of new-mown grass far below, before I was yanked inside, the window slammed shut, one of the attendants swearing at me. All I had wanted was some fresh air!

I opened my eyes to find myself being scrutinised by Mr Sutherland. 'Are you all right?' he asked me.

'Fine. I'm fine,' I told him, without meeting his eyes. 'Shall we walk?'

He looked unconvinced, but he nodded. 'I thought we'd go down through the village,' he said, 'then we can follow the river for a bit, if you like. It's far from scenic, I'll grant you, but we'll also be far from the crowds in the parks taking the air, or walking in their Sunday best from church, and I thought—maybe I'm wrong, but I thought you'd like to see a different aspect of Edinburgh.'

'What made you think that?'

'You see a very different side of the city from the rooms you have in the Grassmarket—compared to the New Town where you work, I mean. I know from what you've told me that you could afford better, so that means it's a choice. Of course it could be that you want to keep yourself to yourself, neighbour-wise, and in the Grassmarket, nobody looks too closely into each other's business. But I reckon you like the buzz of it too, you like to watch and to speculate. You're curious about how other people live. Am I right?'

'You make a great deal of deductions about me, Detective Sutherland. You have a way of making a question of a statement.'

He laughed. 'And you have a way of not answering either. I'll assume I'm right.'

'About your choice of location for a walk, I'll give you that,' I conceded, unable to hide my smile.

We took the steep path down, walking side by side, our paces well matched. The chemical smell grew stronger, and then I ceased noticing it as we picked our way past looming mills, and a huddle of buildings and courts that proclaimed themselves to be Robert Legget and Sons, Tanners. The village was eerily quiet, though there was washing hanging on the lines outside a few of the tenements, and a dog barked as we passed. A narrow bridge spanned the Water of Leith, tumbling brown and foul beneath, yet upstream I was horrified to see a gaggle of ragged children leaping about in the poisonous shallows.

'Poor bairns, they'll be bound to catch something from that water,' Mr Sutherland said, 'and I don't mean a fish for their tea.'

We crossed the bridge to the other side where there were more poorly maintained tenements, what looked like a corner shop on the ground floor of one of them, more warehouses, another works of some sort. Though we saw no one, I was conscious of the presence of the workers and their families silently watching us. I began to feel uncomfortable. We did not belong here. We were intruders, sightseers, like the visitors to the institution from which I had escaped, who wandered through the gardens created by the inmates. Did the workers in this village feel trapped as I had, in a life defined by a never-ending routine? It was not the same, not at all the same, yet there were similarities.

'Aye,' Mr Sutherland said, picking up on some of my thoughts, keeping his voice low, 'it's not much of a life, is it? Mind, they wouldn't thank me for saying so.'

'Is there a school here for the little ones?'

'There is, though whether they attend or not, that's another question. The tenement in Glasgow I was raised in was a few rungs up the ladder from a place like this, but there were still a good few families who didn't think it worth sending their weans to school. My da, he knew it was important, thank the stars, but here—you'd think they'd be asking themselves, what's the point, wouldn't you? Let those wee terrors we saw enjoy themselves while they can before they're put to work, you know?'

He muttered something under his breath, shaking his head. 'I shouldn't make assumptions, but you can't help feeling the good people of Edinburgh are happy to have their industrial lungs and the people who work and live there hidden well away from view. Happy to let them police themselves too. They don't send the law in here, you know.'

'Is that why you chose this location?'

He stopped abruptly. 'Do you think I'm running scared from a few policemen on the beat? The chances are, they wouldn't have a clue who I am or more importantly who I was, but I don't want to take that chance. I'm persona non grata in this city, but it was once my city. I'm known here, which is why I'm careful about where I go, and why I'm constantly looking over my shoulder...' Mr Sutherland took a ragged breath. 'I'm sorry.'

'No, I'm sorry.' The temptation to comfort, to place my hand on his arm, was too much to resist. 'I am truly sorry. I do know what it is like to be constantly looking over your shoulder.'

His hand covered mine. Glove on glove, but I felt the heat of his skin. His expression softened. Inside, I felt a fluttering, anxious, sensation, a yearning to offer more, but more of what? He turned to face me. I wanted him to close the gap between us, though at the same time I dreaded it. He made no move, though I felt—oh, I have no idea if it was my own longing or his or both of us I felt, or indeed how long we stood there, our eyes locked, his hand covering mine, saying nothing but both of us aware—I am *sure* we were both aware—of the longing for more—more closeness. Warmth. Touch. Simple things, but they were far from simple.

He sighed, a long exhale, and the spell broke, enough for the longing to dispel, but not enough for either of us to release ourselves. His hand remained on mine. 'Look,' he said softly, 'the truth is, I wanted you to myself for a while, that's all. I lived and worked in this city for more than ten years. There's a lot of folks I'd rather not bump into, for my own peace of mind as well as theirs. We've all moved on, Mrs Crawford, and I'd like to keep it that way. Do you understand what I'm saying?'

Was it so simple? A moment ago, there had been such anger in his voice. Yet what he said now made a great deal of sense. He had not moved on, not as far as he wished, but who was I to dig up other people's skeletons, when I had enough trouble keeping my own in their cupboard.

Besides.

The truth is, I wanted you to myself.

Wasn't that what I wanted too, only I was not brave enough to say so? 'I understand,' I said. 'Let us enjoy the sunshine and forget the world for a time.'

He heaved a sigh, his frown easing. 'Let's try, any road.'

Chapter Nine

Rory

Edinburgh—
Sunday 5th August 1877

We walked on the narrow path, both lost in our thoughts. I heartily regretted my outburst, yet the mood between us was not as awkward as it could have been. The sun was shining, there were trees in full leaf, and the Water of Leith rushing past us on its journey to the Firth of Forth and out to sea gave the illusion that we were in the countryside.

It would have been the most natural thing in the world for us to walk arm in arm, if we had been what we must have looked, a couple with no more ambition than to take the Sunday air and enjoy a bit of peace and quiet. The fact that I very much wanted to do just that was one of the reasons I didn't suggest she put her arm through mine. I couldn't afford to indulge myself. It was simply wrong.

Even if it had felt right. Even if I had thought that she felt it too, when she'd touched me a few moments ago. Compassion changing to wanting. I wouldn't dare call it desire. I couldn't afford to go down that path.

So what path did I think I was treading then—and I don't mean the one that we were strolling on! Getting to know her? Making her feel at ease with me so I could assess how able she would be to deal with the real reason for my presence here? Aye, a good way to go about earning her trust, that would be, if I gave in to what I was wanting to do, which was to put my arms around her and kiss her. So I wouldn't give in to my impulses, tempted as I was—and I was very, very tempted, which in itself was very unusual. Boundaries are boundaries between my work and my private life, and I'd never before had any problem sticking to them. Likely I was imagining the feeling was mutual. If I could have convinced myself of that, the battle would have been won.

We left the straggling outskirts of the village behind at the bend in the river where the walls of the huge cemetery could be seen on one bank.

'What is that building?' Marianne—Mrs Crawford!—pointed up at the imposing classical edifice on the hill looking down at the village.

'It's the Dean Orphanage.' She had stopped walking, and was gazing fixedly at the building. It occurred to me, a bit too late, that it might remind her of the place she'd escaped from. I couldn't see much resemblance in style, but the fact that it was a large institution with extensive grounds could well be enough to trigger unpleasant memories. 'Maybe we should turn back,' I said.

But she stood her ground. 'It must hold a great number of children. So many little ones without any family.'

'Or alternatively, with family who have not the means to take care of them.'

'Not orphans, but it is what they will be called, just the same.' She gave a deep shiver, then turned her back on the building. 'It's not a happy place. Will we take a walk in the cemetery? At least there, the inmates are at peace.'

It's not a happy place.

I didn't want to spoil the mood, but I wasn't here for my own benefit. It struck me that this was as good an opportunity as any to sound her out about what she knew— or didn't know—of her own background. I was already worried about her. The way she disappeared into herself every now and then, like a light was switched off inside her. The way she snapped sometimes, if I pushed her. Not just touchy, defensive. You could almost see the drawbridge being pulled up. I needed to tread carefully, but I also needed to make progress.

'What is it?' She stopped, and I realised I'd been trailing behind her. 'You were miles away.'

'"It's not a happy place", you said, as if you knew what you were talking about. I was wondering why—were you an orphan?'

I thought she might palm me off, but she surprised me. 'I never knew my father, nor my mother either, which I suppose does make me an orphan, though I've never thought of myself as such and I was not raised in an orphanage.'

We had entered the cemetery through the main gates, but of one accord had immediately veered away from the wide paths to the perimeter. There was a bench against the wall, and we sat down. 'What happened to your parents?' I asked, hoping to fill in one of the many gaps regarding what I knew about her, and more importantly what she knew about herself. I was, I'll admit, also genuinely curious on my own behalf.

'I don't know. I was raised by a couple who had no children of their own. I was well cared for, given a reasonable education, but they did not care very much for me. I knew from an early age, that I was not their child, that they were being paid to look after me. And, yes,' she said, her gaze meeting mine, 'I was curious as to who was paying them.'

I hadn't voiced the question in my head, but it was an obvious one. Her eyes were more green than hazel today. Her hands were clasped in her lap. Her skirts were brushing my leg. We were not touching at all, but I felt as if we were, bodies and minds. I know, it's a ridiculous thought, but it's what I felt. 'That must have been painful though, growing up knowing you were—I mean, it sounds like they were more distant than they had to be.'

'They were kind enough, but I was not their child. At least I was not simply dumped in a place like that.' She pointed in the direction of the orphanage. 'Why should I care, if my family—whoever they were—did not?'

One thing I'd always been certain of in my own life, was that my parents loved me, and that I was very much wanted. If I'd been given away as she had—I simply couldn't imagine how I'd feel. Had Lord Westville, her father, cared? Was that a question she was going to ask when the truth came out? If she did, there was no answer. 'So what about the money then?' I asked, returning to surer ground. 'Did you ask them where the money for your keep came from?'

'A benefactor, that is all they would tell me. He wished to remain anonymous. I assumed it was a man. I assumed it must be my father, though I have no basis for that, it could have been his family, or even my mother's family. I assumed, when I was old enough to make such assumptions, that I must be the result of a—a misalliance, as they say.' Her mouth curled. 'That my parents were not married and that I was not wanted. Anyway, I never depended upon the money. I made my own living.'

'Looking after children?'

'Yes. I helped the school mistress in the local school from when I was about sixteen.'

'So your love of children goes back to then?'

'It does. I love to teach.' She gave me one of her tight little smiles. 'Governesses, nurses, nannies, are supposed to say that, but not so very many of them mean it. There are so few so-called respectable jobs open to women, and men assume that we are born with a maternal instinct. Many of them assume that it is our only talent, our only fate, to be a mother, or failing that, to care for someone else's children.

'But you're quite wrong,' she continued, 'if you're thinking I resent being forced to earn my living as I do. It is the other women I feel for, those who believe they have no choice since expectations of women are so ridiculously low. *That* I resent. For myself, from an early age I have enjoyed teaching little ones.'

'But you have opted to work for private families rather than in a school since you came to Edinburgh.'

'No, since before that. The school mistress was a lovely woman with the patience of a saint called Miss Lomond. It was she who suggested that I become a governess rather than a teacher. I was too young, you see, to be given any more responsibility, and the pay for such a junior position, for a woman, was not enough to support me. I had my stipend, but Miss Lomond pointed out that since I had no idea where it came from I would be foolish to rely on it.'

'That was very far-sighted of her.'

'Far more than I realised at the time.' Her smile faded, but she gave herself a wee shake. 'Sadly, like many middle-aged women from a respectable background with no desire to find a husband, Miss Lomond spoke from experience. Like me, she had had an allowance—from her brother, I believe. When he married, he decided that he could not afford to continue to support her as well as his family. I owe her a great deal.'

'Are you still in touch?' It was unlikely, but one thing I'd always wondered was why no one had made any attempt to have her released or even to visit her in the institution.

'She died ten years ago, of typhus. Now, Mr Sutherland, I've told you a great deal more than you are entitled to know, so I would appreciate it if you ceased to interrogate me as if I was one of your suspects.'

She jumped to her feet and set off at a pace along the path. I hurried after her, noting that at least she was not headed for the exit gate. That allowance of hers had been used to pay her keep in those places where the man who administered it had had her locked up. Even if she'd wanted to claim it after her escape she couldn't have, without giving away her whereabouts.

Did she know who it was that was responsible for her incarceration? It was one of the many things I still didn't know about Marianne Little. There were so many gaps, and I wasn't overly sure which ones mattered. I'd telegraphed my employer to let him know I'd found his relative, but I hadn't heard back from him yet.

I caught up with Marianne—I simply couldn't think of her as Mrs Crawford now. 'It is my turn to interrogate you,' she said. 'Tell me why you became a policeman—aside, I mean, from your enthusiasm for asking questions.'

'Oh, that's simple, I followed in my father's footsteps.'

'Really?' She stopped beside a massive tombstone with

a weeping marble cherub perched on top of it. 'But I am sure you told me he was from the Highlands?'

'They were short of numbers to police Glasgow, back in the day. He was a Highlander from the Isle of Harris, my da—*m'aither*. He was twenty-one when he came to Glasgow, and Gaelic was his native language. He was well built, like myself, and he was ambitious, and like I said, the authorities were desperate as the streets were getting out of control. He worked bloody—he worked hard. He was not long without English, he was clever, and he was good at his job, but he was always a teuchter, a Highlander who had come to Glasgow to put boots on his feet. He never made it past sergeant in twenty-odd years' service.'

'And yet you followed him into the police force?'

'It was all I ever wanted to do. I joined the Edinburgh force, though. A different city, and decades on from my da's time. I had it easier than him, but whenever I stepped out of line, I had the fact that I was a Weegie thrown in my face.'

'And did you step out of line often?'

'I was always on the side of justice.'

She laughed drìly at that. 'As defined by you, and not the law?'

'That's one way of looking at it. It's a question of—of interpretation. I didn't think it was our job to lock up the people that the good citizens of Edinburgh would prefer to be invisible. Is a person struggling to make ends meet a vagrant? Is a drunk man necessarily a criminal? Just because a young woman's out on the streets after dark, does that make her a prostitute? Don't get the idea that I was the only officer who thought that way, we chose our battles, and there were a lot of grey areas between the right and the wrong side of the law.'

'I'm willing to bet you were a minority, however. Few people look beyond what they have been taught to see.'

She spoke bleakly. It took me a moment to understand the connection she must have made, with the upholders of law on the streets, and the upholders of law in that damned institution. She'd been a school teacher and a governess, and then she'd been labelled something else entirely. Now she was a governess again, and just as she was starting to recover from her years of incarceration and settle into that life, she was going to discover that she was another person altogether. It made my mind whirl, just thinking about it all, and I'd known the tale for a good few weeks now. I thanked the stars that the Marquess had as good as gagged me. If I'd lumbered her with everything I knew about her, she'd have collapsed under the weight of it.

'You're miles away,' Marianne—Mrs Crawford!—said, dragging me from my thoughts. Again.

'I was thinking about what you said.' Not exactly a lie, that. 'About people making assumptions, not looking beyond what they're expecting to see. It's easy to make fun of a constable on the beat as a big lump of brawn with no brain, focused on finding a drink when there's nowhere else open, and spending his nights courting chambermaids, but it's a hard and difficult job. You have to be as tough as the men you're policing.'

'You mean you were violent?' she asked me, her tone indicating disbelief that I found reassuring rather than insulting.

'I mean we faced violence. "Fists, feet and teeth" is what we were told to look out for. The teeth belonging to dogs, mostly but not always. I was forced to defend myself on occasion,' I added, because I felt the need to be entirely honest with her to make up for not being completely open, 'but I swear I never did any more than that.'

She gave me one of her looks, making me feel she was picking through my thoughts for the truth. I held her gaze, and it turned out to be the right thing to do, for after a moment she nodded, satisfied, and I felt that I'd passed a test. It made me wonder though, what she knew herself of physical violence. I couldn't bear the idea of it, as if being locked up hadn't been enough of a trial.

I wished then, fervently, that she'd trust me, that she'd let me know her, I mean really know her, and the strength of that rocked me, for it was way beyond my remit. I wanted it for myself, not for the work I was here to do. I started walking again, to give myself a bit of time. Once again, it was she who broke the silence.

'You loved your work, despite the danger,' she said.

Another statement, not a question, and she was in the right of it. 'I loved putting things right,' I admitted. 'I still do. I never saw the point in going after those who were forced on to the wrong side of the law to survive. It was the ones who deliberately chose to make a living that way I was interested in. Turns out I had a nose for sniffing those sorts of characters out, I had the right combination of brain and brawn. I didn't use violence, I told you that, but they had to know I could if I had to. As to brain—it's mostly about knowing who to look for, where to look, as well as trusting your instincts.'

'And you were good at it?'

'Good enough to make a name for myself.'

'Success made you unpopular,' she said.

Yet another statement, I noted. She was good at this, playing me at my own game. 'There are always some who resent the success of others. I've never been the type to so-cialise with colleagues, so that didn't bother me.'

'What then?' she asked, her eyes intent on my face.

I could have pretended not to understand her, or brushed her off, but I didn't want to, even though I'd never talked about what I felt about any of it before. Not even when I was pushed to. 'My cases were picked up in the press, the sen-sationalist ones at first, that report trials with lots of lurid detail. For some reason, they cottoned on to the fact that my name came up a few times, and they made something of that.'

'You were famous!'

I swore vehemently, fortunately in the Gaelic. 'I got a public reputation that I'd rather not have had, and that wasn't fair either, for there were many good men solving crimes in the city. I could have well done without it. All I wanted to do was get on with the job I loved.'

'So what went wrong?'

'The public, the press, the great and the good like it when you catch criminals, provided they come from a criminal class. They don't like it when you try to tell them that their friends and neighbours might be criminals too—and that's what I found when I started asking questions. However what's done is done and there's nothing I can do about it.'

I could feel her watching me. It made me uncomfortable. Even though she couldn't possibly read my actual thoughts, she was uncommonly good at sensing my feelings. 'I don't think you are capable of letting it go,' she said slowly.

I sighed, for it was dawning on me that she was right. 'It's not what I'm here for.'

'No, you have another case now that you can't talk about.'

We'd talked about it plenty, though she didn't know it,

and she'd given me a great deal to think about. 'Not yet,' I said, hedging.

'How long do you think it will keep you here in the city?'

'It can't take too much longer.' We had stopped walking again, though I hadn't noticed. We'd come almost full circle round the perimeter of the main burial grounds. I could see the gates in the distance. How much longer? Was it fair of me to keep what I knew to myself, even though that was what I'd been instructed to do?

I genuinely felt as if I was on the horns of a dilemma. On the one hand, she had a right to know. On the other, to know what, while the question of her inheritance was yet to be decided? On the one hand, she had a family and a name. On the other was what the world would make of it all. If all that was doing my head in, what was it going to do to her?

And in the meantime, there was the fact that I didn't want to think about it any more, not for now. The difficulty was, when I looked into those eyes of hers, and I stood close enough to smell the soap she used, but not nearly as close as I wanted to be, I wanted time to go to hell, and the job I was here to do, along with it. I wanted something more than the life I had, working, eating sleeping, happy to be a lone wolf. Looking at her, what I felt was terribly lonely.

It threw me. I didn't know what to do or to say, so I just stood there looking at her, with doubtless half at least of what I was longing for written on my face. And she just stood there too, looking back at me.

A clock began to chime. It must have come from the orphanage. We both started. 'We'd better get back,' I said.

'I had better go home,' she said at the same time.

And we left it at that, though neither of us wanted to. I knew that for certain.

Chapter Ten

Marianne

Edinburgh—
Wednesday 8th August 1877

The day started as it always did, with the horrible rude awakening, the cold sweats, clammy skin, the terror so all-consuming that I dare not open my eyes. Then the slow creeping in of reality. The Grassmarket view. Flora. Dressing. Breakfasting. As I stood just inside the close, preparing to take my first steps outside, I looked for him standing in the doorway of the coffee shop with his mug in his hand. Rory Sutherland beginning his day by looking out for me to begin mine.

I did not wave or nod or go over to talk to him, but if he had not been there I would have been disappointed. He made me feel not alone. Wanted? Of course I was valued by the mothers who employed me and by the children I cared for, but this was different. He wanted me for myself, not for what I could give him. That sounds strange, but it's what I sensed from him. What I felt for him.

I had dreamt of Rory Sutherland. Deep in the night before my usual nightmares took over, I had dreamt of him. Of us. I dreamt of the heat of his flesh, slick with sweat, merging with mine. His mouth. His tongue. His hands. I dreamt of the shuddering, clenching, thrill of him sliding inside me. I dreamt of my fevered response, so different from my daytime self, urging him on, urging myself on. I dreamt of the confidence of his touch and of mine. Knowing that what we did was what the other wanted. The certainty of it. And the pure, utter delight of letting go.

A sharp cry, a hand on my arm yanked me out of my daydream and back to the side of the road and saved me from walking straight into the path of a horse-drawn tram on Princes Street. I cried out, pushing the hand away, horrified at my own lapse. My saviour was a man, a perfectly harmless complete stranger who was more frightened by my narrow escape than I was. Muttering a rudimentary apology and my thanks, I hurried across the thoroughfare, thrown that I had so easily abandoned my customary caution. Was it really so necessary after all this time? Perhaps not, but I looked over my shoulder again before continuing, slowing to my usual measured stride.

My thoughts drifted back to last night. It was a dream, wish fulfilment, the product of my own suppressed desire, nothing more. Yet it had been so intimate, so intensely felt. I don't have visions, though that was how my insights have been described by some. I see what others don't, though they could if they would try harder. I see through lies and I understand acute emotions.

On occasion this led to something like a dream unfolding in my head, as if my mind was putting it all together into a story for me. The pictures were not always accurate. Sometimes they were what might happen, possibilities rather than certainties. That's what made me susceptible to being branded a liar, when they were used as evidence against me. All I ever wanted was to help people make better choices. If only I had been as perceptive when it came to myself, but I'd had no inkling, not until it was too late. I thought myself infallible. How wrong I was proven to be.

But last night was simply a dream, nothing more. A dream that had awoken a yearning, craving, longing, to have what I had dreamt happen for real. Or rather, it was Rory Sutherland who had awoken that feeling, and now it wouldn't go away. I tried to banish him from my thoughts, tried to calm my mind and cool my body, but had only part succeeded by the time I arrived at Queen Street. My reception at the front door, however, abruptly completed the task.

'Mrs Crawford! Thank heavens.' Mrs Oliphant herself beckoned me from the top of the stairs as soon as I set foot in the marble-tiled reception hall. I followed her into the main bedchamber, where she closed the door behind us and sank down on a *chaise longue*. 'I fear the baby is coming early.'

I untied my cloak and laid it on the bed. 'Have you sent for the midwife?'

'Not yet.' She laid her hand on her swollen abdomen, wincing. 'I wanted to be prepared. Oh, Mrs Crawford, do you think it's a boy? My husband will be so disappointed if it is another girl, when we already have three daughters and only one son.'

My heart sank at her plaintive tone. I could not know whether the baby was a girl or a boy, but I did know that if the child was female, this was not news my employer wished to hear. I sat down on the *chaise longue* beside her. 'You will know soon enough. Boy or girl, you should be preparing yourself for its entry into the world, not fretting about how your husband will receive the child. I will have one of the footmen send for the midwife.'

'Yes, yes, please do so.' Mrs Oliphant, to my relief, regained some control over herself. 'Do you think all will be well?'

'You have no cause to imagine otherwise.' I could not alter the outcome here, and my telling her anything at all would not help to prepare her for whatever nature had in store for her. 'You have had four perfectly healthy births, Mrs Oliphant.'

'I know, but I am forty next month, and this may be my last chance to give my husband the second son he desires so much. But you are right, of course.' She broke off as the pain swept over her, squeezing my hand tightly until it passed. 'You're right,' she said weakly. 'I will know one way or another in a few hours. If you will be so good as to summon my maid, Mrs Crawford.'

'And the children? The plan is for your sister is to take them temporarily, isn't that correct?'

'Yes, but she's not expecting them for at least another two weeks, when you were to take two weeks to yourself. What shall I do?'

'Leave it with me. I will send a telegram.' I gently pushed her back down on the *chaise longue.* Sweat had broken out on her pale brow. Her pains were coming worryingly fast. I rang the bell for her maid and hurried downstairs, calling for one of the footmen.

It felt like a very long day, though I finished early once I had seen the children off with their aunt. All four of them were excited to be going to Portobello and the seaside, heedless of the reason for their unexpected holiday. Mrs Oliphant, like all of the well-to-do mothers who employed me, had made every effort to disguise her condition, it being thought vulgar to appear pregnant, and indecent to talk of the origins of their progeny. The Oliphant children would doubtless be informed, when they returned from the seaside, that a little sister or brother had been delivered by the stork or found under a gooseberry bush.

The weather had held fair all week. It was a pleasant late afternoon when I walked home, and I decided to enjoy a moment in the sunshine, taking a seat in Princes Street Gardens. I don't allow myself to remember the past, for it was too painful, but the encounter with poor Mrs Oliphant had upset me. It shouldn't have, I knew better than anyone that men wield the power in this world and dictate what we should feel and when. I had bowed to convention, once upon a time, willingly. I persuaded myself that I wanted what he wanted. He wanted it so very ardently, or so I believed, and I had never felt wanted before, for myself alone. I trusted him, and I trusted what I sensed from him. Desire. Need. I detected no sense of danger, no sense of his treachery until it was too late. Far, far too late.

Chapter Eleven

Marianne

Five years previously

I had been locked up for nearly three years, initially in a small asylum in York from which I tried to escape, after which I was transferred to this enormous institution in the Scottish Borders. I had attempted to escape from here too, and lost the few liberties I had as a result. Of late, I had changed my tactics, trying to reconcile myself to the version of myself they presented to me. I tried to persuade myself that I was the person they claimed I was, in order to be able to set out on the journey they wished me to take, towards recovery. But buried deep inside me was a small, resistant core. My mind was not unhinged. I was not insane.

The doctor who had been newly assigned to my case was also new to the post of Physician Superintendent to the asylum. He was younger than those who had analysed, examined and pontificated about me in the past, one of those eager men whose good looks and good birth have instilled in them a confidence in their own abilities and charm that was often misplaced.

He set about measuring my head with his metal callipers without any preliminaries, contorting my neck and shoulders to ease his endeavours as if I were a life-sized doll stuffed with straw. When I protested, he seemed taken aback to hear me speak, and when I asked him to explain what on earth he was doing, he looked even more surprised. His ego and his enthusiasm led him to do as I bid him, however. He was without guile, but weighted with prejudice.

'The science of phrenology allows us to understand the workings of the mind,' he said pompously. 'From my readings of your skull, it is clear to me that you are not naturally inclined to evil. Though your nature is undoubtedly degenerate, it is not vicious. Rather, it is the sensual side of your brain which dominates and has contributed to your moral decline.'

This was so different from any past explanations I had been given, that I struggled to comprehend what he was saying. 'What has what you refer to as the sensual side of my brain got to do with my being locked up?' I asked baldly.

'Everything! I admit my approach is not conventional, or not yet, at least,' the doctor said, looking pleased to be able to expound. 'Let us consider your case history, Miss—er, Miss Little. You claimed to have visions of the future.' He drew the thick folder that documented my history in that place towards him, and flicked back through the pages. 'If we disregard the more trivial allegations, it came down to three main incidents. There was the woman you claim to have "saved" from marrying a bigamist.'

'He *was* a bigamist!'

'He always denied that, and the fact is, he did not marry the woman you claim to have saved.'

'He would have done, had I not intervened.'

'Then there was the more disturbing case of the illegitimate child…'

I ceased to listen as he droned on. I had tried countless times since my committal to make them understand what really happened in each instance, but the 'truth' that had been documented and used as evidence against me, the truth as presented by the man who betrayed me, his version of the truth always prevailed. My dossier proclaimed that I believed I could prophesy, and that I had used my prophesies vindictively. I could do no such thing.

The natural powers of intuition and deduction that I had had since I was a child had been turned into lunacy. My pitiful attempts to redress the balance of power, to arm vulnerable women with facts, to allow them to make better choices, had been translated as the vicious rantings of a madwoman. It would have been pointless to waste my breath attempting to defend myself again, and so I remained silent, staring at a point over the top of the doctor's head.

He was too absorbed in expounding his theory to notice my lack of response, or more likely he didn't care. 'I see from my predecessor's notes that you have lately been less resistant to the notion that these visions of yours were a figment of your imagination. That is proof that the regime here has tempered your mind somewhat,' the doctor said. He stroked his callipers as he spoke, as if they were a much-loved pet. The change in his tone alerted me. I started to listen again.

'The problem we have, however, is getting to the *root cause,*' he continued. 'Until we know that, we cannot risk releasing you, lest you lapse into believing you can foretell again, do you understand me?'

I prayed that I did not, but my stomach began to churn

in fear. I had assumed that if I continued with my charade of compliance and acceptance, I would eventually be deemed cured and then released, but this man appeared to be redrawing the rules, setting up new obstacles. I was so tired, so deeply humiliated, I was not sure I had the will to fight on.

'Do not despair.' The doctor misread my expression, putting aside his callipers to pat my hand. 'I believe, Miss Little, that I do understand the root cause, and shall be lauded when I am proved right. My analysis of your lunacy has shown to me that at the heart of these visions you claim to have, is a challenge to the sanctity of marriage.'

At the heart of these insights of mine was a desire for justice. The women I had helped, or tried to help, were being used, abused, lied to, robbed of their wealth, or in one case a child. 'I have no idea what you are talking about,' I said.

'Let me put it in simple terms. Your skull, Miss Little, tells me you have an overly developed sensual nature. This is something which has been overlooked. Though the evidence is there, it was misinterpreted.'

'What do you mean? What evidence?'

'The prophesy you made, that the man you claimed to have been your betrothed, would—let me see, yes, I have it here, "be the death of you".'

Francis. A wave of nausea made me feel faint. I pinched my nails into the tender flesh of my wrist. Pay attention!

'Now clearly, it was no prophesy, unless you are a ghost.' The doctor laughed at his own feeble joke. 'Until now, the main focus of your treatment has been to show you that these prophesies of yours were a figment of your imagination, but it is the content that interests me.

'You elected upon this unfortunate man as the answer to your dreams. You persuaded yourself that the feelings generated by your fevered imagination and overheated brain were reciprocated. The sensual nature which I have detected with my callipers, took hold of you. You could have what you had always wanted, a husband, a child. Then, when he rejected you, when he tried, in the most gentlemanly way, to refute your claim on him, your madness persuaded you that he was trying to kill you. Do you see?'

'I never thought he would murder me. That's not what I said.' Francis had told me he loved me. I thought I loved him. I was convinced he wanted me, convinced of his desire for me, else I would never have given myself so willingly. In the aftermath, for those fleeting few moments, he let his guard down and I sensed his true feelings. If I married him, I knew he would be the death of me. Not literally, but spiritually. As his wife, my life would be lost.

I had tried to explain this countless times. Two years in this hellish place had taught me to keep my mouth shut, for my words were invariably turned against me, but this was too much. 'Francis wanted to marry me,' I said, which was one fact I had never doubted. Not even now. 'I didn't make that up. I wasn't deluded. He was desperate to marry me, in fact. He was devastated when I told him I wouldn't marry him.'

Also true, and one of the things I had never understood. I had asked myself over and over, why had he turned on me, why had he betrayed me, why he had engineered my incarceration and why he paid to keep me locked up? What was his motive? Was it humiliation? Vindictiveness? How could his passion for marrying me have turned to this?

'It was you who were devastated, Miss Little,' the doctor reprimanded me. 'The feelings you attribute to him were your own.' He spoke in the condescending tone of a man speaking to a child. They all used that tone, doctors, orderlies, nurses, but on that occasion it grated almost beyond enduring. 'You were, let me see, almost twenty-six and already past your prime child-bearing years.'

'My what?' My nausea had metamorphosed into a burning anger, but I tried desperately to control it. 'What has my age to do with anything?'

'Hysteria,' the doctor said with a smug smile. 'The result of an empty womb. All of those visions of yours are connected in some way to the institution of marriage. An institution you, a confirmed spinster, despaired of joining. It is a pity,' he continued, looking not at me but at his own notebook, 'for I believe a child may have been the saving of you, a natural release, as it were. Alas, without that outlet your passion turned poisonous. You set out to ruin the happy marriages of others with your so-called prophesies, and when you tired of that, you turned your perverted desires on an entirely innocent man.'

'Innocent! Francis wanted to marry me!' Leaping to my feet, I could no longer contain myself. 'I refused him, and as a result of that refusal, he had me locked up.'

The doctor shook his head and tutted. 'Hysteria and delusion. We have our work cut out, I fear.'

'I am not hysterical. I am not delusional.' My voice rose with each exclamation, but I couldn't stop myself. 'He would have been the death of me. I am dying now, in this place.'

'That is quite enough, Miss Little. Listen to yourself. Have you any idea how ridiculous you sound, claiming that a perfectly respectable man wanted to kill you?'

'Why don't you listen! I didn't say he wanted to kill me, I said he would be the death of me.'

'And here you are, alive and large as life.'

'I am barely alive, thanks to him. Because I didn't marry him,' I said, catching my breath, sounding sullen to my own ears. A child sticking to a lie. But it wasn't a lie. When I refused him, he was beside himself. I was terrified and utterly taken aback by his white-faced fury. That was when my conviction took hold. When he left without laying a hand on me, I collapsed, and did not move for hours.

When I awoke and found myself alone, I thought him truly gone, I thought I had saved myself, but when he returned and instigated my committal, I realised my mistake. I had trusted him completely. I had confided in him, told him what no one else knew of my attempts to help people, of my ability to read them. And he used all of it against me.

The doctor, utterly indifferent to the anguish he had stirred up, was putting his callipers away in a leather case. 'Now, if you will control yourself, I will inform you of my treatment plan. Your case is more advanced than I had thought, but I am still of the opinion that my diagnosis is correct. I shall make my reputation if I can cure you.'

I was shaking, tears streaming down my face, but I forced myself to listen to his plans for me, all the time my mind racing. I would not waste any more time wondering why Francis had taken such a vicious revenge on me. What was clear to me now was that I had been right in a very different sense from what I'd imagined. I thought I had saved myself by refusing to marry him, but I was wrong. If I did not escape this place I would die none the less, either from the treatments or of despair. I would not let it come true. It was a warning, and I would heed it.

'Hysteria,' the doctor droned on. 'Thinning of the blood.

A cooling diet. Isolation to inure you to your cooled passions and empty womb. I do not believe it will come to surgery.'

'Surgery!'

'A most radical solution, and a last resort, for though it will definitely cure you, you may not survive. Hydrotherapy however, ice baths—yes, they might be of great value. Now, you have taken up a great deal more of my time than I expected, but I am confident that I have made progress. In time, a few years perhaps, when we are sure you are past the age where your womb is functional, then your release can certainly be considered. For myself, I have high hopes that my innovative work on you will assist in resolving many similar cases.' He smiled as if I should find that some sort of comfort.

'I shouldn't be here. You have no right to hold me. I demand you release me. I demand…'

He opened the door and the orderly who had been waiting outside took my arm. 'She may require a sedative tonight,' the doctor told him, though I was too faint with horror to require anything but to be supported back to my cell and left alone.

Days passed, and I continued to act out the torpor I was no longer feeling. I appeared to the staff languid, lethargic, co-operative, but inside, a fire was burning. I was not mad, therefore I could not be cured. What's more, I didn't want to be cured. I would not be the *case* that made my new doctor's reputation. I was determined that no matter how long it took me, I would escape the institution and the treatments forced upon me and I would disappear for ever from the clutches of the man who had had me locked up. All I needed was the opportunity.

Chapter Twelve

Rory

The weather had returned to its usual miserable version of a Scottish summer, with a mizzle of rain drifting down. Every now and then the clouds would thin enough for the sun to make an effort to shine, long enough to make the cobblestones steam, and get your hopes up that it might win through, before the rain closed in again. I drank my coffee and pondered my next steps regarding the issue of Marianne—I'd given up completely trying to call her Mrs Crawford.

Sunday had unsettled me. I'm used to being on my own. I *prefer* my own company to anyone else's. Not on Sunday though. I hadn't wanted the day to end. And the things I'd told her, ordinary things about myself, but it hadn't only been facts. I'd talked of my feelings, and I'd told her a lot more than I'd meant to. Nothing that mattered, save that it did, because I never talked like that. It was one of the accusations that Moira was forever levelling at me—that I kept my own counsel on everything.

Moira! Now where had that come from? More than likely she still lived here in the city, which was something that ought to have occurred to me before now. I hoped she was married with a family, for it's what she had wanted. I hoped she was happy, to make up for the misery I'd caused her. I hadn't thought about her in years, which proved she was in the right of it when she ended things between us. Talking to Marianne had raked up a whole raft of memories I had no wish to be lumbered with. Maybe it was unfair of me to blame Marianne. Perhaps it was this city.

On Sunday, I'd put the fact that I shouldn't be here to the back of my mind, which was easy enough to do, far too easy, when I was with her. On Monday, I decided to take myself off to Portobello, think things over, untangle what was important for the case, and what mattered only to me. Even though the seaside had not the bustle of the weekend, there were plenty of women and their weans and their nannies or governesses or nurses or whatever the devil they were. The families who decamp out of the city to their big summer houses during the week, for the men must still go about their important business in the town. Would Marianne be part of the entourage if her current employer headed for the seaside? I still knew so little of her present life. Did that matter? To me it did.

Watching the waves creep up over the broad, damp yellow sand on Portobello beach, I'd let myself think about Marianne in exactly the way I'd told myself I wouldn't. I wanted her. Not in that way—or not only in that way! I wanted to get close to her. I wanted something I'd never wished for from a woman before. A friend? No, not that. A companion? That sounded far too staid and platonic. I didn't want platonic, even though that's all I could have.

I didn't know what I wanted, that's the truth, and that unsettled me all the more.

It was the waiting that was doing my head in, I decided. I wasn't used to waiting to be told what to do. On Tuesday I took another walk up the Crags, with the city spread out beneath me from the top, New Town, Old Town, all the way to Portobello where I'd been yesterday, and over to the other side of the Forth, and the East Neuk of Fife. Standing on the edge of one of the cliffs, I could trace the location of the many crimes I'd solved, including the ones that had made my name.

The view was like a map of my career as a policeman, the station, my old digs, the narrow, meandering streets of the Old Town where poverty and crime lived cheek by jowl, the wide boundary that was Princes Street and the gardens, the organised grid of the New Town, where I'd been employed privately when I was off duty to solve the crimes that never made it to the police.

It was a clear day, so I could see the sprawl of the docks at Leith where I'd found the body that put an end to my career here. All the old bile came flooding back before I could stop it. I'd been kidding myself, thinking I'd put it behind me. I'd been kidding myself, thinking I'd got over the shame of it, the sheer bloody pain of being exiled from the city I loved, from the work I'd loved and done so well. Too well for some.

It was the injustice of it that really stuck in my craw, when I let myself start thinking about it again. A dead woman whose murder was not even acknowledged, dead because she was somehow embroiled in something that the great and the good wanted kept hidden. No, I wasn't over it. I hadn't put it behind me, even though I knew that

I was teetering on the brink of ending up as she had, just for being here.

I'd walked away once. I could walk away again, I told myself. I was here for another case, and I didn't have the time to dally on resolving that old one. Not only was I risking my neck being here in Edinburgh, I was being paid good money to get the Marquess's case done and dusted. My reputation—the one I'd made for myself in the last seven years, with sheer hard graft—depended on my doing what I'd been employed to do.

And there was the rub. I was being employed to wait while Lord Westville tried to sort out the legal tangle, which left me too much time on my hands. Time to think about the old case. Time to think about Marianne. Time I could be using doing what I was most inclined to do, which was get to know her. Which was why I had tried to stay away from her.

Though I couldn't stay away from her entirely. I kept an eye out for her. Wednesday morning found me drinking coffee in a tavern in the Grassmarket. The woman Marianne called Flora came in and ordered her usual breakfast of bread, cheese and ale. She was a pretty lass, though she wouldn't be for much longer. Work such as she did would take its toll, one way or another. What chance had she to make a better life for herself? It had always been a sticking point with me back in the day, the way women like her were treated, but I'd never thought too seriously about what else they could do to survive. I'd never thought myself fortunate, simply because I'd been born a man and not a woman.

'There are so few so-called respectable jobs open to women.'

Marianne's words stuck with me, calling me out as thoughtless. For women like young Flora over there, falling asleep over her breakfast, there was plenty of work of the menial kind, but very little that would make any sort of decent living. If matters did get resolved, and Marianne had her inheritance, the last thing she'd do with it was set herself up in the lap of luxury. She was the daughter of a marquess, but she wouldn't play the lady, I was willing to bet. She'd go her own road. I'd like to see that.

That brought me up short again. It was none of my business what she did. I had no business in being interested in her. More than interested! I finished up my coffee and was on the brink of leaving, thinking that I'd catch her up as she walked to work, when *he* walked into the tavern.

I swore under my breath, for I recognised him straight away. He stood there in the doorway, surveying the room as if he owned it, which for all I knew he might well, by now. Judging by his clothes, Billy Sinclair had obviously gone up in the world since I last encountered him at the High Court, where he'd been in the public gallery for the trial of the docker who ran a very successful gang of thieves.

I'd suspected at the time that Billy was the brains behind them, and his appearance on the day confirmed it for me. There hadn't been time to follow up on that one though. Only a week later, I'd been giving my marching orders.

Billy sauntered over, stopping at Flora's table to drop a coin on to it—a coin that looked to me like silver. With a sinking feeling, I realised I'd been caught out. Billy, pulling up a chair to sit down beside me, nodded in confirmation. 'Katy over there has her head screwed on,' he said. 'She's planning her retirement from her current profession, if you know what I mean, and I'm her pension.'

The proprietor appeared with a cup of coffee and a bottle

of whisky. 'Just a splash,' Billy said, waiting for the man to return to his counter before addressing me. 'Mr Sutherland. I can't tell you how sorry I am to see you here.'

'Billy.' I smiled tightly, my mind racing. 'You're looking well.'

'I'm doing well enough,' he said. 'It's Mr Sinclair these days, but you can call me William.'

'What is it you want from me, William?'

'Straight to the point. I always respected you for that, Mr Sutherland.' He took another sip of his coffee laced with whisky. 'I'm here to give you a friendly warning. I don't know what it was you really did to get yourself in the bad books. I never believed what they put in the papers about you. Taking bribes!' He rolled his eyes. 'As if.'

'Thank you for the vote of confidence.'

He grinned. He had come up in the world, but he'd lost a few more teeth in the process. '*I* know you were set up. I don't know *who* was behind it, though I could take a good guess. Thing is, Mr Sutherland, seven years isn't long enough to make this city safe for you. You shouldn't be here.'

'I don't need you to tell me that, William.'

He laughed shortly. 'That's what I thought to myself when I was told you were back. He's too smart for that, I thought to myself. So he must have a good reason.'

'Is that what you're here to find out? Or are you here to find out for someone else?'

He bristled. 'I don't take orders from anyone these days. I came here out of the goodness of my heart, to give you a friendly warning.'

'It's news to me that you have a heart. Is that something else you've got your hands on while I've been away?'

'Very funny. I'm being serious. You rattled cages you shouldn't have rattled. They framed you, I know that, they dragged your name through the mud, but they left you with your heart beating. See, I happen to know that unlike me, you do have a heart. I reckon you'd like to keep it beating, too.'

'I appreciate that, William, and believe me, I share the same goal, but I've business here to conclude.'

He glowered. 'I hope you're not going to go about lifting up any old stones. Unfinished business, so to speak, especially if it involves me. Things here are ticking along nicely, since you left. We all keep our noses out of other people's business, and we all know when to keep our mouths shut. Something you never did learn, did you?'

'What was it you just said about keeping your nose out?'

He held his hands up as if in surrender, but his face hardened. 'Have it your own way, but don't say I didn't warn you. I'll give you this for nothing, because you and I go back a long way, and I owe you a few. As far as I know, I'm the only one who knows you're here. How long that will last I can't say, but no one will hear it from me. I'd be a bit less regular in your habits though, if you get my drift.' Billy scraped his chair back and got to his feet. 'Good luck to you, Mr Sutherland. I hope you don't need it.'

I paid for my coffee and hurried to the doorway, but there was no sign of him in the bustle of the Grassmarket. No one tells me what to do, I thought to myself, while at the same time thinking, I'd be an eejit to ignore what he'd said.

Back at my digs, there was a telegram from Lord Westville informing me to await further instructions. Fortunately the instructions in the form of an express letter had also arrived. Now that he knew his cousin was alive and unwed, the Marquess was determined to secure her inheritance. The process was complex, but would be complete within the next two weeks. He was, he assured me, as determined as I to bring Eliot to account, and was taking pains to ensure the man was fully occupied with estate matters, and under the impression that he was valued. In the meantime, I was to ensure his cousin came to no harm.

Chapter Thirteen

Marianne

Edinburgh—
Wednesday 8th August 1877

Those vile memories of the asylum had caught me unawares as I sat in Princes Street Gardens earlier that day. Usually I never allow them to creep up on me in the daylight. Was there a reason for that particular memory to have forced itself upon me? A reminder to trust no one? Or more specifically, not to trust Rory?

Rory was not Francis, the comparison was repellent, but I forced myself to compare them all the same. I had to, for the sake—literally—of my own sanity. Francis was the first and only man I had ever trusted, and that had proved a catastrophic decision. My judgement, my intuition, the tried-and-tested ability that I had relied upon my whole life had failed me.

I had trusted him with my heart and my body. I was on the brink of trusting him with the rest of my life when I finally saw through him. He betrayed me, yes, he did, but he could not have done so had I not failed myself. I had confided in him, I revealed my true self to him, and he turned it all against me.

Was I making the same mistake again, in thinking I could trust Rory? From the first, I felt I *could* trust him. With Francis—oh, I could not remember. Did I even ask myself that question? I was a different person then, singularly lacking any experience of being loved and embarrassingly ready, on reflection, to fall head over heels. Francis had desired me. He wanted to marry me. I sensed both those things so fiercely, and yet I must have been mistaken. He had kept his true, vindictive nature hidden from me until I refused to marry him and he revealed his true colours.

No, Rory wasn't like that. I felt none of that desperate need there had been from Francis, nor did I feel that I was being carried along by the force of his feelings. It was the force of my own feelings for Rory that confused me. He was an attractive man, why shouldn't I be attracted to him? But it was more than that. He listened to me—another thing that Francis had never done. He was interested in what I had to say—too interested, sometimes. He unsettled me, but not in a threatening way.

And then there was this persistent conviction I had, that I was meant to know him. I could trust him, but that didn't mean I would confide in him. I could acknowledge my attraction to him, but that certainly didn't mean I would give in to it, and I most certainly would never, ever fall in love with him or any man for that matter. So why should I not do what I believed I was meant to do, and indulge this compulsion I had for his company? My release from my duties with Mrs Oliphant for two weeks was fortuitous timing.

Having decided to surrender to my destiny, I was not in the least surprised to see Rory loitering near St Giles. I spotted him from the other side of the Lawnmarket, at the same time as he spotted me. 'I was hoping to bump into you,' he said, when I crossed the High Street to join him.

'I was hoping the same thing, though I'm not sure I wish to hold another whispered conversation inside the Kirk.'

'Nor I. It's a pleasant evening. I know somewhere close at hand where we won't be disturbed.'

He led the way down Victoria Street, and then at the head of the Grassmarket, turned left on to Candlemaker's Row and through the gate which brought us into the lower reaches of the graveyard attached to Greyfriars Kirk. Behind the walls, the noise and bustle of the city disappeared, leaving us alone in the peace of the old burial ground.

'I used to like coming here for a break when I found myself in the vicinity back in the day,' he said, leading the way along a path that led to the right. There's a spot up by the old Flodden Wall that I particularly liked. There's an odd little crypt, simply built like a stone outhouse. Trotter of Mortonhall, it says. I've often wondered who or what the family were.'

We reached the place a few moments later, and stopped to perch beside each other on one of the many overturned tombstones. Behind the walls of the cemetery some of the older tenements loomed, but inside the walls it was silent save for the birds and the rustle of the leaves in the few trees. I was angled towards him, my skirts brushing his leg. He had pulled off his hat and gloves, setting them down behind him, and was frowning down at his hands. His nails were neatly trimmed, his hands were very clean, but the knuckles were rough and scarred. 'Is life as a private detective as violent as it was as a policeman?' I asked him.

He shook his head. 'These are all old,' he said, indicating his hands. 'The people who can afford to employ me are very different from the types I was once employed to capture.'

'What sort of cases do you solve?'

'A multitude of different things, but in the end, it nearly always comes down to money. Money stolen. Money contested. Money made. Money lost. Though it's not nearly as boring as it sounds,' he added with a twisted smile. 'Usually there's a puzzle to be solved, and that's what I like. As well as putting things to rights, of course. I've an orderly mind.'

'Does your current case involve putting things to rights?'

I thought at first he wouldn't answer me, but after a moment he sighed heavily. 'I sincerely hope so.'

'Are you making good progress?'

He gave me a look I could not interpret. I had the feeling that he was on the verge of saying something, but then changed his mind. The man who solved puzzles for a living was a puzzle for me, and that, I confess, made me more determined than ever to try to understand him. 'It's been put on hold for a couple of weeks as a matter of fact,' he told me. 'There's a piece of the puzzle that needs clarifying. Until it is, the man who is paying me wants me to hold fire.'

'You find that—frustrating?' It was more of a guess than a supposition.

'A wee bit, because I don't like it when I'm having to wait on someone else doing something, but it's more— ach, I don't really like being told what to do, I suppose it's that,' he said, smiling ruefully. 'Though in this case, it makes sense.'

'But you are troubled, all the same?' I ventured, feeling on more certain ground.

'It matters. I want to get this one right. I mean, I want

to get every case right, but this one—it matters more than it should.'

'Are you worried that you will fail?'

He gave me another of those strange looks. 'I'm determined not to.'

'Is there a chance—?'

'I've said more than enough,' he interrupted, his tone making it very clear that the subject was closed. 'I don't fail. I never fail. That's why I'm in such demand.'

'You make a good living, then?' I asked, accepting the change of subject.

'More than I know what to do with, considering there's only me.'

'That might not always be the case,' I said, surprised to discover that I wasn't very keen on the idea I had mooted.

No more was he, for he shook his head vehemently. 'I'm not the marrying kind, if that's what you mean. I'm already married to my work, there's no room in my life for anyone else.'

'But what about family? You must have some?'

'None that I'm in touch with. I was an only child, and so too were my ma and my da.'

'*M'aither?*' I ventured.

'Not a bad attempt, but it's softer, and the "r" rolls. *M'aither.*'

I repeated the word, but with no greater success. 'Have you ever been to the Highlands?'

'Once, when I was wee, I went for a few weeks to stay on Harris with my—*m'aither's* cousins. I remember the beach, the sand like silver and the sea the colour of turquoise, with a mountain range on the horizon that was the mainland. I couldn't get my head around that, that I was looking down on Scotland. The sun shone the whole time we were there—or that's what I remember, any road. My da told me that was almost unheard of up there.'

His face had taken on a distant look. His smile had softened. Happiness warmed him, as if he was basking in the sunshine of the Highlands again. I wanted to step into that world with him. I wanted to feel the warmth of happiness make my skin glow. 'It sounds wonderful,' I said.

'There was a wee gang of us weans that played together every day. We built a fire on the beach, and cooked the biggest crabs you've ever seen in your life in an old pot filled with sea water. I hadnae a clue how to go about eating it, and they all laughed at me for trying to bite through the shell. Have you ever tasted crab? It's not a bit like fish. Sweet as a nut, it is. And mussels too, so soft, like a burst of the sea in your mouth, have you ever tried them?'

'You're making me want to.'

'Then there was the fish we caught from the end of the harbour wall. You could swim in the harbour too, the water was much warmer there, that's where I learned, but you had to be careful not to get caught out when the tide turned. That's one of the many things all the other weans knew but I didn't. I didn't know how to light a peat fire, or how to stack the stuff, or how to shear a sheep, or even the right bait for the fish, depending on what we wanted to catch. They made me feel a right eejit, a peely-wally wee runt from the city, but I learned fast. Not that I've had occasion to practise any of it since, mind.'

'It sounds idyllic, even though you were a—a peely-wally…'

'It means pale. I was wind-burned and sun-tanned by

the end of the holiday, so I stood out just as much, when I went home.'

'Why have you never gone back? You clearly loved your visit.'

His smile faded. 'School. Then work. Life got in the way. When my ma died, my da always said that we should pay another visit, but I never found the time.'

'You wish you had,' I said, though once again I didn't mean to say so aloud.

'But I didn't,' he said bitterly, 'and I try not to waste my time on what might have been. Look, Marianne, I don't know how we came to be talking about my childhood…'

Marianne. The way he said my name warmed me, though he didn't seem to have noticed the slip. Was it because I occupied his thoughts? Did he dream of me as I had of him—no! I could not allow myself to go down that path. 'I asked,' I said. 'I am interested.'

'I never talk about myself like that.'

The admission reassured me, for he loosened the guard I usually had on my own tongue. 'What did you wish to talk to me about then? You were waiting for me at St Giles. Couldn't it wait until the morning, when you take your coffee in the Grassmarket?'

To my surprise, he scowled. 'I won't be taking my coffee there in future. I've been spotted,' he added, in answer to my unasked question. 'Your Flora, whose name is actually Katy, reported me to a former acquaintance.'

'What!' Instinctively, I grabbed his arm. 'She told the police you are here? But how did she know who you are?'

'Not the police. She didn't know anything about me, save that I was a stranger and had become a regular at the tavern. She told a man called Billy Sinclair. He had his finger in a good many criminal pies during my time here, but essentially he was a thug. He's moved up in the criminal world since I left Edinburgh, though. These days, I reckon he pays others to do that aspect of his business.'

That Flora, who was actually Katy, was some sort of informer, I put to one side for later consideration. 'Did he threaten you, this man?'

'No, he had come to give me a bit of friendly advice, for old times' sake. To get out of Edinburgh, before someone else found out I was here, in other words.'

My fingers tightened around his arm. 'Mr Sutherland...'

He took my hand from his arm and enveloped it in his. 'Won't you call me Rory? I've already called you Marianne.'

So he had noticed! 'Rory.' Our eyes met, and I forgot what I was going to say. Through my skirts, I could feel his knee pressing against my leg. His head bent towards mine. My heart began to pound.

'Marianne.' With his other hand, he touched my cheek. The lightest of touches, tracing a path down to my jaw. 'I've been thinking.'

'Yes?' I leaned closer, the better to hear what he was going to say.

'What is it about you?' His fingers fluttered down my neck, settling on my nape, at the gap between my gown and my hair. 'You make me say things—tell you things— talk to you.'

I could feel his breath on my cheek. 'I've been thinking about that too.' My body was urging me closer, an irresistible force was tugging at me, so that when I spoke our mouths were almost touching. 'This is going to sound odd, but I feel we were meant to meet for some reason.'

'It doesn't sound odd.' His lids were heavy. His breath

was like mine, rapid, shallow. 'I mean it does sound odd, but it doesn't feel odd.'

I gave in to the temptation to place my free hand on his cheek, smoothing the palm of my glove over his skin, my heart beating faster as my touch made him shudder. 'I have two weeks' holiday, as of today.'

He groaned softly. 'I wish you hadn't told me that.'

'Don't you want me to…?'

'Oh, there's lots of things I would like you to do, Marianne.'

He said my name so softly. He leaned into me, closing the last tiny little gap between us. I felt the warmth of his lips on mine, the merest brush, and then he took my hand and leaned back. I was crushingly disappointed, but he didn't let go, unbuttoning my glove, peeling it back, finger by finger, and I forgot everything save the anticipation of what he would do next.

When he lifted my hand to his mouth, I almost cried out my pleasure at the softness of his lips on my palm, the gentlest of kisses, my fingers drawn into his mouth, relishing the heat that shimmered from his touch, making my stomach clench. I could see my wanting reflected in his eyes. I could feel my own yearning reflected back from him. What on earth was I doing? I asked myself, but I didn't really care.

Save that he had obviously asked himself the same question. He let me go reluctantly, but he let me go. 'We simply can't be doing this!' he said firmly.

Chapter Fourteen

Rory

Edinburgh—
Wednesday 8th August 1877

We simply can't be doing this!

Talk about an understatement! But by the sun and the stars, I wanted to. It took me all my willpower to let her go and to get to my feet, pulling on my gloves, as if they would somehow keep me safe. 'I'm sorry,' I said, my voice sounding as shaky as I felt. 'I truly didn't mean that to happen. I can't be letting that happen again.'

Marianne looked as flustered as I'd ever seen her, which was no consolation whatsoever. Her cheeks were flushed. There was a look in her eyes that told me she was as carried away as I had been, and as taken aback. Heaven help me, what I wanted to do was put my arms around her and kiss her and forget all about all the very, very good reasons why that was impossible. 'I'm sorry.'

I could see her visibly changing, pulling herself together, as she put her gloves back on. 'There is no need to apologise. It is not as if you forced yourself on me.'

'I would never…'

'I am aware of that.'

She stood up, shaking out her skirts. She was wearing the green dress again. The colour suited her. This was hardly the time for telling her so.

'All the same,' I said, because I couldn't get over how far I'd strayed from my own rules, 'I didn't mean to…'

'Nor did I, but I did!' She drew a breath, then continued in a softer voice. 'Forget what happened just now, it doesn't matter. I mean it's not relevant to why—to what I was trying to say.'

'You've lost me. No, wait. You mean when you said we were meant to meet?'

'Yes.'

We had met because I was looking for her. I couldn't say that, and even if I could have, it wouldn't have been completely true. I deal in facts, but I couldn't deny I had an inkling of what she was talking about. 'I felt it too, I'll admit, but I'm not sure where this conversation is going, Marianne.'

She wrinkled her nose and furrowed her brow. It made me want to kiss her, so I took a couple of steps away from temptation to look at the inscription on one of the nearby gravestones. *Here lies the mortal remains of…* The date was 1752. It was adorned with a skull and cross bones.

'They were more honest, back then,' Marianne said, joining me. 'Not a weeping angel or a grieving cherub in sight.'

'My thoughts exactly.'

'Really?'

She raised her brow. Just the one. I wished she wouldn't do that, I found it ridiculously alluring.

'What are you planning on doing for the next two weeks,

Rory, while your other case is in limbo? Will you remain in Edinburgh?'

'Where else would I go?' I asked, taken aback.

'I don't know, but since Edinburgh is dangerous...'

'No, no. I've no plans to go anywhere.' I was under orders to stay put. Then I remembered this morning, and Billy Sinclair's suggestion that I get out of town. 'I've been thinking about my old case.'

'Have you?' Marianne gazed at me, wide-eyed.

'I have, but I didn't mean that I was thinking of doing anything about it.'

'But don't you think that might be it? The reason we— that fate—no, I don't believe in fate—but don't you think all the same, that's why we met? I *knew* that you have not been able to forget about it, you as much as told me so on Sunday. And now you have two weeks, and I have two weeks. It is beginning to make sense.'

She smiled at me, one of those rare real smiles, the ones that reached her eyes, and her eyes were hazel that evening in the burial ground, and I wanted to kiss her again.

'Shall we walk?' I said, suiting action to words, and thinking fast. She was right, in a way. Ever since I'd come back to this city, that old scar had been itching. Even before, I'd made the connection between the unclaimed victim in that case and the victim in my current case walking beside me. Two lost women, only this one, thank the sun and the stars, was alive and kicking and very much determined she wasn't a victim. What a woman! I really admired her. Among other things.

We had come right round to the part of the graveyard that fronts the church itself. There was a bench, just on the other side of the door, and so I headed for it. If I did pick up the old case again, I could kill two birds with one stone, so to speak. Have one last go at finally finding out what had happened all those years ago, and at the same time, I could do what I'd been told to do, and keep an eye on Marianne. Which was also what I wanted to do, very much. Which rang a warning bell. Faintly, mind.

'Funnily enough,' I told her, as we sat down, 'I didn't take kindly to having Billy Sinclair warn me off this morning.'

'I gathered that.'

'Did you, now? And here was I thinking myself a man of mystery to you.'

She laughed faintly, frowning at the same time. 'You are, most of the time.'

'Not always though, clearly. You're very good at reading people, you'd make a good detective.'

'So you think I could help you, then?'

'Hang on, I didn't say…'

'But it's what you want, isn't it?'

I sighed. 'It wasn't my intention when I came here, but being back in this city made me realise how much grief that old case is still giving me. I thought I'd put it behind me. I don't think I have.' I hadn't meant to say that, but the relief of it! It shook me, I mean really shook me.

Marianne touched my hand. Glove on glove, and just for a second, not long enough for it to mean anything more than a bit of comfort, and it was. 'I want justice for her,' I said. 'The woman who was murdered. And for me, if I'm honest. Maybe justice isn't the right word. I want to find out what happened, I want to know why.'

'It's the not understanding that's the worst, isn't it? Why

me? What did I do to deserve this? And not being able to do anything about it. I know what that's like, Rory, I really do.'

I knew what she was referring to.

Why me! What did I do to deserve this!

My heart went out to her, and I couldn't say a word to let her know I understood. It wasn't only that I was under orders to keep my mouth shut for the time being, I knew, though I didn't like to admit it, that the Marquess was right. Better a whole story to tell her than half a tale. It touched me though, deeply, that she'd said that much. She understood. That touched me too. 'Thing is, Marianne, I'm not sure that I'd be able to get any further than before.'

'But if you don't try—though perhaps I shouldn't be encouraging you? How dangerous would it be, Rory?'

I tried to ask myself that, honestly. The problem was, I still had no idea who was behind what had happened all those years ago, who it was I'd be upsetting if I did resume my investigations.

'It's undoubtedly a risk,' I said, which was not a lie. 'And seven years is plenty of time for a trail to go cold. The dead body wasn't reported in the papers. All the stuff that they printed about me, that was all a smoke screen invented by someone. None if it had anything to do with what I was actually investigating.'

'You were wronged,' Marianne said, putting her hand on my arm again. 'For seven years, you've wondered why. You have the opportunity to put your mind at rest, Rory. Why wouldn't you take it?'

Her words went straight to my heart, for they were so obviously spoken from hers. She had also been wronged, and she didn't know why but she would, soon, she'd know that and so much more. My hand had wrapped itself around hers of its own accord. Our eyes were locked on each other. There was a stillness between us, as if we were scared to move. 'Marianne.' I said her name so softly, just because I wanted to say it.

'Rory,' she said.

Our lips touched. I hadn't meant them to. I hadn't meant to kiss her. I knew I shouldn't kiss her, but our lips touched, and she sighed into me when they did, and I felt my breath leaving me in a whoosh. A butterfly kiss. It took all my resolve to pull back. It was nothing, I told myself, though it wasn't.

'I can help you,' Marianne said. 'I don't know exactly how, but at least I'm a fresh pair of eyes and you've admitted yourself that I'm intuitive.' Our hands were still entwined. Our lips were still only a few inches from each other. 'Please, Rory. I'd like to—I want to.'

Two weeks, with the perfect excuse to be in each other's company. The Marquess might even approve. I couldn't have cared less about the Marquess at that moment. Two weeks with Marianne. The alarm bell sounded again, slightly more loudly this time. Was I playing with fire? But it was only two weeks. Two weeks to finally find out why someone had tried to destroy me. Marianne was right, that was the crux of it. And at the end of two weeks, she'd find out why someone had tried to destroy her. And who he was.

'You'll do it,' she said, though I'd said nothing. 'And you'll let me help you?'

I nodded slowly. 'But I'm not taking any risks, not with regard to your safety, do you understand?'

'Yes, yes.'

'No, I mean it. If I tell you something's dangerous. If I tell you not to do something. Or not to talk to someone. If

I tell you that it's not safe to stay involved, you listen and then do as you're told. Do you hear me?'

She opened her mouth to protest, no doubt to tell me she was perfectly capable of taking care of herself, but she met my eyes and thought the better of it. 'Why don't you start by telling me what happened, all those years ago?' she said.

So that's what I did. 'It began when a woman's body turned up in the docks at Leith,' I said. And that's how we decided to return to the scene of the crime the next day.

Chapter Fifteen

Marianne

Edinburgh—
Thursday 9th August 1877

The rain that morning was no more than a light drizzle, and by the time we reached the waterfront at Leith, it had all but ceased. We had taken the tram, rattling down Leith Walk from Princes Street, disembarking at Commercial Street, where we walked along towards the bridge over the Water of Leith.

It was a very different river here from the one we had followed tumbling along the banks of Dean Village. Wider, more like a canal, and emptying out into the vast complex of docks that surrounded the main basin and the harbour. I had not been here before. I had had no notion that the place, so near to the city, was so enormous.

'Stay close,' Rory said, 'and mind what I told you, keep your head down. The docks are rife with criminal activity. The chances of me being spotted by a former customer are far higher down here, which is why I've taken the precaution of changing my appearance. We'd stick out like a sore thumb otherwise.'

I was wearing my cloak with my hood pulled up. In a change from his usual understated neatness, Rory was wearing workman's boots, a rough jacket and trousers, a collarless shirt with a muffler, a cap rather than a hat, and no gloves. It ought to have looked incongruous on him, but I thought it suited him. He had not shaved, I noticed, his chin was dark with stubble, which also suited him.

I had dreamt of him again last night, my dreams even more real than before, for now I knew the softness of his lips, the warmth of his mouth. Enough to inflame my imagination. Enough to make me wake, racked with longing. Enough, looking at him then, my face shielded by the hood of my cloak, to make me want more.

We simply can't be doing this, Rory had said yesterday, though I was sure that he wanted to kiss me, kiss me properly, as much as I had wanted to kiss him. This conviction I had, that we were meant to be together had inconvenient side-effects. Was that all it was? What mattered most, and I was sure of this, was giving Rory something I would never have, peace of mind.

I would never really understand why Francis had me locked up, but yesterday it was so clear to me that Rory suffered as I did, with endlessly posing the question, *why?* If we could find the answer, what a huge relief that would be for him. The black cloud that I sensed hanging over him, the anger and the frustration would be gone. Someone had tried to destroy him. If we could discover why—oh, I so desperately wanted that for him.

So wanting to kiss him, wanting more than kisses from him, feverishly dreaming of what that would be like, must be a side-effect of my fervent longing to help. That made sense to me. Now that I understood it, I could control it.

The tingle I was feeling then, the excitement of being with him, the way I was so acutely conscious of the man beside me, that too was merely symptomatic of my fervent desire to help him.

If that manifested itself in desire for the man himself— then what if it did! It wasn't as if I was in any danger of acting on it. Fate—yes, I would credit fate with a role— had brought us together for one reason only, and we had two weeks to complete the task.

I turned my mind away from Rory to our surroundings. Behind us, Commercial Street was extremely busy, with drays, carts and carriages of all sorts jostling for position. People swarmed about, clerks with bundles of papers, dockers directing the carts in and out of the huge doors that were the entrance to the quayside, the occasional well-dressed man picking his way from his carriage to the steps of one imposing building or another. There were women too, with baskets and aprons, like everyone else rushing about their business.

'That's where all the port offices, custom house, all that sort of thing are,' Rory said. 'The commercial heart of the city. Where the money is.'

'So this case, do you think it is "all about the money" too?' I asked, following him in the opposite direction, to cross over the river.

'Somewhere along the line, it's bound to be, though I've no idea how. She was found on this side, but we'll get a better view if we cross over to the Shore. Are you sure you're wanting to do this?'

'Provided you are sure you will not be in too much danger?'

'Don't worry about me,' he said, which I knew was not an answer.

The waterside was lined with buildings, old and new, and there were a huge variety of ships, old and new, tied up alongside. Steam ships, paddle steamers, barges, and older clippers looking decidedly shabby and tired, surrounded by an army of little boats. Men were crying out to each other, we had to stick close to the buildings to avoid the endless flow of traffic, but above the noise I could smell the sea, and I could feel the salt of it on my face.

Rory's hair was wind-blown, fairer in the light down here, with streaks of gold I had not noticed before. His arms swung at his side. I hate to be held, but I wanted to take hold of his gloveless hand. I edged closer, so that my cloak fluttered against his legs.

He caught my eye, and smiled. 'You're enjoying yourself.'

'It's exciting,' I agreed, and it was, in a way I was not accustomed to. I was excited to be with him. I was excited to be out and about in a part of Edinburgh that was completely strange and new to me. I was excited by the thrill of the chase, even though we weren't chasing anyone yet, merely going back to the start of the trail, as Rory had put it.

I was excited by the prospect of helping him. I was exhilarated by his company, not being alone, not being lonely, engaged on something so very different from my usual line of work—much as I loved that. I was thrilled by the challenge of it all. My spirits lifted, and I smiled broadly at him.

He stumbled on the cobblestones. 'Have you any idea how much I want to…?'

Kiss you. Neither of us said the words, but we were both thinking them. Remembering yesterday. The kiss that was not nearly enough. We had come to a halt. Our eyes met again. I felt it again, that breathless tension, dangerous and exciting, pulling me towards him. I stood rooted to the spot.

He blinked, shook his head, started to walk again. 'Did I tell you that you've the makings of a good detective.'

I suppressed the completely irrelevant elation I felt at having my own tumultuous feelings returned, and followed his lead. 'You did. Yesterday.'

'So I did. You're good at reading people, that's what I said. You're a good judge of character. It's something I pride myself on, it's something I have to be good at in my line of work, but I like to have my judgement backed up with facts. With you it's more—more instinctive. You've a sense of whether or not people are telling the truth. Honestly, sometimes I feel like you can see right inside my head.'

'I cannot!' I exclaimed, immediately on the defensive. 'I told you yesterday that I find you almost impossible to read.'

'Most of the time, is what you said.'

'It's true. You keep your feelings closely guarded, most of the time.'

'And some of the time, with you I mean, when I should be keeping them to myself, I can't,' he said wryly. 'Though I should. I'm determined that I will.'

He was looking out at the docks, not at me, but I knew exactly what he was thinking, because I was thinking of it too. I spoke simply to break the spell. 'I have always been good at reading faces, even when I was a child. I remember one occasion when I was helping to serve tea to my foster mother's friends. I was handing round a chocolate cake, but when one of the women reached for a piece I said, no, you can't have that, you'll be sick again.

'At the time, I had no idea why everyone was embarrassed or why I was sent to my room. I presume she was expecting a child, though it may not have been that, but it's stuck in my head because I was punished so unfairly, simply for saying what was obvious to me. My foster mother accused me of listening at doors. She was never unkind to me, but she didn't like me. To use your phrase, it was all about the money for her.'

'She told you that?' Rory said, looking appalled.

I shook my head. '*I* told her that. Although she hid it well, I knew that it mattered more to her than me. She was furious.'

How could you possibly know that?

I winced, for her voice was loud and clear in my head, the first time I'd thought of that scene in years. I had said far more than I'd meant to or had ever said before. Not even to Francis had I confided this pathetic little tale. He had never shown any interest in my childhood. 'Anyway. I didn't know how I knew, but I knew and it was a very long time ago, and I don't know why I'm telling you.'

'Some people such as yourself, they're just better at piecing together what's in front of everyone's noses. I do the same, in a different way. I take all the facts I know, I add a bit of glue based on experience, and I get a picture. It's not a dark art, I don't *know* more than anyone else, but I'm better at working it out and making sense of it. I reckon you do the same, only it's not facts you use it's more what you feel from people. Would I be right?'

He was so perfectly right, I was temporarily lost for words. 'Do you find—have you ever had—has it ever got you into trouble?'

'Mostly, it's got other people into trouble. Criminals, I mean. What about you?'

I teetered on the brink of telling him. I came very close, because no one had ever understood that aspect of my character in that way, and it was such a relief, a pleasure, being understood. My intuition gave me the pieces. On occasion my sleeping mind was the glue that put them all together into a picture. It sounded so benign, yet it was those pictures that I had used to try to help people. Those pictures that I had described to Francis. And he had used those pictures, labelled them visions, and had me committed.

Horrified, I saw how close I had come to giving Rory the same ammunition. 'Why would you ask that?'

'It got you into trouble with your foster mother. I meant were there other times…?'

'We're here to try to find out why you were hauled over the coals for trying to piece together a picture of a murder, not to poke into all the incidents in the past where I have been hauled over the coals for—' I broke off, putting my hand over my mouth. What was wrong with me! I never lose my temper. I never speak without thinking! I took a calming breath. 'Your being hauled over the coals resulted in your exile from this city. The blackening of your name. A crime left unsolved. It's why we are here.'

I started to walk again, heartily regretting my outburst. Had I overreacted? This constant comparing of Rory with Francis in my head, I found it vile. Rory didn't deserve to be compared with that man, and I would happily never, ever think of Francis again. It was the institution that haunted my dreams, and my suffering there. Only since Rory had appeared had Francis also come back to haunt me.

Rory wasn't like Francis. Not even in the way he wanted

me. It was a longing that I felt from Rory, raw desire, but—
but reined in, somehow, and—and sweeter? No, not that.
I hadn't the words, but it was different. Or perhaps what I
was actually trying to describe were my own feelings, not
his. I couldn't read him when his guard was up. But when
he touched me, or looked at me, when our lips had met—
no, I wasn't mistaken, whatever I was feeling, so was he.

And just now, when *I* let my guard down, he hadn't de-
rided me or mocked me. And yesterday, when I'd said that
I was meant to help him, he'd accepted that. He wanted
my company, he was glad of my offer of help, but would
he wish either if he knew that for four years I had been
incarcerated in an asylum? He was an unusual man, but
I doubted there was any man unusual enough to consort
with a woman who had been branded a lunatic. I had to
be more careful.

'Marianne, slow down. Wait a minute.' Rory stopped at
a gap between two ships on the quay. 'The spot we're looking for is over there,' he said, pointing at the opposite side.
'Do you see that inlet with the swing footbridge, just before where the main docks broaden out? It's known as the
Rennie's Isle bridge. Her body was found lodged in there.
Someone chose the wrong place to put her in the water.'

I shuddered. The screech of a steam train thundering
past towards a much larger railway bridge further down
made me jump.

'That line wasn't there in my day,' Rory said, shading his
eyes to look at the engine. 'The docks it serves were only
just being built. Do you see what I mean about the money
that's pouring into this city?'

'It's the same in the New Town. In the three years I've
been here, it has expanded at an incredible rate. It seems

that every other day, a new circus or place is opened up, a new park or garden railed off. What now? Should we go over and take a closer look?'

'I don't see that we'd gain anything from it, I just wanted to remind us both what this is all about. She wasn't drowned, you know. She was already dead when they threw her in.'

'Poor woman.'

'Aye, no one deserves that fate.' He sighed, gazing over at the inlet and the little bridge. 'I wish you would trust me. You can, you know.'

'I do.'

'Then why is it you keep clamming up on me?'

I opened my mouth to contradict him, but could not.

'You can't deny it, because you can't tell a lie. It's been as clear as day to me from the start. You can dance around the truth, or you can keep something back, but you can't tell a lie. Your foster mother should have believed you when you said you didn't listen at doors, and she should have asked herself how a wee lassie in her care came to know that she wasn't actually cared for.'

'I was always treated…'

'Well enough,' he concluded for me, his lip curling. 'You deserved to be treated a lot better than that. Every wean deserves a bit of affection.'

His words brought a lump to my throat. 'You can't miss what you don't know, Rory.'

He frowned, looking deeply troubled. 'Do you ever wonder…?'

'What?'

'Nothing.' He reached towards me, then changed his mind. 'Like you said, we're not here to dig into your past, but mine. Or rather the poor woman that was found over there.'

Do you ever wonder...?

What? Better not to know. I followed the direction of his gaze, looking at the little bridge and the inlet it protected.

'She was caught up in the bridge itself, when it was swung open,' Rory said. 'I reckon whoever murdered her dumped her body in the docks over there, the big ones that were under construction at the time, and the tide moved her. She wasn't meant to be found but she was.'

'Are you sure she was murdered, Rory? It wasn't an accident, or—might she have jumped?'

'I *know* she was murdered. I'll explain later.'

'And she hadn't been missed? That's what you told me.'

'That's what got me at the time. No one cared. No one had even reported her missing.'

No one had reported me missing either. No one had wondered where I was, why I had disappeared. No one had cared enough. No, that was unfair. Those who might have cared were the women I had helped, but even had they been aware of my fate, they would have been helpless. 'You cared,' I said to Rory.

'Aye, and look what happened to me. Have you seen enough here? We're making ourselves a mite conspicuous. We'd best get a move on.'

'Must we take the tram back? The sun is out, why don't we walk back to the city and talk about our next steps?'

'Because I haven't worked out what they are, yet. But if you fancy a walk, we could head along the coast to Newhaven, it's not far. It's a wee fishing village. We'll be safe enough there.'

Chapter Sixteen

Rory

Edinburgh—
Thursday 9th August 1877

We walked back along Commercial Street, Marianne keeping a steady pace with her head down, me beside her keeping a look out just in case, though my mind was on other matters. The woman herself, specifically.

She was prickly as a hedgehog one minute, blurting out stuff she clearly didn't mean to tell me the next, and what she did tell me was making me feel like I'd been put through a wringer.

You can't miss what you don't know.

It made my guts twist, thinking of everything those words implied, and I'd come bloody close to blurting out that stupid question.

Do you ever wonder who your parents were?

Despite her avowal that she didn't care because they had given her away, I found it difficult to believe she hadn't wondered. But what was the point in stirring it up right now, when I was honour bound not to tell her what I knew, and anyway, their names weren't the point. It wasn't *who* her parents were that would matter to her, but why they didn't keep her. A dead mother was only one side of it.

What had her father been playing at? I could understand him getting someone else to care for his motherless child, but to have nothing more to do with her—that I didn't get. It didn't matter to me, I told myself for what seemed like the hundredth time, or rather it shouldn't matter. If the Marquess tasked me with the telling of the tale, I would be the bearer of facts, hopefully of good financial tidings, that was all.

Aye, right. I was getting in deep. Not too deep, not so deep I couldn't extricate myself when the time came, and I'd have to. I was committed to keeping an eye on her for the Marquess—which admittedly, I could do from more of a distance. But I'd committed to letting Marianne help me with this old case, and if I changed my mind it would look odd. What's more, I didn't want to change my mind.

Two weeks, that's all we had. I could almost hear the clock ticking, and I told myself that I was glad of it. There wasn't time, in just two weeks, for me to get myself in any deeper that I already was. Even if every moment I spent with her made me want more. Even if what I felt for her had a strength and a depth I hadn't felt before for any woman.

Two weeks wasn't going to be nearly enough with her, I felt it in my bones, but it would have to be. At the end of two weeks I'd lose her—literally. Marianne would become Lady Mary Anne. Titled, connected, rich and well above my station. I'd do well to remember all of that. And I would, I decided. Starting right there and then.

'You would never know that the docks are so close,

would you, or that the Firth of Forth was out there?' I said, pushing all of that to the back of my mind.

'I was thinking the same,' Marianne told me, smiling. 'Buildings on both sides, and the walls so high, I can't even see the masts of the ships over them.'

'You'll get a bit of a view back from Newhaven. Have you ever been there?'

She shook her head. 'I've never had cause. The families that employ me go to Portobello or North Berwick when they want to take the sea air.'

'I was at Portobello on Monday. I was thinking of you, watching all the weans with their nannies and governesses.'

'It is where Mrs Oliphant's children are now, taking a holiday with their aunt. She has her own nanny, which is why I am not required.'

'And you'll have another bairn in your charge, will you, when you go back to Queen Street in two weeks?'

'She will be in the care of a wet nurse for now, poor little thing. Her mother wanted a boy,' Marianne explained, 'for Mr Oliphant considers he already has a surfeit of daughters.'

The commercial buildings and warehouses had given way to a mixture of tenements and small shops. 'You don't like him, do you?'

'I make better work of disguising my feelings when I am with the family,' Marianne said, with one of her wry smiles. 'It's nothing personal, I have very little to do with him. I dislike the way he takes his wife for granted, and I heartily dislike the contempt in which he holds his daughters, at least two of whom are considerably brighter than his precious son, who will have the education *they* deserve.'

'They have you, though.'

'Only until their own governess returns, and when they are old enough, they'll be sent off to a school to learn how to be young ladies. I am not qualified to teach them those skills.' She pushed her hood back, smoothing her hair as she gazed around her. 'Ordinary families going about their business, though some of these children should surely be in school.'

'That would be a real challenge, if you were up for it,' I said. 'Getting them there and keeping them, I mean.'

'Oh, I would certainly be *up for it,* if what you mean is, would I relish it. It wouldn't only be a question of making the lessons interesting and challenging enough that they would want to stay, it would also be a case of persuading the parents that it was worth their while sending them there in the first place. In many cases, they would be giving up the few pennies the child could bring from doing other work.'

'You've thought about this.'

'A great deal. It's one of the ways I have of passing the time when I don't sleep. I could make such a difference to so many lives, given the chance. You probably think that arrogant of me.'

Don't sleep, I noted. What kept her awake? Memories? Fear of the dreams she might have? Or had she lost the habit of sleep in that place? Most likely all of it. 'I don't think you arrogant at all,' I said. 'I think it's admirable and pretty unusual that you have considered it. You've no knowledge of places like these, people like these. Don't take this the wrong way, but people raised as you were, in a respectable family, not the working type of family—families like these—people like you don't…' I bit my tongue, realising I was getting into a total fankle, and in danger of being offensive.

But she didn't take offence at all. 'Unlike people like you? You're right,' she said. 'And if I had stayed on at the school with Miss Lomond, I would have remained oblivious. I wouldn't have come across the women who opened my eyes. Women forced to earn a living doing the most appalling work.'

Her words gave me goosebumps, for I thought immediately of what Nurse Crawford had confided in me of the work she and women like her did to keep the institutions that employed them going. While those in charge played at god, these women swabbed down, mopped up, slopped out, fed, soothed and restrained the inmates. How they could endure it, hear the cries, witness the suffering, sometimes assist in inflicting it, and then go home to their own families with any peace of mind at all, I had no idea. No wonder some of them lost their humanity. And as for Marianne! That she had come through it all, and had brought a dream with her, put me in awe of her. And if the Marquess got his way, she could have her dream realised.

Don't worry. You'll have the money. You can make that dream and every other you've had come true.

The words were on the tip of my tongue. For the first time the sheer scale of possibilities that would be open to her took my breath away, putting all the other difficulties and emotional upheaval into the background. She'd come through so much, she could come through this and out the other side. She deserved this.

'What is it? What are you smiling at, Rory?'

'You're quite a woman,' I said, 'and if you look over there, you'll see the fishing harbour at Newhaven.'

Chapter Seventeen

⦿⦿⦿

Marianne

Rory's smile was infectious. For no other reason than that I was here with him, breathing in the fresh sea air, in a place I'd never before visited, my spirits lifted. I gave myself over to the moment. The fishing village of Newhaven was only a few miles from the city, but as we walked along the quay with the shuttered fish market behind us, it felt like another world. The air tasted of salt, and there was no pall of smoke hanging over us. The sun had still not made an appearance, but the sky was milky white and not dirty grey.

The tide was coming in, little waves creeping in through the neck of the harbour to lap at the hulls of the fishing boats that were stranded there, lying almost on their sides some of them, in the mud and silt, which gave off a stench of fish and seaweed. The empty boxes stacked outside the big doors of the market smelled of the day's catch—or maybe the previous day's. Across from us, on the harbour arm, there were nets drying, a clique of men working on them. The wind was blowing the wrong way for us to hear them talking, if they were talking.

It was peacefully quiet. We walked along the jetty to the neck of the harbour, where there was a commanding view out over the Firth of Forth. The flat kingdom of Fife was spread out before us, looking close enough to swim to.

'It's a shame it's not a clearer day, you can see all the way to Stirling from here sometimes,' Rory said. 'I reckon if I asked nicely, I might be able to persuade one of those men over there to gift us a crab, since it looks as if they're boiling up something to eat. You stay here, I won't be long.'

I watched him make his way back down the jetty to the harbour arm, not rushing but covering the ground quickly enough. I had the distinct impression that he'd been on the brink of saying something important to me just before we reached Newhaven, but then he'd changed his mind.

I couldn't fathom what he was feeling, never mind what he might be thinking, for his guard was up. Often, it seemed to me, he cut short his words, or changed them to say something else. He was careful. I supposed that must come from being a detective, or it might be that he had always been careful, and that was why he had become a detective.

There were times when my ability to read people irked me. I could be walking past someone and find myself assaulted by their anger or their foul temper. Grief was less common, but weariness and misery were sadly everywhere, and there was nothing I could do to alleviate any of it. I tried not to intrude, but it's difficult for me to switch off.

In the asylum there had been countless, terrible times when I wanted to cover my ears and scream for oblivion, to hide under the meagre covers and to stop listening to the outpourings of suffering and horror from the other inmates.

I ached to help them, to tell them, I hear you, for some of them could not even articulate what they felt.

I dared not speak though. Anything I said would be seen as further confirmation of my insanity. So I kept silent. In that diabolical place, I came to hate my intuition, for it multiplied my suffering, and burdened me with guilt for my enforced inaction. Only once, I had dared to use what I knew, and then I had acted without thinking, reacting to the threat, the immediate danger, screaming out the warning that stopped Nurse Crawford in her tracks as she began to unlock the cell door. I saved her life with my warning, and the risk I took in telling her was repaid in full when she gave me my life back.

Since my escape, I kept to myself everything I intuited, sensed, or unwittingly pieced together in every household I have worked. The women who employed me thought me perceptive, sensitive, trustworthy, but that is all.

How could you possibly know that?

I made sure that no one could ever throw that question at me.

You can't miss what you don't know.

My words this time. My hurt, that Rory's question had dredged up. I had forgotten it. It was his doing. He had a way of making my feelings spill out, things I didn't even know I was feeling, opening up wounds I thought long healed. Every time I thought I had myself under control, he overset me. He made me feel out of control. He made me want to lose control. But I wouldn't. I would never be such a fool again. I simply couldn't allow myself to.

I watched him chatting with the men on the other side of the harbour, his hands in his pockets, gesturing over to me. I was worrying too much. We were nothing to each other save two people with a shared purpose. In two weeks, he would go back to London, never to return. I resolved to stop worrying, to enjoy the moment.

He looked quite at ease, and not in the least in a hurry. I wondered what he was saying about me. Was I his wife? His sweetheart? His sister? No, not sister, and not wife either. As for sweetheart—no, we were not two innocents wooing. Acquaintance would be the most accurate, but we were surely far beyond mere acquaintances—had been since we first met. He was not employing me to help him, and we were not friends. Or were we? The only friend I ever had was Miss Lomond, but friendship felt far too safe a term for what I felt for Rory. One did not dream of making love to a friend.

He was coming back with a bucket. I had dreamt of him again the previous night, naked underneath me, inside me, making fierce, frantic love such as I had never made before. In my dream we were equals in passion.

'Success! And look, we're in luck, it's a beauty.'

My face was hot. Extremely thankful for the brim of my hat, I was happy to peer into the bucket and hide my face. Inside was the most enormous crab I've ever seen in my life. 'Good grief! Is it dead?'

'Cooked. It will be easier to eat if we leave it to cool.'

He set the bucket down. 'Do you think you could sit here? I have it on the authority of the fishermen over there that the sun will come out in a bit. Here, take hold of my hand and dreep down.'

I burst out laughing. 'I'll do my best, if you tell me how to—to dreep?'

'You don't really need to dreep. I just wanted to see your face when I suggested it. You dreep down a wall from the top, you know, sort of dropping and clinging at the same time to make the fall shorter. Here, take my hand and sit down there.'

I could have managed perfectly well, but I chose to let him help me, sitting down with my legs and skirts dangling over the wall. He sat beside me, close but not touching. He took off his cap, and pushed his hair back from his face. 'There, we're comfy now.'

'As *comfy* as we can be, perched on rock.'

'And look, the sun's coming out right enough.'

'And we have a crab for our dinner.' I was still struggling to compose myself, with him being so near. 'What more could we want?'

'A hammer for the claws, but I've found us a stone. You have a lovely smile, Marianne, did you know that? There, I didn't mean to make you blush, but it had to be said. When you smile—I mean properly smile, not that smile you use when you are pretending to smile—it makes your eyes glow.'

'Like a cat in the dark, you mean?' I said, trying to disguise my surprise and delight at the compliment.

'Like your eyes are smiling too. It warms me, when I'm on the receiving end of it which has not been often, mind you.'

The way he was looking at me was heating me from the inside. His own smile was so warm. 'You think I am ill tempered?'

'Crabbit, you mean? Like our dinner would have been when he was caught. Don't be daft. I think—I wish you could be happy, that's all.'

I could tell he had for once failed to guard his tongue,

and spoken what was on his mind. It took me aback as much as him. 'I am happy.'

Rory covered my hands with his. 'Are you, truly?'

He asked so earnestly that I took his question seriously. 'I am not unhappy.' I was not locked up. I was free. Provided I was never found, I was free. 'No, I am certainly not unhappy.'

His hands tightened on mine. 'That's pretty much what I would have said. I'm happy enough. I'm not unhappy. In fact, it wouldn't even have occurred to me to ask myself the question.'

'The why did you ask me?'

'I don't know. You make me think things I don't usually think. You make me want to do things I shouldn't want to do. I shouldn't be holding your hands. I shouldn't be sitting here beside you, thinking about kissing you. I shouldn't have told you that's what I'm thinking.'

'But you did.' And now I was thinking the same thing, when I should not be. It meant nothing. It couldn't mean anything. It was the day. The sea. The sun which was shining. The strangeness. It was Rory.

'When you look at me like that, I don't want to let go of you,' he said.

It was a question, though he didn't phrase it that way. 'Then don't,' I said to him.

I leant towards him. He leant towards me. My eyes drifted closed. I could feel the sunlight on my face, and his breath, and my heart was pounding so hard, and my belly was fluttering. And then his lips rested on mine, and I stopped thinking and gave myself over to sensation. It was a careful kiss. One I could escape from if I chose. Soft. His lips shaping themselves to mine without moving. And then it was less careful. Still soft, but more urgent. His tongue lightly touching mine. Our lips locked, kissing, and the kisses making me feel like I was melting, that I was liquid inside.

A whistle from one of the men on the other side of the harbour put an end to it. We sat staring at each other, our hands clasped, our breathing synchronised. The wind ruffled his hair.

'I can't believe we did that, in full view of those men,' I said, though I really couldn't have cared less.

'I can't believe I did that, when I've told myself countless times that I can't.'

I shouldn't have been pleased by this, but I was. It wasn't only me who was—not obsessed, but distracted. Often. 'Countless times?'

'A good many, at any rate. And when you do that thing, raise just the one eyebrow like that, you can have no idea what it does to me. I wish you weren't so bloody gorgeous.'

That made me laugh, breaking the spell, breaking our touch. 'I am thirty-three years old, and long past aspiring to be gorgeous. Not that I ever did.'

'Well, I'm forty, and long past the age of having my head turned, you'd have thought, but you're a fair way to doing it.'

'Has it been turned before?'

Rory pushed his hair back from his face again, and set his cap back on. 'I was engaged to be married once.'

I was entirely unprepared for that confession. 'You said you were married to your job.'

'I was. That was the problem. She was a good woman, far better than I deserved. That old case, it wasn't the reason for our parting, but it was the final straw.' Rory sighed, looking suddenly weary. 'We should talk about it, shouldn't we, the case, I mean? Not let ourselves get distracted. Let me see what I can do with this crab first.'

Rory made short work of dissecting the crab with the help of a stone and his pocket knife, throwing the waste to the gulls. It was utterly delicious, sweet and delicate white meat from the claws, stronger dark, juicier meat from the body which we scooped up with our fingers. We ate silently, each lost in our thoughts. If he was thinking about the old case, I was not. I was thinking about the kisses we had shared. I was thinking that he had matched my desire when he kissed me, just as he had matched my desire in my dreams. My desire roused him. His desire roused me.

'It's good, but not near so good as the ones I had on the beach on Harris.'

His words cut into my reverie. Mundane words, but the look he gave me made me wonder what he was thinking, if he knew what I had been thinking. It was another trick of his—not trick, I don't mean trick. Technique? He said one thing while thinking another.

'Sometimes I feel like you can see right inside my head,' he'd said to me.

I wished that I could do so more often.

'Here, use this.' He handed me his handkerchief, which I was obliged to use for my own was sodden. 'Did you enjoy it?'

'Isn't it obvious? It was wonderful.'

'It's even better when you have butter.' Rory threw the last of the shells from the bucket into the water, which had reached the wall on which we were sitting. The tide had come in, far enough for the fishing boats to bob about as if they were nodding. Across from us, on the other side of the harbour, the men looked as if they were preparing to go to sea. 'Will we stretch our legs while we talk? We can head along to Granton Harbour. It's only about a mile— unless you've walked far enough already?'

'No, I'm happy to walk and anyway, I've never been to Granton.'

'It's a port like this one, though much bigger. There's a new harbour that serves the fishing boats and the steamers out to Burntisland in Fife.' He got to his feet, holding out his hand. I took it and was pulled up effortlessly, though immediately released.

'You're not worried about being seen there?'

'I don't think so. I only told you the bare bones of the case the other day, I'll fill in the blanks while we walk.'

Chapter Eighteen

Rory

Edinburgh—
Thursday 9th August 1877

I was kicking myself for giving in to temptation, not even five minutes after I'd decided I wouldn't. I suggested we walk because if we continued sitting down together, I was pretty certain I'd give in and kiss her again. In public! With a crew of fishermen for an audience into the bargain! It wasn't so much the fact that I'd kissed her at all that shocked me to the core, it was how much I'd enjoyed it, and how much further I had wanted to go. It was the way she had kissed me back too, as if she felt the same. And there was no way it was wishful thinking, I was sure of it.

The old case was why we were here, I reminded myself as we made our way past the fishermen at the other end of the harbour, me giving them a look that made sure none of them made any comment on our behaviour. The sun had disappeared again, and there were clouds on the horizon. The breeze had picked up a bit too, as we began the walk along the front towards Granton. Marianne's skirts whipped around her ankles, but when I asked her if she'd changed her mind about the walk, she shook her head vehemently.

'Go on,' she said, in a way that made me think she was as keen as I was to distract herself. 'Forget what you've already told me and start from the beginning. Try to imagine you're writing a report or whatever it is policemen do. Did you have a notebook?'

'I did.' Concentrate, I told myself. Focus! 'They took it from me, but I wrote down what I could remember afterwards.'

'So your instinct even then, was that it was important and that you might need it one day?'

'I just knew the whole thing stank to high heaven. My policeman's instinct, if you like.' I tried to put myself back there. Tried to remember the man I'd been all those years ago. 'I told you I'd acquired a bit of a reputation for solving tricky cases. I was good at my job, and I *did* get to the bottom of the cases I was given, but I never liked the way the press reported them, as if I had a special talent or skill, as if I had some kind of magical powers, when all I did was use my head.'

'To make pictures that others couldn't.'

'Or didn't take the time to.'

'I think you are too modest,' Marianne said. 'Clearly you have a talent for detecting.'

'I have, I'll take that, but what I'm saying is, to me it's not anything extraordinary, and I didn't like that the press made out that it was.'

'So when the press made those false accusations, did they also cast aspersions on your previous successes?'

I took my time answering her, since it was clear she was making connections with the accusations that had been levelled against her. It made my heart ache, thinking what might be in store for her if the press got hold of that story. I'd been there, and if there was anything I could do to prevent the same thing happening to her—but what? And what business was it of mine? None, I knew that, but it wouldn't do either of us any good for me to lie to her. 'They implied that I must have been getting a helping hand, somehow,' I said. 'That I had been too good to be true.'

She nodded, a deep frown furrowing her brow. 'And the good you had done, or the harm you had prevented, the fact that you'd brought criminals to justice?'

'You're right, all that was forgotten, washed away,' I said bitterly.

Her lip curled. 'And your talent was used against you.' She turned away from me to face out to the Firth, where one of the Burntisland steamers was puffing its way across to this side. 'I know how that feels, Rory.'

Her voice was tinged with anger. Her gloved hands were curled into fists. I could see the memories chasing each other across her face as she turned to face me again. 'Years ago. Nine, ten years ago, long before I came to Edinburgh, I was employed as governess to two little girls in one of two large houses in a small town. I was on good terms with the governess from the other house. She was a little older than I and had unexpectedly come into a small inheritance. It was much discussed, as such things are, and everyone assumed that she would stop working but like me, she loved children.

'What she actually wanted was a child of her own. She met a man, personable, respectable looking, a stranger, though he claimed to have some connection with the town. I knew from the first—sensed from the first—that he was lying, though it took me some time to understand the extent of his deception. In a nutshell, he was after her money, nothing else. She wanted a husband and a child. But he already had a wife.

'I don't know,' Marianne said, when I opened my mouth to ask the obvious question. 'I cannot tell you how exactly I came to that conclusion. Things I'd heard him say, things he didn't say, things my friend told me about him. The way he hedged his bets when she spoke of where they would live. The persistent sense I had that he was holding something vital back. As I said, I don't know, but I woke up one morning and the picture was so clear in my head, I felt compelled to tell her.'

She drew a ragged breath. 'The courage she showed in confronting him—knowing that she was destroying her opportunity to have a family—oh, Rory, I almost wished I had kept silent.'

She turned away to face out towards the water again. I watched her struggle to control herself, desperate to put my arm around her, but knowing that was the last thing she wanted. All I could do was hand her my handkerchief, thankful for the small mercy that I always had a spare, for the other one had been used as a napkin earlier.

'I'm fine now,' Marianne said, looking far from it. 'I beg your pardon. I never talk about the past, it is too upsetting, but the parallels are so strong, I felt—because I do understand. As I said, my friend confronted him and he turned on her so viciously that she let fall it was I who had been the architect of his downfall. Needless to say, he then turned on me. He warned me that he would neither forget nor forgive what I had done, and then he disappeared, presumably back to his wife.'

'Poor woman. At least she was spared a bigamous marriage.'

'Yes, but at such a cost. It was a big scandal for a small town, and she found herself at the centre of it.'

'What happened to her?'

'I don't know. She left the area, her reputation in tatters, poor woman. It was so unfair, but at least she had her legacy.'

'And you?'

'Yes, I suffered too. The man found a way to tell the tale that made him the maligned and innocent victim, and I—I was accused of maliciously making it all up.'

I swore, invoking one of my da's most vicious Gaelic curses. 'It's outrageous. No wonder you have such a poor opinion of my sex.'

'Not all of you. I have a very high opinion of *you*.'

That stopped me in my tracks, and despite the sorry tale, it gave me a warm glow, distracting me for a wee bit. 'It's entirely mutual,' I said. 'It must have cost you to tell me. I appreciate it, I promise you.'

Her face crumpled, and she cursed under her breath, the first time I'd ever heard her do so. 'I wanted you to—you see I do understand.'

'And I can see you do. We've both suffered for having the courage of our convictions. You did someone a good turn, and it was turned against you.' I understood a lot more than she could have dreamed. It sickened me, for this sorry story must have been part of the evidence against her, the facts twisted and distorted to make her out as deluded. There was a gaping hole in the story as she told it, and that was how the tale got to the ears of the man who had her committed.

I wasn't going to ask her, she was in such a fragile state,

and it wasn't exactly pertinent. I couldn't help wondering though. Was it from the bigamist? A big scandal in a small town would be easy enough to dig up, but that meant Eliot must have known where to look. From where he paid the stipend to—right enough, that would be it.

Marianne straightened her shoulders and dabbed her eyes. 'I beg your pardon, you won't believe me, but usually I am not in the least emotional.'

'No more am I, save when I'm around you.'

'I'm not sure if that's a compliment or not.'

'It's a statement of fact,' I said ruefully. 'Shall we try to direct our emotions back to the murder case?'

'An excellent idea. Please proceed, Detective Sutherland.'

We had reached the long harbour arm at Wardie Bay, and I steered her towards it, away from the increasing bustle of the Granton seafront. 'I was on duty when we got a report that some weans had thought they had spotted a body caught under the bridge,' I told her, returning to the past. 'I took it with a pinch of salt but it turned out they were right. We had no idea who she was when we pulled her out, and she didn't fit with anyone we knew was missing, but that didn't count for much.

'She was pretty, she was young, and she was very obviously expecting a child. There was a gash on her head that looked suspicious to me. I put all of that in my report that night. The next day, I was called in and told it was an open-and-shut case. She was simply an unfortunate lassie who had found a way to deal with the shame of her condition, and the blow to her head happened when she fell in. Case closed, they said.'

'But you were determined to find out who she was?'

'They couldn't stop me doing that. It was my duty to try to put a name to her, let any family know, but they said it was best to let sleeping dogs lie. If anyone came forward to report her missing then fair enough, but until then she was just another tragic statistic. I thought that was unbelievably callous. At the very least some man somewhere must have contributed to her condition. It felt all wrong. Where she was found, it seemed to me that she'd been washed round by the tide from the new docks they were building and was likely put there by someone who intended to make sure she'd be lost for ever.'

We had reached the point on the harbour where the steamboat docked from Burntisland. There was a waiting room where we could have got a cup of tea, but neither of us were inclined to go in, so we started to retrace our steps. The weather had closed in. It had started to spit rain. 'I was told there were more important matters for me to investigate.'

'More important than a murder!'

'A woman, found in the docks, pregnant and with no wedding ring. The implication being that she wasn't respectable, perhaps a prostitute, and so not worthy of investigation. I know, it's wrong—'

'But it's how it is,' Marianne interrupted bitterly. 'Go on.'

'Another thing that makes a detective—or any policeman, for that matter—good at his job, is information. Knowing where to find it, I mean. The better you are at that, the quicker you are at solving crimes. The woman wasn't one of the street walkers in Leith, I knew who to ask to make certain of that. Besides, her clothing was well made, she looked to be in good health, and she wasn't under-nourished—so that was another dead end. Once again, I was told it wasn't worth bothering about. Then I was ordered to leave it, and given another couple of cases.'

'But you couldn't, because you smelled a rat, and because the more someone tells you not to do something, the more determined you are to do it?'

'That's about right. To cut a long story short, since we're running out of pier to walk and time's getting on, I went to my superior officer and made my case for murder. By then, she'd already been buried in a pauper's grave—mighty fast too. My superior was a good man, I could trust him, or so I thought. He promised he'd look into it. Two days later, he told me there was nothing to look into. Case dismissed.'

'But you didn't dismiss it.'

'I couldn't let it go, even though I was supposed to be—ach, it doesn't matter. Like you said, despite the lack of evidence, I was convinced I was right.' It was tipping it down all of a sudden. All around us, people were running for shelter. 'If we head up to Trinity we can catch the train back to the city. It's only a few hundred yards.'

We got to the station, standing under cover on the platform to wait for the train, which was fortunately due in a few minutes. 'You're drookit,' I said to Marianne. 'Soaked, I mean.'

'Drookit. I like that. What's wrong, Rory?'

I could have brushed her off, but I didn't want to. 'Raking it all up like this, it's a double-edged sword. I want to find out what happened, who murdered that poor woman and why, but it's making me think about myself. What if I'd done as they said, kept my mouth shut and stayed here? I was up for promotion again. I was earning enough from my private work to put money aside—that's one good thing about the papers making a fuss over me, it got me a lot of private work, and it paid very well. The plan was to buy one of the smaller houses in the New Town. I was due to get married. The day my superior told me the case was closed, I was supposed to be sorting out the final details of the wedding.'

I took off my cap to shake it out, and pushed my sodden hair back from my forehead. 'Looking back, it's obvious that I wasn't suited to settling down, but it was expected and I never questioned it. My ma had passed away a few years before, so my da was delighted at the thought of grand-weans. I was doing well. I was of an age to be thinking about taking a wife.

'And we got on, Moira—my betrothed and I. We were well suited, that's what everyone said. Her family was quite a step up from mine, but they never made me feel as if that mattered. Yet I simply couldn't see past that case. I became obsessed. It became an issue between us. In the end I— we—agreed there would be no wedding.' I winced, not wanting to recall that painful scene.

The train whistled, and a belch of steam preceded it as it screeched into the station. We had bought third-class tickets, right at the back in the last carriage. Marianne took my arm as we walked down the platform. We took our places on the hard wooden seats. The rain was coming in through the open windows. It was cold, my cheap woollen jacket was starting to smell damp.

'Is it a terrible thing to say, to think it might have been the making of me, rather than the ruining of me?'

Marianne turned towards me, frowning. 'How long have you been thinking in that way?'

'It's only just occurred to me.'

'And would it have occurred to you, if you hadn't come back here?'

'Probably not. And I still want to find who the woman was, if she was missed. Her family, if she has one, deserve to know her fate, at the very least. '

'Shall we give her a name, since no one else has? What shall we call her?'

I thought about it for a moment. 'Lillian,' I said.

'What about Lillian?' Marianne said at the exact same time.

We looked at each other and smiled. I leaned my head back, closed my eyes, and felt the tension leave me. I knew I shouldn't be here in this city. I knew I shouldn't be with this woman. But at that moment, all that mattered was that I was.

Chapter Nineteen

Marianne

Edinburgh—
Friday 10th August 1877

'She's beautiful,' I said to Mrs Oliphant, looking down into her new daughter's scrunched-up little face. It wasn't exactly true, I've always thought new-born babies look like a very tiny, very stern Queen Victoria, but it was a small enough lie for me to be able to pass it off. 'Have you chosen a name?'

'She is merely Baby at present,' my employer said. She was sitting up in bed draped in a selection of shawls, her hair hanging limply down from her nightcap. Though it was mid-morning, the curtains were drawn over the windows and the gas sconce was lit. There were dark shadows under her eyes, testament to what she had endured giving birth, and the sleepless nights that had followed despite having a wetnurse to attend to the little one.

The poor woman looked every day of her forty years, and despite the perfect little girl she had given birth too, quite miserable. 'My husband had decided on Simon, after his grandfather,' she told me. 'He is too disappointed to choose a girl's name.'

'Then why don't you name her?'

Mrs Oliphant sighed. 'You think me very feeble, don't you?'

'No!' I instantly regretted letting my impatience show. She had clearly endured enough of it from her husband, who had behaved exactly as I had predicted, when presented with another girl. 'I think your ordeal has taken a great toll on you, but look at what you have achieved.'

I settled the baby into her arms, and took the liberty of perching on the bed beside mother and daughter. 'You have brought a new, perfect life into this world. That's something your husband cannot do.

Her smile trembled. 'I have done that, haven't I?'

You can't miss what you don't know.

I was suddenly besieged with memories of my own childhood, memories I had no idea were locked away. 'Children sense far more than we realise,' I said, delicately touching the little baby's toes. 'I was raised by foster parents. I will always be grateful for the home they provided for me, but I knew, I always knew, that I was not loved.' I struggled on, a lump in my throat and my cheeks burning. 'I instinctively knew I was not wanted, Mrs Oliphant,' I said, forcing myself to meet her eyes. 'Though they were never cruel, always did the right thing by me, I could tell it was from duty, not love.'

'My dear Mrs Crawford, I had no idea. You are such a confident woman, so self-assured. And you are so good with the children, you always seem to know exactly how to deal with them. Even Ronnie heeds you, and the girls dote on you. To be honest, I have always been slightly in awe of you. I don't know how you do it, always knowing a step ahead what it is they want or need.'

'What they need before anything else is to know that they are wanted. That they are loved. Each and every one of them.'

'Including this little one, you mean?' Mrs Oliphant gazed down into her daughter's sleeping face, and gently stroked her plump cheeks. 'You're quite right, she is lovely. I will not have her brought up thinking herself unloved or unwanted. Even if her father does not care for her, I do. Oh, dear.' She fumbled in the sheets for her lace-edged handkerchief and dabbed at her eyes. 'I have become such a watering pot.'

'It is perfectly normal,' I told her, patting her hand—another thing I never usually did. 'Rest, peace and quiet from your very boisterous brood, will make all the difference. I take it that your husband…'

'He is staying at his club for a few weeks. He needs his sleep, and does not wish to be disturbed in the night by the baby crying.'

Since the baby would be spending the night in the nursery on the next floor, I doubted Mr Oliphant would be disturbed. 'Then you should make the most of this time to recuperate,' I said, 'and to enjoy this little one while you have her to yourself.'

'I shall call her Octavia,' Mrs Oliphant said, with a sudden smile, sitting up in bed, careful not to disturb her baby. 'After Octavia Hill, have you heard of her? She is a philanthropist who rents housing to the poor in London. I know of her only because I heard my husband telling one of his fellow businessmen that he was relieved that no decent Edinburgh woman would follow her lead.

'My husband owns a large portfolio of property in the Old Town. Slums, for want of a better word I am ashamed to say, and like to remain so, if he has anything to do with it. "Tenants find their level", that is what he is forever saying. His tenants don't deserve better, in other words. I can see I have shocked you.'

I couldn't deny that. 'I had no idea.'

'Why should you, your business is with me, and my business in domestic. The irony is that he won't for a moment guess *why* I have named her Octavia. It simply wouldn't occur to him that I would have taken it upon myself to find out about her namesake—for that is what I did. I went to the library.'

'Goodness, did you?'

'Now I have surprised you. I must say, I surprised myself. It was the day that my husband told me this was my last chance to give him a son. I had forgotten until now.' She reached over to clasp my hand in hers. 'I am glad you came to visit. You have reminded me of how fortunate I am to have little Octavia, and her sisters, and even her brother.'

'Perhaps your little Octavia will take inspiration from her namesake, when she grows up.'

'Perhaps.' Mrs Oliphant looked unconvinced. 'All my mother ever wanted for me was a good husband and a family. It's all I ever wished for too. I am fortunate, I have a beautiful home and am well provided for, I want for nothing, materially. Until now, like my husband, I have assumed my children will follow in their parents' footsteps. Ronnie is destined to take over his father's business, though it is already clear to me that Lizzie has a far better brain. And the girls will be found good husbands. Is it wrong of me—foolish of me—to wish for more for my daughters?'

'Neither wrong nor foolish,' I said, though I had little confidence in her wishes coming to fruition. Mrs Oliphant had been raised to bend her will to her husband. She knew nothing else. 'Lizzie is a very independent-minded little girl,' I said, brightening.

'Her father thinks her impertinent. I wish I had your strength of character, Mrs Crawford. You would know how to set a better example to my girls.'

'You have more strength of character than you realise,' I said, getting to my feet. 'Little Octavia is evidence of that already, for you have taken the naming of her into your own hands.'

'I have! And I shall stick to it too.'

'Excellent. Shall I put her back in her crib?'

'No, leave her with her mama.' Mrs Oliphant kissed her daughter on the forehead, then held out her hand to me. 'Thank you, Mrs Crawford, for the trust you have shown in me, and for giving up your own time to visit. I won't take any more of it, but if you could ask someone to send me up a tray of tea on your way out, I would be obliged.'

Rory and I had agreed to meet in Queen Street Gardens, because we could hope for some privacy there, the only other regular users of the garden, Mrs Aitken's family from Number Forty-Two, having decamped to North Berwick for the remainder of the month. When I arrived, he was already waiting on the bench where I had first encountered him, once again hiding behind a newspaper.

'Is there something wrong with the bairn?' he asked me, seeing my scowl.

'No, but there is something wrong with the baby's father.' I sank on to the bench, allowing my annoyance to take hold of me. 'Poor Mrs Oliphant dared to have a daughter and not a son, and her husband has had a tantrum and taken himself off to his gentleman's club.'

'At least while he is there, his wife will have respite from his company.'

I was obliged to smile. 'That is more or less what I said to her. Oh, dear, now you are thinking once again that I dislike men, which is not true, Rory. I like you.'

'That's what they call serendipity, for I very much like you.'

I could see from his face that he hadn't meant to say so, and though I knew I ought to wish he hadn't, I was very glad he had. 'I have never met anyone like you.' The words tumbled out before I could stop them.

'Serendipity again. I've never met anyone like you either. I think that every time I see you.'

'So do I.'

We were quite alone in the garden. My hand rested on his shoulder of its own accord. Then my lips met his of their own accord. Since yesterday, I had been longing for another kiss. The taste of him. The melting feeling inside, and the heat spreading through my body. I leaned in to cup his chin, smoothly shaved, sliding my fingers to the back of his neck to curl into his hair. His hat tumbled off.

Our kiss deepened, became more urgent, demanding, wanting. I gave myself over to the taste of him, the sweet, aching desire that was building inside me, making me feel as if my clothes were too tight, making me feel as if I couldn't breathe. One kiss merged into the next, into the next, and I was lost in a whirl of desire, wanting, aching for him to touch me, totally forgetting where I was.

Then his arms slid around me, locking me firmly in his embrace, and I jerked back, jumping to my feet. 'No!'

'Marianne! I'm sorry. I'm so sorry, I shouldn't have…'

I wrapped my arms around myself, taking another step back. 'It wasn't—I didn't mean…' I was shaking too much to continue. I turned my back to him, trying to banish the memory of those other arms roughly pinning me while the second man secured my arms behind my back. Of the reek of sweat and the stench of fear coming from the restraint jacket as they strapped me into it with ruthless efficiency. Of my helpless fall to the padded floor when they pushed me into the cell. 'Try escaping from that,' one of them shouted as the door slammed. Then came my screams, drawn from my depths, echoing over and over until I was hoarse.

But I didn't let them break me. That's what I reminded myself when I came to my senses again. It had been my first attempt to escape. It wouldn't be my last. And I had succeeded. I was free. I was in Edinburgh, and the only bars were the railings marking out Queen Street Gardens. I could smell new-mown grass. There were birds singing. I was free.

My heartbeat slowed. The memory faded. I turned around to face Rory. He was still seated on the bench, his eyes riveted on me. I thanked the stars he had not attempted to touch me. Mortification took over from horror. What must he think of me? 'I'm sorry.'

He said something under his breath I couldn't catch. 'I beg of you, don't apologise. Just tell me what I should do.'

'Nothing.' I studied him, clasping my hands together for they were still shaking. All I could sense from him was concern. He met my gaze frankly, allowing me to read him—at least that is what I felt. No disgust. No contempt. Just warmth and concern. 'You must think I am m—' I bit back the word.

'No!' He jumped to his feet and took a few steps towards me, then stopped. 'I don't think—you are not—I didn't mean to, but I frightened you.'

I don't think you're mad. You are not mad.

Was that really what he was going to say? 'It wasn't the kiss,' I said.

'I shouldn't have put my arms around you, is that it?'

He asked the question so gently, so carefully, yet still I had no sense of him judging or condemning, and though there was anger there, it was directed at himself. I wanted, suddenly, to tell him the truth. I wanted desperately to tell him, because I couldn't bear him to take the blame for what others had done to me. But even in my vulnerable state, I knew that would be a huge mistake. Knowledge was power. I did not think that Rory would abuse my trust, but I hadn't thought Francis would either. I had too much to lose. The life I had made for myself here. My sanity, if I was ever taken back to that place again.

'I'm perfectly fine now,' I said, returning to sit beside him. I had myself completely under control again. 'I don't like to be held, as you said.'

Why not?

I waited for him to ask the question, hoping he would not for I had no explanation I could give him. 'I'll remember that,' he said.

I was completely at a loss. Didn't he want an explanation?

'When you want to talk, I'll listen,' he said, 'I've told you, Marianne, you can trust me.'

His gentle tone and his understanding made my eyes smart with tears. This time I hadn't spoken aloud, yet he had still intuited what I was thinking. I wanted to trust him, I wanted to pour out the sad, sorry, horrific tale of my suffering. To what end? To label myself an escaped lunatic? To have Rory tactfully, but completely, withdraw from me? I wanted to help him. I wanted to be with him, though I knew I ought not to.

Totally conflicted, I changed the subject. 'Mrs Oliphant has named her baby Octavia, after a woman called Octavia Hill.' I recounted the tale, hands folded in my lap but not too tightly clasped, though I could not quite meet his gaze. 'I don't doubt her desire to give her daughters a different life, but nor do I hold out much hope that she will succeed. Do you want children, Rory? At some point in the future, I mean?'

He blinked, taken by surprise at my turning the subject, but as ever he took my question seriously, taking his time to answer. 'Like you, I think there are already too many children in need in this world.'

'Did I say that?'

'You implied it when you were talking about setting up your own school.'

'But when you were engaged to be married, it must have been in anticipation of having a family?'

'It's what Moira wanted, and my da was desperate for grand-weans. I wanted to please them, but I'm ashamed to say that I didn't think about it too deeply.'

'Did you love her?'

I thought he would tell me it was none of my business, which it wasn't. It didn't matter, I told myself, but I knew it did.

Rory looked troubled, picking up his hat and turning it around in his hands. 'I hadn't thought of her in a long time. Only since I got back to Edinburgh, and then last night, after I told you about her, I was going over that night when she broke it off. She said to me that if I loved her I would put her first. I'd forgotten that.' He put his hat back on. 'Truth is, she was right. I put my work first, always, and I couldn't see that changing. It was when I told her that, she gave me the ring back, and she was in the right of it. It seems I'm not the marrying kind. I didn't know myself as well as you did.'

'I'm not sure I know what you mean.'

'You told me you'd never wanted to marry. If I'd taken the time to think about it, I'd have reached the same conclusion but I didn't, I was too caught up with my work. And you know what's worse, Marianne? When I left Edinburgh, I was still too caught up with my own concerns, the injustice that was done to me, the injustice that was done to the woman we've named Lillian, that I barely gave the injustice I'd imposed on my da and Moira and her family a thought.

'They had expectations of me. They looked to me to make them happy, and I let them down.' He stopped, looking quite taken aback. 'I don't know where that came from. I didn't even know it was lurking there.'

'That's exactly what happens to me when I'm with you. I say things aloud that I mean to keep to myself, and I find myself thinking of things that…' Now it was my turn to fall silent.

'Thinking of things that you thought long buried? Is that it?'

'I didn't say that I had *never* wished to marry,' I told

him, proving his point. 'I said that I am now certain I never want to marry.'

'Meaning you did once?'

I was already heartily regretting saying anything, I certainly wasn't going to say any more. I didn't want to talk about Francis to Rory. I didn't want Rory to know about the needy, naive person who had been so desperate for love. I could tell myself that Rory's opinion didn't matter, but it would be a lie.

'Time is getting on. The clock is ticking,' I said. 'Tell me what progress you made this morning.'

Chapter Twenty

Rory

Edinburgh—
Friday 10th August 1877

I was gobsmacked, and by the looks of her, so was Marianne, at what she'd just confessed. She didn't want to tell me any more either, and I didn't know what I felt, but I couldn't leave it. 'Are you saying you were engaged to be married too?'

She sighed. 'A long time ago.'

'What happened?'

'Like you I realised, much later than I should have, that it was a mistake. I terminated the engagement.'

Did you love him?

I couldn't ask her that. I didn't want the answer to be that she had, but I wanted to know what had happened all the same. I was still shaken by the way she'd reacted when I'd put my arms around her. One minutes she had been kissing me passionately, lighting a fire in my belly, making me ache with wanting her, and the next minute she was looking at me as if I'd tried to strangle her. Had that been his fault? Had he hurt her?

'I don't know what you're thinking, Rory, but I would remind you, we're here to talk about your old case not my old love affair.'

The words hit me like a punch in the gut. 'It was a love affair, then?'

'I thought so at the time.' She lifted her eyes to meet mine, gleaming more yellow than green, and I recalled that phrase, *cat-like,* that the doctor I'd spoken to had used. 'I found I was mistaken,' she added, her tone strained, 'but not before I had surrendered—no, that's not right—not before I had indulged in the passion which I mistook for love. Now you have the truth, I expect you are shocked.'

'I don't know what I'm feeling.' I was struggling to take in what she was telling me, and more importantly, why.

'You must have known that you were not the first man I had kissed.'

Still that odd tone, and she was holding herself tight as a bow. 'I didn't care, Marianne. When I was kissing you, I wasn't thinking about who else you might have kissed. I wasn't thinking at all.'

'But afterwards…'

'Are you wanting me to criticise you for it?' I felt a flicker of anger. 'Are you wanting me to tell you that I think less of you?' My anger took root. 'Do you think that I'm a bloody hypocrite?'

'I don't!'

'No? Then why did you take that tone with me, when you told me that you're not a virgin—for that's what you meant, I take it? You were just waiting for me to judge you.'

'I was…'

'You misread my reaction. Do you know what was actually bothering me? I was wondering whether it was him who hurt you. Was it him who made you terrified of having someone's arms around you? That's what was bothering me.'

I knew I was reacting out of all proportion. It wasn't like me to get angry like that, but then everything I felt for Marianne was nothing like me and I was all over the place. Kissing her like there was no tomorrow one minute, and forgetting everything except wanting to go on kissing her. Then being stared at as if I was murderer. And now, when it hadn't even occurred to me to judge her, for I was very much intent on judging him, she was ripping up at me for doing just that.

I threw myself to my feet, cursing under my breath, angry and frustrated by the pair of us. 'I make my own mind up about people, I thought you knew me well enough to understand that. Do you think *I'm* a virgin? I'm forty years old, of course I'm not, and the women I've made love to—do you think I'm one of those men who thinks that only harlots can be passionate?'

Finally, I caught myself and bit the tumble of words back. 'I'm sorry. It's not like me to lose my temper. I didn't mean—I don't know where that came from. Again.' I caught my breath, trying to steady myself. 'I'm sorry. You'e right. What you did, who you did it with, it's none of my business. I just don't like the thought of you being hurt, that's all.'

You know that alarm bell that had clanged faintly a couple of days ago, when we talked about spending the next two weeks together? Well it clanged again at that, and I noticed it this time. I didn't like the thought of her being hurt. I wanted to be the one that stopped her getting hurt further. But if I wasn't careful…

I took a deep breath. I had to be careful or we'd both

make a mistake we might well rue for the rest of our days. She wasn't for me. I wasn't for her. That's the way it was, and that's the way we both wanted it to stay. We'd lay off the kissing. And I'd send another telegram to the Marquess, asking him to get a move on. The sooner Marianne knew the truth about herself, the better for both of us.

And if I kept telling myself that, I might start to believe it. 'Sorry,' I said. 'Rant over. Right then.' Time to do what I always do, and get back to work. I patted my coat pocket and drew out my notebook. 'Let me fill you in on what I've been up to, assuming you still want to know.'

She nodded. I sat down, making a point of keeping some distance between us, and opened the notebook, but her hand on my arm stayed me.

'I just want to say that I don't think of you like that at all, I promise you, Rory.'

'It doesnae matter.'

'Doesnae,' she repeated, with a valiant wee smile. 'Your accent becomes so much broader when you are emotional.'

'Aye, well, then I reckon I must speak broad Weegie or Scots when I'm around you, but I really am sorry I lost my temper.'

She had her hands clasped again, so tightly it was stretching her gloves at the knuckles. 'I am usually quite calm and collected too, but when I am with you, I am...'

'All over the shop?'

'Does that mean up and down? Yes, I'm all over the shop. I have known you just over a week...'

'Eight days. It's only been eight days.'

'It feels much longer, doesn't it? And we have less than two weeks left. Is that it? Do you think it's because we have so little time that we are *all over the shop*?'

'I don't know, it might be,' I said, because it was a straw I could clutch at. Twelve days left, maybe less if the Marquess could grease the legal cogs and get them to move faster. Twelve days, and we'd be going our separate ways. I didn't like the twinge I got in my guts at the thought. Part of me was thinking it might be a good idea to damn the Marquess and his orders to hell and just tell her the truth now. It would scupper any inappropriate hopes and desires I might be harbouring about us good and proper.

I wasn't just thinking of what it meant for her, but I was thinking of what she'd think of me, keeping it all to myself for so long. But I kept coming back to the fact that I'd not a whole story to tell her. And I was under orders to keep my gob shut. And they were sensible orders, what's more. So I turned back to my notebook once more, and the old case that had never failed to distract me, and I told Marianne what I'd turned up.

'The thing that always bothered me, as you know, was that our Lillian was a missing person that no one seemed to have missed. Widening the search, getting in touch with the police in the other big cities in Scotland, see if they knew anything about her, that was going to be my next step when my career came to a sudden halt. But this morning I had another chat with one of my own contacts here, the one who gave me the friendly advice a few days ago.'

Marianne, who seemed to be trying as hard as I was to forget, put her mind on the case, nodded. 'Billy Sinclair? You told me that he "owed you" a few favours, have I that right?'

'You have. He wasn't happy, but I told him this would be the first and last time. What he told me was what I'd already surmised. "You're looking in the wrong city," were

William's exact words. "You should look closer to home, Mr Sutherland."'

'Closer to home? Glasgow!'

'Exactly. And there's more. The reason William was persuaded to talk was because the man we're looking for is dead.'

'The murderer, you mean?'

'The man who put her in the docks. "An amateur, and a mere pawn". Again, I'm quoting William.'

Marianne's brow knitted. I had her full attention now. 'Does that mean someone was paid to do it?'

I closed my notebook again and stretched my legs out, still taking care not to brush against her. It was there all the time I was with her, that sense of her, awareness of her, even when I was totally focused on something else—well, almost totally. 'I think I was right all along. There could be only one reason for the pains they took to stop me investigating Lillian's murder, and that was because somehow, she was involved with someone important.'

'So it really was all about the money?'

'Almost certainly. The question is, whose money?' I said. 'And my nose tells me that we're getting close.'

'So we are headed to Glasgow?'

I hadn't meant for us both to go. But she was smiling at me, that real smile, and her eyes were warm and she'd shifted on the bench towards me, and though I meant to say no, *I'm* going to Glasgow, what I said was, 'Monday, if you're up for it. I've contacts there through my father who might help, I'll send off a few telegrams today, set the wheels in motion.'

Chapter Twenty-One

Marianne

Glasgow—
Monday 13th August 1877

The journey on the steam train from Edinburgh took two and a half hours. Rory said little for most of it, sitting quietly on the bench beside me, lost in his own thoughts. I had no idea what they were. Just outside Glasgow, our carriages were hauled up a steep incline by a rope powered by a stationery engine. I must confess, it made me extremely nervous, and I chose not to lean out of the windows with the other passengers to watch as the ropes were attached. I was simply glad when we reached the summit and could continue through the tunnel into the station under our own power.

Glasgow's Dundas Street station was smaller than Edinburgh's Waverley, and the platform swarmed with people from the busy train. The roof over the station prevented the steam from escaping, and as each new train pulled in, a cloud of black smoke was released, making the train, the people and the platform in the near vicinity disappear into darkness.

'You'll need to stay close,' Rory said. 'Do you mind putting your arm through mine? And hold on to your purse, for there are pickpockets everywhere here intent on making the most of the blackouts.'

I was more than happy to take his arm. 'I must confess, I'm feeling a bit overwhelmed. I'm not used to crowds like this. I feel as if I'm in danger of being swept along and separated from you.'

For answer, he pulled me closer. 'Are you regretting coming along?'

'Don't be daft,' I said, in a terrible attempt to mimic his accent. 'I want to see the city where you grew up.'

'It's five years since I was last back to attend my father's funeral, I wonder if I'll still recognise the place.'

We emerged from the station and Rory led the way to what he informed me was George Square. It was not the small, private garden I had imagined. On the contrary, it was a huge square set out with style and symmetry, featuring neatly kept lawns with small railings, and wide, paved walkways. There were trees and numerous statues, orderly flowerbeds and neatly spaced benches, and there were gas lights too, all around the perimeter.

A wide cobblestoned road separated the square from the mansions, hotels and commercial buildings which surrounded it. Hackney carriages loitered outside the Queen's Hotel. Horse-drawn trams and private carriages rattled along, but inside the square seemed an oasis of calm. Nannies strolled with their baby carriages. Men sat on the benches with their newspapers and pipes. A group of women stood gossiping. Above us, though the sky was dirty grey, the sun was streaking through.

'You're seeing it at its best today,' Rory said. 'Don't be

fooled though. A few hundred yards that way you'll find some of the roughest and most dangerous parts of the city. A few hundred yards in that direction is the River Clyde and the docks, and a bit further down river again, they build the ships and the steam engines that help Glasgow power the modern world.'

'I thought you loved Edinburgh the best.'

'Wheesht, don't be saying that here.' Rory grinned. 'This is my home town, of course I love it the best. While I'm here, any road. Come on, we've time to spare, will we take a stroll through George Square? When I was wee, it was a private garden. It's supposed to be open to the public now, but judging by the clientele, I reckon they mean only those and such as those.'

It seemed to me that he was right, when we crossed the road and entered the square. The men were all well-to-do in their business suits and top hats, the women clad in silk gowns and twirling frivolous lace-trimmed parasols that I couldn't help thinking would be filthy and painfully difficult for their maids to clean at the end of the day. Rory was attired with his usual understated elegance. I was wearing my green summer gown and with my favourite shawl and bonnet, an assembly that I had always considered my best, but as we meandered arm in arm around the square, I felt under-dressed, on the verge of shabby. I withdrew my arm from Rory's.

'What's wrong?'

'You're right, this square is for those and such as those. Shall we go?'

'You can't possibly be thinking that you look out of place. That gown suits you. I've always thought so. It brings out the colour of your eyes.'

'You have never said any such thing to me before.'

'I've thought it though, a few times.'

'It's the only summer gown I own.'

'Considering this is one of about ten days in the year that you would get the opportunity to wear it, to own another would be wasted.'

'If this one was a little smarter—' I broke off, embarrassed. 'Never mind.'

'I didn't think you set much store by clothes.'

Honestly! I wanted to roll my eyes. Sometimes Rory's powers of perception were irritating. 'I don't, usually. It would be wholly inappropriate for me to be better dressed than my employers.'

'But if you had the money...'

'I would spend it on more important things than silk gowns.' Looking up from the brim of my bonnet, I made the mistake of catching his eye. Blast the man, I could not lie to him. 'I'm not a governess today, but I'm dressed like one and you are not, and for the first time we are out in public in very respectable surroundings, not lurking in our usual haunts of graveyards and mill villages and dusty churches, and I feel I'm making you look conspicuous.'

I quailed as his face set, remembering his outburst in Queen Street Gardens when I had presumed he was judging me. 'I'm not saying that you are embarrassed by me, Rory, I'm saying that I am—I am uncomfortable. Though I know I shouldn't be. It's only clothes.'

'I've told you before that I think you're bloody gorgeous.'

My cheeks grew hotter. 'The point is, I don't think so. Now you'll tell me that it doesn't matter, but I think it does. Today, at any rate.'

Mortifyingly, I found myself on the brink of tears. Rory

ushered me over to one of the wrought-iron benches. 'We'll be late for your appointment with Mr Munro,' I demurred.

'This isn't like you.' He sat down, giving me no option but to follow suit.

'I know it's not.' I was nervous, jittery, and I couldn't understand why. It wasn't really my gown, that much I knew.

'Are you worried about meeting my da's friend?'

It wasn't that, though that might be part of it, in which case it wasn't a lie. 'How do you plan to introduce me?' I asked. 'Don't you think my presence might complicate matters, or make him more reticent? He's doing you a big favour, won't he be more likely to speak to you openly if I'm not there?'

I must have sounded convincing. Rory, in fact, looked relieved. 'I wouldn't be too long. I must admit, there's merit in what you say.'

'I will sit here and wait for you.' With the nannies, I was thinking. If only I had a charge of my own I wouldn't feel so out of place.

'Come on, I know where we can find you somewhere more comfortable.' He got up, holding out his hand and I allowed myself to take it. 'It's only five minutes away just off Ingram Street. I think you'll like it.'

He left me at the gates of a graveyard, with the promise that he would join me within the hour. St David's, the church which guarded the entrance, was in the Gothic style, squashed into a tight space that made it appear inordinately tall. There were three sections to the burial grounds, the main one long and narrow, enclosed by a high wall, with two smaller walled areas on either side of the church. The walls shut out the noise of Ingram Street. It was a quiet, gloomy place, but I felt immediately more at ease.

Rory had told me it was known as the Merchant's Grave-yard. Reading the gravestones, I could see why. Sugar, to-bacco, wool, the huge slabs of stone that covered the crypts proclaimed the merchant's trade, his wealth, his philan-thropy and his stature. His wife and children were after-notes. There were other slabs laid neatly around the walls. Also buried here, Rory had told me, was the man that Mad-eleine Smith was accused of murdering twenty years before.

I had not heard of the case, but at the time it was appar-ently notorious, a respectable and very young woman who poisoned her lover, and whose love affair, documented in her passionate letters, scandalised Glasgow society at the time. Respectable young women didn't take lovers, they didn't declare their passion in writing, and they most cer-tainly didn't commit murder. Madeleine Smith was not found guilty, though the peculiar Scottish verdict of not proven implied that the jury believed her to be so.

Rory said that Madeleine Smith's family stood by her, though the scandal forced them to move away from Glasgow. Her letters though, sounded like exactly the kind of thing that could have been used against her. I could eas-ily have encountered Madeleine Smith in the asylum. We had both in our own way escaped that fate.

Unlike Greyfriars kirkyard, there was a uniformity to the tombs in Glasgow, and an austerity to the gravestones. I decided against looking for Madeleine Smith's lover's grave, and instead found a spot in the sunshine at the far corner of the burial grounds, and a convenient stone bench set against the wall. I was still on edge. In George Square, walking arm in arm, despite my shabby gown, Rory and I could have been a married couple taking a stroll together. We were not looking over our shoulders, either of us, and I was not having to mind someone else's children. For a moment, just a moment, I had allowed myself to dream that the illusion we were creating was real. That was what had set me on edge.

I was tired of looking over my shoulder all the time. What was I afraid of? Who could possibly be looking for me now, after all these years? Why should I feel safer in Glasgow than in Edinburgh? Was it an illusion, or was it Rory who made me feel safe? Rory, who was also looking over his shoulder for an enemy he couldn't name. Rory, who in ten days, possibly less, would be walking back out of my life to pick up his own. If we discovered Lillian's true identity, he might even resolve what I had come to think of as *our case* even sooner. And his other, suspended case? Was that what was preying on his mind during his silences? I knew so little about his real life, but why should I? When he was gone, it would be better for me not to be able to imagine. And he would be gone soon enough.

When he was gone, I resolved, I would be less afraid. Restlessly, I began to circle the burial ground in the opposite direction. When he was gone, there would be no more blood-stirring kisses. I wouldn't have him to look forward to seeing, to talk to, but I could make another friend, couldn't I? Not one like Rory, but…

There was no one like Rory, that was the problem. I stopped in front of a tomb commemorating Andrew Buchannan, tobacco merchant and Lord Provost of Glasgow. I could not possibly be so foolish as to imagine myself to be falling in love with Rory. I forced myself to try to recall how I had felt that one fatal time I had fallen in love.

Anxious. I was always anxious. Eager to please. Thrilled when I did please. Devastated when I did not, and anxious—anxious again!—to make amends.

There must have been more to it than that. Passion? I sat down on the obliging tobacco merchant's grave and tried to remember. There must have been passion. There had been, on his side, and I had wanted what he wanted. Until afterwards, when I had wanted the opposite of what he had wanted.

Sighing, I pushed these unpleasant memories to one side. It sickened me to compare Rory and Francis, so I would not. I must have loved Francis, for I had agreed to marry him and I had made love to him, but what I felt for Rory was very different. Passion? Undoubtedly. Just thinking about his kisses set me on fire.

The restraint that he showed too, the sense that he was holding himself on a tight rein, made me want to unleash him. But it wasn't only passion. Rory listened to me. Rory was interested in what I had to say—too interested for comfort at times. And he was careful with me too. He knew when to stop pushing me, when to restrain his curiosity. And he didn't judge me. Though he didn't know me. And I'd make sure he never would.

Ten days, perhaps less. Not enough for me to care too much, not enough for me to miss him too much, not enough for him to become a part of my life. Not that I wanted that, any more than he did. I was in no danger from Rory, so there was no danger in my being with him. In my wanting him. And my longing for his company, that was precisely what I'd said the other day, a side-effect of the clock that was counting down the days until we went our separate ways.

A signal to make the most of them? My edginess gave way to a different kind of tension. I got up and began to make my way towards the entrance. Rory was walking towards me. He waved, and my heart leapt.

Chapter Twenty-Two

Rory

Glasgow—
Monday 13th August 1877

When I saw Marianne walking towards me, my heart lifted, and that worried me, but then she smiled, and I forgot to worry, and hurried towards her, smiling back.

'Do you have good news?' she asked me. 'Could Mr Munro help?'

'I'll tell you in a moment. Are you feeling better now?'

To my surprise, she slipped her arm through mine. 'It's odd, isn't it, being in a very different city together. You don't have to worry about being seen by the wrong person in the wrong place, and I—oh, I think it is time that I stopped worrying and began to enjoy my freedom.'

Freedom. I waited, wondering if she'd even noticed the slip, but she didn't. 'Go on then,' she said, 'tell me what you have found out, it's why we're here after all.'

'Is there anywhere we can…?'

'Sit and be private? Yes.'

She led the way to a stone bench on the back wall, in full

sun. I took off my hat and gloves and handed her the slice of fruit cake I'd brought her, wrapped in paper. 'I thought you might be hungry. You can eat it while I talk.'

'Thank you! I didn't think I was hungry, but now you mention it.' She took her gloves off, crumbled a bit and popped it in her mouth. 'Delicious.'

She crumbled another bit and held it out to me. I don't like fruit cake, I've always found it claggy, but I took it, surprising us both by guiding the cake and the tips of her fingers into my mouth. Her eyes widened. She withdrew them slowly, letting my lips linger. I turned her hand over to kiss her wrist, feeling the flutter of her pulse on my lips, feeling my own heart thump, and her fingers ruffling through my hair.

There were birds singing somewhere. There wasn't a breath of breeze. The sun baked down on us through the grey-blue sky. I looked up to find her eyes fixed on me. Her lips were parted. I think it was she who moved towards me, but I wouldn't swear to it. Then we kissed. Sweetened by fruit cake, warmed by the sun, it was a delicate kiss, though not careful. I knew how much she wanted me, from that kiss. I ached with wanting her. Which was why I ended it, though slowly, mind. Very slowly.

We stared at each other. Entranced, mesmerised, I don't know what it was. I didn't want to break the spell. I wanted to kiss her again. If she'd made a move, just the tiniest move—but she didn't. So I took a long overdue breath, and I sat back, but it was Marianne who spoke.

'We've not got long left,' she said.

'I know.'

'*Ah know.*' She smiled, one of her real smiles. 'You feel

it too, don't you, just as strongly as I do. The clock ticking. The need to—to...'

'Make the most of it. How could you doubt it?'

Her smile faltered for a moment, but then she rallied. 'I don't. I wish...' She reached for me, taking my hand and placing it against her cheek. 'Oh, Rory, I wish that we could stay here for just a little longer. In this city, I mean, away from Edinburgh. Where we are safe.' She kissed the palm of my hand, and I should have been glad that she let it go then, but what I wanted—well, it's obvious what I wanted. 'We've become distracted again,' she said.

'It's too easy done. I've never had that problem before. Let me think.' I moved away from her to do so. Then I re-counted what Gordon Munro had told me. 'The problem is,' I said, 'the family he thinks are Lillian's have been on holiday doon the watter. On the Clyde Coast, that is. They're not due home until tomorrow morning, so we'll have to come back another day.'

Marianne was silent for a moment, biting her lip—which I had to stop watching for what it was making me want to do. 'We don't have long,' she said. 'Going back to Edinburgh, then coming back here again, it seems such a waste of time.'

'What are you thinking?'

She was blushing faintly—though that might have been the sun. 'I'm thinking that fate might have taken a hand. We could stay here in Glasgow.' She was definitely blushing. 'If you thought it was a good idea.'

I thought it was a terrible idea—or that's what I told myself I was thinking. My body, on the other hand, leapt at it, in every embarrassing way. And was it such a terrible idea after all? We would save ourselves a journey. We could take

separate rooms in a hotel. We could take separate rooms in
a separate hotel—that would be safer. Then I remembered
that Marianne had been a bit overwhelmed when we arrived, that Glasgow was completely new to her, and it not
being new to me made me wary of leaving her in another
hotel, no matter how respectable it might be. So the same
hotels, but different rooms, then?

'What do you think, Rory?'

'The Queen's Hotel,' I said, my mouth running way
ahead of my mind. That's the one on George Square, right
beside the train station. It has a good name.'

'Is it expensive?'

'This is my case, so I'll take care of it. And I won't have
you arguing. Think about it, Marianne, you're more or less
working without a fee. Unless Mrs Oliphant is paying you
for your holiday...'

'She is very generous, but it wouldn't even occur to
her to do so, and even if it did, I doubt Mr Oliphant would
agree.'

'Forget about him, and everything else. I'll take care of
any expenses while we're here, and that isn't up for dis-
cussion.'

'Can you afford it?'

'Easily,' I said, ridiculously touched. 'I'm not rich, but
I'm very comfortable. I do well for myself.'

'And there is only you,' she said, with an odd smile.

Only me. I'd always relished that before. Only me, without Marianne—was I kidding myself, staying overnight
here with her? In separate rooms, I reminded myself. And
I might be comfortably off, but compared to the wealth that
was hopefully coming her way, I was a pauper.

If anything happened between us, would she think I was

making a play for her money? It hadn't occurred to me until then, but now it did—like that man she told me about, the bigamist who had tried to marry her friend. But then I had no intentions of asking her to marry me. The very idea of it made me laugh. Or would, if I thought about it. Which I wasn't going to do.

I got up, holding out my hand to help her. She took it, and she slid her hand into my arm, as if she'd been doing that for weeks. We hadn't even known each other for two weeks. No one could fall in love in two weeks. I had never been in love. I was forty years old. If I'd been going to do it, I'd have done it by now.

'Do you fancy coming with me on a wee trip down memory lane?' I asked her.

She gave a skip, beaming up at me. 'You read my mind. That is exactly what I would like to do.'

Glasgow was changing under our very noses, was how it felt to me. My eyes were out on stalks on the journey to Partick, I couldn't get over the number of big new tenements that were popping up, at the way the streets had broadened and bustled even more. We got off the tram at Partick Cross, and I stood for a moment, Marianne on my arm, looking about me in amazement. More tenements, a mix of red and blond sandstone, with shops under them, their awnings out, goods stacked outside, all the way along Dumbarton Road.

We walked along, dodging the multitude of people going about their business, and I filled Marianne in on the changes. She was like me, her eyes darting from one place to another, wide with interest, and every now and then she'd look up at me, check up on me, then nod to herself, as if I'd passed some sort of test.

'I'm fine,' I said to her, catching her out, just as we turned into Keith Street, and then I was brought up short. 'Is this it?'

'It is, and it isn't.' I began to walk slowly down the street. 'That flat there, on the second floor, was ours.' It looked shabbier than I recalled, against the newer buildings that had gone up since. 'And here,' I said, standing in front of the next block, 'this used to be a wine merchants, and there was a dairy further down.' The old buildings, thatched cottages and two-storey houses were falling down, their roofs sagging, their windows boarded up. The church was still there, and the old Quakers Graveyard, but all around it the buildings were falling down or being pulled down.

'Your father isn't buried there, is he?' Marianne asked, looking at the tumble of ancient graves.

'No, that's not been used for about twenty years,' I said. 'He's over in Govan with my ma. Across the other side of the Clyde.'

'Do you want to pay your respects?'

'I'd rather recall happier times. We *were* happy here, you know.'

'Yes.' She smiled, pressing my arm, which she hadn't let go the whole time we'd been walking. 'Show me more.'

So I did. The big police station on Anderson Street where my father was stationed for a while when he was with the Partick Burgh force. The school I went to. The grocer shop where my ma used to send me for bread and milk in the mornings. The cricket ground at Hamilton Crescent. 'Though that wasn't there when I was a wean. We played out in the back courts, along the banks of the Kelvin, and what is now the West End Park.'

I didn't want to go further along to Thornhill, where my da had moved when my ma died. Instead, we retraced our steps to walk into the park, over the old Snow Bridge, with the massive edifice of Glasgow University rising up in front of us. The day had turned sultry, but the weather had still brought out the Weegies in force.

We passed couples like ourselves, who nodded a greeting as they passed. Men doffed their hats. Weans screamed and shouted on the banks of the Kelvin, just as they always had. The river was too low for the mills to be running. Further in, at the pond, there were nannies and governesses from the posher bit of the West End, and on the steep banks of the grass rising up to the terraces that were being built there, younger people sitting taking in the sun from all walks of life.

The view from the top of the hill was as breathtaking as ever, with the sweep of Park Circus behind us, the West End Park spread below us, and over on the other side, the University. 'My goodness,' Marianne said, 'it is quite beautiful. And so grand.'

'Here, it is. If you look over there, you'll see the Clyde, and the shipyards I was telling you about. That's what all the new tenements in Partick are for, to house the ship builders.'

'It's quite a contrast, isn't it.' She was looking at Park Circus, the elegant town houses, the imposing porticoes. 'This is like Edinburgh's New Town. And the park there, acts as the border, like Princes Street Gardens, save that people here seem to mix more than they do in Edinburgh.

I like it here. I mean this city. I don't know why, but I feel comfortable here in a way that I don't in Edinburgh.'

'Glasgow's a friendlier city, but you weren't at all comfortable this morning.'

'I was overwhelmed.' She walked away, over to the edge of the hill where we were standing, and leaned on the railings, looking out over the west of the city. 'Don't you miss it, Rory?'

I hadn't, until she asked me. Joining her at the railings, I focused on the ribbon of the Clyde, where the cranes for the engineering works were spread out, more of them than I remembered, bigger than I recalled. 'I left for Edinburgh to join the force twenty years ago. I've never worked here, never made my own life here, never thought to either.'

'Is there a demand for your sort of work here?'

'Funnily enough, my da's friend from the force said there was good business to be had, for the right man.'

'And are you the right man?'

Glasgow was only two hours from Edinburgh by train. Two hours from Marianne. But why would Marianne remain in Edinburgh, if she had the funds to go wherever she chose? And why would I imagine Marianne's whereabouts would be of any interest to me, after she'd found out…

'Rory.'

She tugged at my sleeve, raising her eyebrow at me. Just the one. And I lost my train of thought. 'Have you any notion what that does to me?'

'I don't know what you mean.'

'This.' I traced her brow with my finger. Then I let my fingers flutter down her cheek. Then I leaned over, and I kissed her. Her lips were warm. Sun-kissed, I thought hazily, the thought rousing me even more. She lifted her hand to my cheek. Smoothing it down, the palm of her glove cupping my chin.

I whispered her name. I didn't know it was a question. I hadn't meant it as a question, but she answered me all the same. 'Yes,' she whispered. 'Oh, yes.'

Chapter Twenty-Three

Marianne

Glasgow—
Monday 13th August 1877

I barely recall the journey back from the West End Park to the Queen's Hotel. We walked until Rory found us a hackney carriage. We sat side by side. I looked out of the dusty window, but I didn't see anything. My hand lay on Rory's leg. He unbuttoned my glove and eased it off slowly, finger by finger. He had removed his own glove. He traced circles on my palm.

All of my attention was on his hand, on the circles he was drawing, circles that were sending shivers up my arm, making my body thrum, making my nipples ache for his touch, making me feel as if I couldn't breathe. Making me want to moan my pleasure. I bit my lip, and he continued stroking my hand. I didn't dare look at him. I never wanted that journey to end. I was desperate for it to end.

When we arrived, and it did end, I did moan, softly. I heard the intake of his breath in response. I dare not look at him. I knew he was as aroused as I was. I knew, though I hadn't touched him. I don't recall descending from the coach or him paying the driver. I waited, barely aware of our surroundings.

But when the carriage pulled away and we ascended the shallow flight of marble steps to enter the hotel's reception area, Rory pulled me to one side. 'Marianne, I want...'

'So do I.'

He laughed shortly, his cheeks warm. 'Two rooms. I'll get two rooms. Then it's not too late to change your mind.'

'I won't, Rory.' Now that my decision had been made, I felt so certain. 'I won't change my mind.'

I thought he would kiss me there and then. He shuddered. He shook his head. He made to say something. Then he headed over to the reception desk. Five minutes later, we were being escorted up the stairs by a liveried porter who seemed to take our lack of luggage quite for granted, muttering about the shocking state of the Edinburgh railway, the vast numbers of passengers and the lack of railway porters.

Rory nodded in agreement, though I knew his mind was on me, almost entirely on me. He barely contained his impatience as the porter showed us the two adjoining rooms, one for Mr Sutherland, one for his good lady wife, and the little sitting room that separated them. Happy that he had earned the tip Rory slid into his waiting palm, the man finally departed.

And finally, belatedly, my nerves began to make themselves felt. 'I've never in my life been in a hotel before,' I said, going over to the sitting room window and staring out at the view of George Square. 'Do you think they believed that we are married?'

'If we'd been any younger, they might have been more sceptical. I'm not much interested in what anyone else thinks, however.'

'But you're nervous!' I exclaimed, unthinking.

He laughed shakily. 'Do you think I make a habit of this sort of thing?' He set his hat and gloves down on the table, and pushed his hair back from his brow. 'I've never in my life—not like this. And I'm thinking—or at least I'm trying to think—to tell myself—that we shouldn't.'

But I felt that this was meant. Our one chance. Fate had intervened. And I wanted so much, so desperately, for this to happen. Now. As did he, I was sure of it.

I set my gloves down beside his. I took off my bonnet. I draped my shawl over a chair. I went to him, putting one hand on each shoulder, and I leaned into him. 'I want you, Rory,' I whispered. 'I have never wanted anyone like this.' The truth of it made me light-headed. Whatever this was between us, it was like nothing ever before. The delight of that, and the relief made me giddy. 'And you want me too, don't you?'

'You know I do Marianne, every bit as much. And I've never...'

'Never,' I said, leaning closer.

'Never.'

Our lips met. This kiss was different. I felt the jolt of connection, joining, merging, the rightness of it, deep inside me. It was a kiss like nothing I'd ever felt before. Elemental. I didn't speak, but I said his name in my head, over and over. And he spoke to me in the same language. Mouth, minds, touching, melding.

Rory, I thought, raking my fingers through his hair.

Marianne, he said, pulling the pins from mine, running

his hands through my thick tresses, uncut for so long now that they hung down my back almost to my waist.

Rory. Pushing his coat back, I felt the heat of his skin through his shirt and waistcoat. The flex of his shoulders as I stroked, then the hiss of his exhaling breath.

Marianne. His mouth on my neck, kiss after kiss, fluttering down my skin, while he pushed back the neckline of my gown, and there were more kisses, on my collarbones, across the top of my breasts, making me sigh his name again.

His coat fell to the floor followed by his waistcoat, his collar and necktie. Kissing, we made our way to one of the bedchambers. Still kissing, we pulled the curtains closed. In the soft afternoon light, we stopped to look at each other for a moment, just a moment.

More?

Yes.

Oh, yes.

Passionate kisses now, but he was careful not to embrace me, his hands on my arms, on the fastenings of my gown, smoothing over my breasts, making my nipples harden and peak beneath the layers of my undergarments. I yearned for him. I ached for him. I was frantic for him. My desire for him staggered me, it was so new, so different, as if this was what I had always been waiting for. This man. This moment.

'Marianne.' His voice took me aback. His eyes were dark, his lids heavy, his breathing ragged. 'I need to know—are you certain?'

'You know I am.'

'If you change your mind…'

'I won't, Rory.'

He studied me for a long moment. Then he kissed me again, slowly this time, taking his time, but when I tried to deepen the kiss, he drew back. 'There's no hurry,' he said, and it confused me, for I thought there was always a hurry. There always had been before. My body was clamouring, roused. I remembered what I had forgotten. That I had reached this point but no further. That the rush there had always been had left me disappointed. I had been so sure that there was more, but there never was.

"Trust me,' Rory said, kissing me softly again. 'Will you trust me?'

I knew I could. I *knew.* I nodded, overcome, unable to speak.

He turned me around, pushing my hair over my shoulder to kiss my neck. He began to unbutton my gown, his mouth feathering kisses on each bit of skin he revealed. I gave myself over to him. He unwrapped me, layer by layer, and I stood pliant, though every touch, every kiss aroused me more. My gown slid to the floor. He reached around me to unfasten my corset, carefully working to untie the knots. Behind me, he was all but fully clothed, careful to keep a distance.

Trust me.

I resisted the urge to lean into him.

My corset fell to the floor. His arms were around me, but carefully, his hands cupping my breasts, his thumbs stroking my nipples through my chemise, drawing a long moan of pleasure from me.

Marianne. Marianne. Marianne.

The way he said my name roused me more. I could no longer resist leaning back into him, my petticoats against his thighs, his soft cry of pleasure as I nestled closer, emboldened by his arousal. My petticoats were next. I stepped out of them. He turned me back round to face him at last, and our mouths met again. Frantic this time. Not slow. Frantic. Still he did not embrace me, but I wanted to be closer. Pressing against him again, I felt him hard against my belly. His hands cupped my bottom, pulling me closer. Hot. I was so hot.

I tugged at his shirt. He pulled it over his head. I studied him. Taking my time. This was new. All of this was new. The way he watched me watching him. The anticipation, sharp between us, shared between us. I smoothed my hands over his skin, encouraged by the sharp intake of his breath, feeling the ripple of his muscles under my touch. Smooth skin. Rough hair on his chest. The dip of his belly. A scar, a long thin scar on his abdomen.

'Knife,' he said, as I traced the curve of it.

His skin was burning. I wanted to feel his arms around me, but I was afraid, and so I wrapped my arms around his waist instead. I burrowed my face into his chest, my smooth cheek, his rough hair, his nipple peaking under my palm, the smell of his soap, a faint tang of sweat. His hands smoothed my hair. He said my name and I looked up, seeing such tenderness in his expression. I slid my arms up around his neck and burrowed closer. Then our lips met again and we fell back on to the bed, still kissing. But though he had kicked off his shoes he was still wearing his trousers. I was frantic, but I wasn't sure what to do. What he wanted.

'Nothing,' he said to me, pushing my hair back from my face. 'I don't want anything. Trust me.'

I did, but I didn't understand, and I must have said so, for he smiled, a smile that I had never seen before, a smile that made my insides tense further with desire. Then he began to kiss me. My lips. My neck. My breasts. Taking my nipples in his mouth, teasing, sucking, licking, driving me wild, and stilling me with his hands. My belly. He knelt down and eased my legs apart. I grabbed his hair. He looked up. Another of those smiles. 'Do you want me to stop, Marianne?'

'No. No, no, no.' And as he kissed me again, his mouth soft and hot between my legs, 'Yes, yes. Oh, Rory, yes.'

His kisses made me feel like molten metal, melted chocolate, bubbling, burning sugar. I was a tightly coiled clock spring, I was a bow stretched too tight, I was clinging to a cliff face, my whole body tensed, and then I was shattered int a million pieces of pure and utter delight, spinning and spiralling out of control, as wave after wave of pleasure picked me up and tossed me in the air and then let me fall.

I was calling out his name, I was clutching at his hair, at his shoulders, my legs were wrapped tightly around his body, and then I was trying to pull him up towards me, to find his mouth. Such kisses. Such bliss. I was lying on top of him, my breasts flattened against his chest, kissing him frantically, saying his name urgently, his hardness pressed to the throbbing heat between my legs. He was still half dressed.

'Rory.' I tugged at the waistband of his trousers. He removed my hand and eased me on to my side. 'Rory?'

'I can't.' He sat up. 'It's not any lack of desire. I've never wanted anything so much in my life, but I simply can't—must not.'

'Why not?' I sat up too, pulling the sheet over my nakedness. 'What did I do? What's wrong?'

'There's nothing wrong. This couldn't feel more right, and that's the problem.'

The words frightened me, for they echoed what I was feeling. Instinctively, I shrank away from him.

Rory rolled out of bed and pulled on his shirt. 'I'm sorry.'

'You're *sorry*?'

'I don't mean that, not the way you think.'

'Then what do you mean? No, never mind. It's best if you leave me alone now.'

He took a step towards me then changed his mind. 'You're right.'

The door closed quietly behind him. I felt as if I'd been dropped violently from a very high, blissful place, to a very cold, rocky one. Tears burned my eyes. I burrowed my way under the sheets, digging my nails into my palms. I wasn't hurt. I wouldn't cry, but I had been *such* a fool.

Chapter Twenty-Four

Rory

Glasgow—
Tuesday 14th August 1877

Mr and Mrs Soutar lived in one of the newer, larger tene-ments in Shawlands on the South Side of the River Clyde. Mr Soutar was employed as a senior clerk in the local Cam-phill Bakery, while his son, Oscar, was an office junior in the Bank of Scotland in Queen Street. It was a delicate situation, and though Marianne and I had discussed how we'd set about it, as we reached the entrance to the close, I was on edge.

'After seven years, if we are right, we may be able to give this family some answers if not all,' she said to me, as I raised my hand to knock the door. 'This is the reason we are here in Glasgow, we must give it our full attention.'

It was the first oblique reference she'd made to last night. Though I'd ordered a dinner to be sent up to her before I went out for a walk to try to sort out the mess my head was in, she hadn't eaten a thing by the time I returned. I hadn't seen her until this morning, when she'd emerged from her room carrying her bonnet and gloves, and determined to talk to me about this visit and nothing else.

I introduced Marianne as my female assistant, for she'd had none of it when I suggested she could pretend to be my wife, and the Soutars seemed to accept this, son Oscar chiming in that he'd been reading all about Mrs Paschal, in Revelations of a Lady Detective. It took me a moment to work out he was referring to a work of fiction.

It was a heart-wrenching hour that we spent with the Soutar family. We already knew from my da's friend that Ada Soutar, their eldest child, had been reported missing around the same time as Lillian's body was found. Mr Soutar told us how much Ada had loved her job at Copland and Lye, one of the posh department stores on Sauchiehall Street that specialised in ladies' apparel.

She was always well turned-out thanks to the staff discount she got, her mother said. She was vain, her father said, and spent too much on frippery, but we must not be getting ideas, his daughter was a respectable young woman. Then he got upset, poor man, though he tried to hold himself together, blowing his nose and coughing, and saying he'd caught a cold paddling in the Clyde at the West Bay lido in Dunoon, which, to be fair, was highly plausible.

Mrs Soutar insisted on making us tea. After she brought in the tray, her husband produced the photograph of Ada, taken on her twenty-first birthday. She was looking primly at the camera, as they all do in those photographs, but you could see she had been a bonny lassie. The same bonny lassie that we'd pulled from Leith Docks, cut off in her prime of life, bearing another life that would never see the light of day. I had to clench my fists to mask my anger. A glance at Marianne showed me she was feeling the same surge of emotion. The waste of it. The pity of it. The sense-less loss.

Which made me forget what I was feeling and turn my attention back to the ones who had suffered far more. We sombrely told them, the Soutar family, of their loss, and it was one of the hardest things I've ever had to do. The tea remained untouched on the tray. We sat with them as the shock gave way to grief. We told them only what we'd agreed, Marianne and I, almost exactly what I'd been told to think had happened all those years ago. Ada had died by accident. She'd tripped and fallen into the docks. She'd hit her head. She hadn't suffered. This last element wasn't true, but there was nothing to be gained by hurting them further. They didn't ask too many questions, the family, and for that I was grateful.

When we left them, Mrs Soutar and Oscar were crying unashamedly. Mr Soutar, with his eyes red-rimmed, took both my hands in the fiercest of grips. 'Thanks, Son,' he said. 'We'll be able to get her a headstone now.'

Both Marianne and I were silent on the journey back into town, and I knew that she was thinking, like me, of the bereaved family we'd left behind. In the waiting room at Dundas Street station, I ordered us both another cup of tea we didn't want, and buns I knew we wouldn't eat. We were both of us aware of the conversation we knew we had to have too, but neither of us had the appetite for that either.

I told myself it was because I wasn't sure of my state of mind, but it was the opposite of that, and I was equally sure that the last thing I should do was discuss it. As to Marianne, for once I hadn't a clue what she was thinking, and as she was clearly determined that I shouldn't, I knew her well enough not to push her.

'Well, we've done what we had to do,' I said. 'I'm glad you were with me. I reckon it made all the difference to Mrs Soutar.'

'We did the right thing, didn't we, in telling them their daughter was dead?'

'I had the proof the minute I saw the photograph.' I shivered, remembering the same woman lying prostrate on the side of Leith dock.

'Don't dwell on that, Rory,' Marianne said. 'Ada's family can grieve for her now. You heard her father. They will have a headstone erected for her in their church graveyard. She was much missed. She won't be forgotten. You have given them that much.'

'*We* have.'

'I have contributed very little.'

'That's nonsense. I wouldn't even have gone back to the case if it weren't for you.' I reached for her automatically, it had become a habit with me so quickly it was scary. Midway, I remembered, and I picked up my teacup instead.

She pretended not to notice. 'What next though, Rory?'

'I don't know. We know more about Ada, also thanks to you.'

'The "fancy rich gentleman admirer" that her mother told me about when we were in the scullery together. They must have had somewhere where they met regularly, don't you think?'

'It could be he had a flat, or rooms in the West End. Ada let fall to Oscar that she'd been taking walks in the Botanic Gardens. He couldn't understand why she'd go all the way from the South Side to the West End, when there was a big new park on her doorstep.'

'And Mrs Soutar was convinced that he was a successful

business man, something to do with property. She couldn't tell me how she arrived at that conclusion. It must have been something that Ada let drop, or that she overheard, and she put two and two together.'

'A bit like you do yourself,' I said. 'And you managed to get Mrs Soutar to admit she knew her daughter was expecting a baby. Neither the father nor the son had any idea about that.'

'Mrs Soutar was very keen that they never do. She has kept that secret for so long, if her husband found out now, it would make matters between them unbearable.'

'Soutar won't hear a bad word against his daughter,' I said. 'Every time I tried to ask him if she was walking out with anyone he bristled. Too much, actually. I reckon he must have some idea, after all. Maybe he noticed more than his wife realised and like her, kept silent.'

'Poor Mrs Soutar is heartbroken. The last thing Ada told her was that she was going to find the baby's father and force him to take care of her. She made her mother promise she'd keep the situation secret until she came home. But of course she never did come home.'

Marianne's eyes filled with tears. I wanted to comfort her, but she was already dabbing at her eyes, glaring at me as if to say, don't you dare. 'Did Mrs Soutar rate her daughter's chances of success?'

'The fact that Ada wouldn't tell her the man's name made her suspicious. I think that both she and Ada suspected it was not his real name.'

'So he was likely married?'

Marianne nodded. 'I'm afraid that makes horrible sense. It was Ada's words. She wanted him to "take care of her".'

'Not marry her, do the decent thing? You're right, the words are telling.'

'What do you think she did expect though, if not marriage?'

'Money? Somewhere decent for herself and the bairn to live? I don't know, it could have been anything.'

'But what she actually got—oh, Rory, she didn't deserve that.'

'No. My sex never cover themselves in glory, where you are concerned, do they?'

She flinched, paled. 'I don't blame you for last night, if that's what you mean. There is no need to inform me once again that you are sorry.'

'I didn't mean—I was referring to the bigamy case you told me about. As for last night…'

She shook her head violently. 'We are discussing Ada.'

We would need to discuss Marianne and Rory soon, but she was right. 'So, we've got a man who's more than likely married, who might be a property developer, who did a bunk when he discovered that Ada was expecting his child.'

'Does did a bunk mean he ran off?'

'It does.'

'But if he was well to do, why didn't he "take care of" Ada and the child before he left?'

'It's a good question. Perhaps he didn't know about the child. What's clear to me now that we've met them is that the Soutar family are not likely to benefit from knowing that their daughter was murdered.'

Marianne had been turning her cup around in its saucer without drinking the contents. At this, she looked up. 'Even if we discover who did it?'

'It's not going to bring Ada back, is it? As things stand,

no matter what they suspect, they can paint a picture for themselves and their family and friends too, if they want, that doesn't slander their wee lassie. Think about it, Marianne, they didn't ask us what she was doing in Leith, or even Edinburgh, for that matter. Mrs Soutar told you some of her thoughts, but Mr Soutar went out of his way *not* to ask. That's what been bothering me, now I come to think of it. It was his lack of questions.'

'So he does know more than he admitted to?'

'Like I said, he probably noticed Ada was pregnant, but he was sticking his head in the sand, hoping that someone else would deal with the situation.'

'Which poor Ada was trying to do. But what about poor Rory?' Marianne asked with a sad smile. 'You still want to know the truth, don't you? To know why your name was blackened? After all this time...'

'After all this time,' I said slowly, 'I'm beginning to think it doesn't really matter that much at all. We've given the family some peace of mind, so they can stop wondering. Right now, I'm thinking that might be enough for me too.'

There were other things on my mind. One in particular, sitting opposite me. Whatever we said at the time, what happened between us yesterday mattered a great deal more than it should have, and it had to be dealt with. I checked my watch and saw to my relief that our train was due. 'It's time we went. Mind now, the platform will be busy.'

'I am prepared for it this time, thank you.'

She marched off, making it clear that she too had been thinking about last night, and she wasn't' ready to talk about it either. I threw some coins down on the table, cursing under my breath for she was almost immediately enveloped in a cloud of smoke. I grabbed hold of her, just as she clutched at me. 'Rory.' She sounded relieved but un-surprised. She tucked her hand into my arm.

We travelled First Class. It was a calculated risk, for there might be a fellow traveller that recognised me, but I hadn't slept a wink last night, and I doubted Marianne had either. The last thing we needed was two hours on a wooden bench exposed to the driving rain that was falling that typical summer's day. We had the carriage to ourselves.

Marianne pretended to be asleep. I passed the journey trying to decide what to do or not do about the tangle I'd got myself into, and in the end I opted to wait until I got back to my digs. If there was a telegram from the Marquess then that at least took one of the decisions out of my hands. It was procrastinating, but I told myself it wasn't, and turned my mind back to Ada Soutar's murder.

Money, as usual, was what it almost certainly came back to. Someone from Edinburgh with enough money to invest in building property in the West End of Glasgow. Someone who maybe had installed his lady friend in one of them. Someone who had completed his business in Glasgow, and scarpered back home, maybe in the knowledge that he was leaving his lady friend carrying his child and his empty promises behind, maybe oblivious to the situation. Someone wealthy and powerful enough to pay someone to make the problem go away. And to have me dealt with as well, when I looked like I might be getting too close—not that I had, but I would have if they'd let me, they had been right to worry.

Edinburgh was a big city and I'd been away seven years, but I doubted the cream at the top of society had changed much. By the time we reached Waverly, I had drawn up a list in my head of possible candidates. Would I do anything to pursue it? Seven years, I'd been waiting to get this close.

Seven years, I'd been nursing a grudge, letting it gnaw away at me, and wondering why what had happened to me had happened. The list in my head was a short one, but what good would it do me? There was no evidence. What's more, after seven years I was scunnered thinking about it. I had other, more pressing matters on my mind.

Marianne wanted to make her own way home. Like me, she clearly wanted to be alone with her thoughts, so I didn't protest, much as I wanted to. I knew I had some life-changing decisions to make, and we'd reached a temporary impasse between us, but the moment she started to walk away, all I wanted was to have her by my side.

I didn't go straight back to my digs. I decided that after all I didn't want a telegram or lack of a telegram from the Marquess to decide my fate, I wanted it to be my own decision. So I took myself off, up Salisbury Craggs in the rain.

I reached the top in record time, head down, marching up, until I arrived out of breath and soaked to the skin. There was no view to speak of today, you could hardly see Duddingston, never mind Leith, so there was nothing to distract me, and not a soul about save for the gulls and the crows.

First things first. There was no denying it, no dancing around it, no more trying to kid myself on. I was in love with Marianne. Deeply, head over heels, desperately in love with Marianne for ever. How did I know, when I'd never been in love before? I just did, simple as that. What happened to all my, I'm too old to fall in love, I'm not the type to fall in love reasons? Easily answered. I'd never fallen in love before because I hadn't met the right person. If I hadn't met Marianne, I would still be the type that didn't fall in love. She was the only one for me. No one else would do. Like I said, simple.

Simple if only it wasn't such a bloody tangle. I was in love. The one straightforward thing I could say to her. I love you. God help me, I'd near enough said it yesterday when I was making love to her. And I'd been making love. That was the thing that hit me like a ton of bricks afterwards. I mean, really making love, to the woman I was in love with. I closed my eyes and lifted my face to the rain, and I let myself wallow in every perfect moment of it.

And it had been perfect, for her as well as me. That's not me bragging, that's just something else I knew in my heart, as if she'd told me herself. It had been perfect. Like nothing else before for either of us. It was it being so perfect that made those other times so irrelevant. I didn't want to think of her with another man any more than I wanted to think of myself with another woman, but it didn't matter. For me, she was the only one, as if there hadn't ever been anyone else before. And there wouldn't be anyone after.

Not even her?

Especially not her! I came out of my dwam to find it was tipping it down again, so I cowered under the crags for shelter. Time to come back down to earth. What the devil had I been playing at yesterday? Or with? Fire, that's what, and now I'd been well and truly and deservedly burned, for I'd paid no heed to the many warnings I'd issued to myself.

I'd known that it was a mistake to stay over in Glasgow, but I'd done it anyway. I'd known that I was lying to myself, when I agreed we were only 'making the most of the situation'. How many times since we first met had I sworn to myself that I wouldn't kiss her again, then by some tortuous logic, allowed myself to carry on in her company until

I couldn't resist her. Me, the detective who prided myself on being able to second-guess everyone's motives, I'd been blind when it came to myself.

But there's only so much self-lacerating you can do. It was done, and I'd done it to myself. Question was, what to do for the best. No, the first question was, what was Marianne thinking? How did she feel? She didn't love me. Did she? She certainly didn't want to love me. And even if she loved me now, at this moment, would she still love me after she found out the truth? Would she think I'd been pretending to fall in love with her when all the time I was actually in love with her inheritance?

No way! Bloody hell, surely she couldn't believe that of me. But if I asked her to marry me before I told her about the money—no, I couldn't do that. Then if I asked her to marry me after I told her about the money—no, I couldn't do that either. What's more, I was losing sight of something even more important. This was about Marianne, and who she was, and the shock she was going to get when she found out. When I told her. That was one decision made. Whatever the Marquess decreed, I was going to be the one who told her. I owed her that.

In the end, it actually was simple. There was no hope. Even if she would have considered marrying me right now, with none of these other things hanging over us, I doubted that she would consider it. She'd been crystal clear that she didn't want a husband, just as I had been crystal clear that I didn't want a wife. Unless it was Marianne.

I was going round and round in circles, and my head was aching as if I'd dunted it on the crags. And here's the thing—yet another thing. Marianne wasn't Marianne. She was Lady Mary Anne Westville. Heiress. Who, if all went well, would do wonderful things with her money, and who deserved to be free to do whatever she wanted, after all she'd suffered. Whatever her plans were, I would play no part in them.

Yesterday, I shouldn't have made love to her, but having done so, I shouldn't have said I was sorry afterwards. I wasn't sorry. It was wrong of me, and the memories would likely eat me up later, but I wasn't sorry. In my own way I'd demonstrated how I felt. I'd always have that.

There was a crack of thunder, followed quickly by a fork of lightning over Duddingston way and another long roll of thunder. We were in for a spectacular storm. The sensible thing now would be to sit it out, but I seemed to have turned into someone incapable of being sensible, lately. I pulled up the collar of my already sodden coat, and began to head back down the hill.

Chapter Twenty-Five

Marianne

Edinburgh—
Wednesday 15th August 1877

Ever since Monday in Glasgow, I had had a crushing sense of an imminent ending. Now we knew that it was Ada Soutar who had been murdered, and at least part of the reason why, we were close to resolving Rory's old case. Soon he would have answers to the questions that had tortured him for seven long years, or he would know that he would never have answers. If he chose to pursue the matter, that was.

In the tearoom at Dundas Street, he had not seemed particularly eager. After all this time haunted by his failure to solve the case and the blackening of his name, Rory had seemed almost dismissive of his own involvement. Ada's family could grieve. That was enough, he seemed to be saying. He could stop searching for answers. He could leave Edinburgh. Which would be for the best. That's what I told myself over and over during my sleepless night. It would be better for both of us if he left Edinburgh.

I did not love Rory. I would not love Rory. I would never, ever, let myself fall in love again. But I had come perilously close. It terrified me, how close I had come. And he had too. His face, when he left the hotel bedroom on Monday, spoke of how much he felt, and how much he regretted. And his words.

I've never wanted anything so much in my life.

This couldn't feel more right, and that's the problem.

Those were *my* thoughts, though I hadn't known I was thinking them until Rory spoke them aloud.

The man I thought I loved had turned on me because I would not marry him. I would not surrender my freedom to Francis, bind myself in marriage, become his. But he had made me his anyway, his prisoner, his madwoman. Love had almost killed me.

I would not love Rory. I did not love Rory. Rory did not love me. On Monday, in the hotel in Glasgow, I thought he might. I thought he was on the point of speaking of it. I *wanted* him to speak, and that's what terrified me more than anything, that I wanted what would destroy me. Rory wasn't Francis. Rory *wasn't* Francis. All of my instincts told me that I could trust Rory, had told me so from the start. When Rory kissed me, I *felt* his longing for me. When he was with me, I was sure it was because he wanted to be with me.

This couldn't feel more right.

I felt exactly the same.

And that was the problem. My instincts had let me down with Francis. The one and only time I had been utterly wrong, and the one and only time when I relied upon them to guide me. I couldn't trust myself. I couldn't take the risk that I might be wrong again.

At least my wakeful night had spared me my usual dreams, my usual waking terror. In fact, it had been two or three days since I had woken with the smell of the institution in my nose, my sheets clammy. My dreams had been of Rory these last few nights, not the asylum. A few weeks ago, two weeks ago, as little as a week ago, I'd have given a great deal to pass one night without my dreams of that place, without having to wake terrified, clammy, imagining myself back there. I had done so for the last few days, and I hadn't even noticed!

I rolled out of bed and opened the window. It was still raining, though softly now after last night's storm. The cobblestones on the Grassmarket were shining, slickly wet and treacherous. I was later than usual, for there was Flora, plaid wrapped tightly around her, hair in soaking rat's tails, heading into the tavern. Surely she could not have had much business in last night's foul weather? Poor woman. If I was in her situation, I would be sorely tempted to earn money from Billy Sinclair.

My stomach rumbled. I closed the window and made my coffee, forcing myself to eat some bread and cheese. There was a possibility Rory might be thinking himself in love with me. And oh, if he was—my heart fluttered wildly.

But if Rory found out he was in love with an escaped lunatic, that would quickly put an end to it. I would never trust anyone with the truth about myself again. Rory already knew far more than I should have told him. I would not give him any more power over me. No more kisses. No more thinking about kisses. No more dreaming about making love to him, or remembering those perfect, wonderful, blissful hours in Glasgow when it had been just the two of us. The lovemaking that had been such a revelation. The lovemaking that had introduced me to a whole new world of sensation. The love that Rory had made to me, giving without taking.

Oh, Rory.

Oh, Marianne, get a grip of yourself!

I set my coffee cup down, and jumped to my feet. I needed him to leave Edinburgh. I needed to tell him to go. I sat back down again. Wouldn't it be better if I never saw Rory again? My heart sank. Never?

One last time. Then goodbye. Resolved, I dressed myself and prepared to seek him out to tell him so. I still had no idea where his lodgings were, but Flora might be able to help me. I was pulling on my cloak when there was a rap at my door that made my heart leap in fear. No one ever knocked on my door except the landlord, and my rent was not due. I stood stock still, willing whoever it was to go away. They rapped again.

'Marianne. Don't be afraid. It's Rory.'

Relief flooded through me. I threw the door open, but seeing him standing there, I was flooded with a very different emotion. 'What do you want?'

'I need to talk to you. I know you don't want me here, I know this is your sanctuary, but I need to talk to you, and in private. It's important. May I come in?'

I didn't love him, I told myself as I stood back to allow him in. But my heart was telling me I did. Deluded heart.

He was looking about him, though he was pretending he wasn't. My rooms that were mine and mine alone, were being surveyed. 'You have quite a view from here.'

I crossed my arms. 'I was on the point of going out.' To look for him as it happens, but I wasn't going to say so.

'What is so important—oh! Rory, have you found out who the father of Ada's child is?'

'What? No. I've a list of possible suspects, but I've decided not to pursue it.'

'Not pursue it! You've spent the last seven years wondering...'

'And I reckon I'll never know. I can suspect all I like, but we've not a scrap of evidence to link anyone to Ada's death. We've given her family an ending, and they can grieve now. Whoever was behind it...'

'Is getting away with murder! And with blackening your name. Destroying your career. You've been wondering and wondering why and who, Rory, for all those years.'

'I've realised it doesn't matter any more. I've made my life somewhere else. I don't want to go backwards. Whoever ordered Ada Soutar's death will pay in the end. Bad things eventually happen to bad people. But me—it's time I put the whole thing to bed for good. I'm done with it, and I actually feel relieved.'

'So you're leaving.' I had what I wanted, and now I didn't want it. He said nothing for a moment, words forming and being rejected as he gazed at me, and my stomach roiled, for it was such a look. 'What is it, Rory?'

'I've had a telegram. It's not Ada Soutar that I'm here to talk to you about, Marianne. It's my other case. The case that brought me here.'

My legs turned to jelly. I had no idea what he was going to say, but I knew I didn't want to hear it. 'You said it was suspended for two weeks. You said that you were waiting on something. A piece of the puzzle that needs clarifying, that's what you said.'

'It's sorted now. Marianne, the case...'

'Has something to do with me.' It was his face. The tone of his voice. No, it was more than that. All the pieces slotted together, all the clues that he'd given me that I hadn't realised I'd picked up, filed away, until I could make sense of them. The odd times when I'd thought he was on the brink of telling me something important. And the questions he'd asked me. I'd even accused him of interrogating me once. I sank on to the chair. My coffee cup still lay half-full on the table.

'Marianne, you're white as a sheet.'

I had been right to be wary. I had been right not to trust myself and right not to trust him. I had been looking over my shoulder all this time and it turned out the person they had sent to find me was Rory!

Chapter Twenty-Six

Rory

Edinburgh—
Wednesday 15th August 1877

I'd already decided there was no future for us, of my own accord. When I read the telegram from Lord Westville, that confirmed it. When I came here, I knew it. But seeing Marianne's face when she realised she'd been my quarry all along—that was when it really sank in. That was when I realised that right up until that point, I'd still been hoping there was a way for us to be together, fool that I was!

'Who sent you?' she asked me, whey-faced, her lovely eyes wide with fear, her hands gripped tightly together, knuckles white.

'It's not bad news,' I said hastily, appalled by the notion that must be crossing her mind, that I'd been sent to lock her up again. 'I promise, you're not in any danger.'

'You promise!'

The look she gave me then. She'd trusted me, and as far as she was concerned, I had been lying to her all along. I drew up a chair and sat down opposite her. I was really struggling not to tell her what I was feeling. I mean, really struggling. As if that would make things any easier. More like a bloody sight worse.

I'd been awake all night trying to work out the least painful way to explain, but I decided that the best thing was simply to get it over with. So I told her, about my meeting with Lord Westville and about the woman he had employed me to find. 'She'd be a distant cousin of his—of my client's I mean,' I said, trying to keep my voice level. Trying, too, to keep my own feelings in check, for I didn't want her sensing them, and I didn't want what I was feeling getting in the way of what I was telling her. This wasn't about me. Or us. It was about Marianne.

She had herself in check again, holding herself painfully rigid. 'He had no idea she existed, this distant cousin, is that what you are telling me?'

'None at all. I was sceptical when he told me at first, but what he told me of his own father convinced me.' I waited, giving her plenty time to sort through what I'd told her before moving on. I'd never seen her so tightly wound.

'So your Lord Westville's father knew of her, but he had no interest in her fate. And *her* father had no interest in making her acquaintance, even after he had paid someone else to go to the trouble of raising her. Am I correct?'

That cold tone. Those measured words. I wanted to tell her she had it wrong. I wanted to tell her that her father had cared, but I didn't know what he'd felt, and it wasn't my place to make her guesses or suppositions for her. 'Yes, but *my* Lord Westville, as you call him, employed me to find her.'

'And how did you set about doing that?'

I told her all of it. Asylum to asylum. Then Nurse Crawford. My voice cracked a couple of times. Marianne was retreating further and further into her shell before my very eyes. I swear, it was like she was turning to stone. 'That led me to Mrs White at the employment agency in Edinburgh. I pretended that I was looking to employ a children's nurse hoping to find more information, but I was given short shrift. She was clearly protecting you.'

'I owe Mrs White more than I can put into words.'

'It wasn't difficult though, to find you in this city without her help. There was the name you'd assumed. And as you've told me yourself, you're good at what you do.'

'As are you, clearly, Detective Sutherland,' she said coldly.

'Marianne, do you understand the implications of what I've told you so far? Your real name is Lady Mary Anne Westville. You're the legitimate daughter of a marquess.'

'You have discovered that I am also an escaped lunatic.'

'There's nothing wrong with your mind! You must know that I've never for one minute thought that you were locked up for genuine reasons. I think that you're the strongest, bravest woman I could ever wish to meet. Even before I set eyes on you, I was in awe of you. To have come through what they did to you, to keep your mind perfectly sane, to have the confidence and belief in yourself—Marianne, I swear to god, that's what I think, and more. You're an amazing woman. I told you that before, and I meant it. I still mean it.'

I could see her throat working. I could feel tears smarting in my own eyes, but I held her gaze. I wasn't ashamed of what I was feeling. I wanted her to know that. Finally, she gave a little nod, picked her cup up and found it empty.

'Shall I make another pot?'

'Please.'

I was glad of it, something to do for her and a breather for both of us. I'd always known this would be difficult, but watching her was proving an agony. And there was a lot more to come. 'Do you want me to get you something stronger?' I asked, setting the fresh cup down. 'I could nip across to the White Hart.'

She shook her head. She lifted the cup, her hands shaking, and took several sips. 'You know that if it ever came out that I was committed to an asylum…'

'That you were wrongly held against your will…'

'Does he know, this man who has employed you to find me?'

'He knows the bones of it.'

'And what did he…?' Her mouth wobbled, and she took another sip of her coffee. 'It doesn't matter. I am not interested in meeting him, any more than he will be interested in meeting me.'

'You're wrong, Marianne. He's your family, and…'

'My mother died giving birth. My father gave me away. His heir was so indifferent he never even mentioned my existence. I was not wanted, Rory. The message could not be clearer.'

I wanted to argue with her, but it would be a distraction, and I wasn't at all sure of my employer's feelings. The Marquess was set on justice, for getting Marianne her inheritance and making Eliot pay for what he'd done to her, but of his intentions regarding the woman who was his kin, he'd said nothing since I'd told him she was alive. Why should he? As far as he was concerned, to me, Marianne was merely a case to be solved. If he ever knew—I shuddered. He wouldn't, and it was beside the point.

'Lord Westville, your cousin, is on your side,' I said, which was true enough. And what's more, he was going out of his way to get her legacy for her, which must mean something.

But Marianne's lip curled. 'Lord Westville, my cousin! Mrs Oliphant will be delighted to discover that she has a marquess's daughter for a governess, don't you think? Lady Mary Anne Westville! That's not me. I have a name, I chose it myself, and I intend to keep it. Are you finished with your revelations, Rory? Now I come to think of it, why did you save them for now?'

It was the question I'd been dreading. I had resolved to stick to the facts, but I couldn't help but tell her something closer to the truth. 'I was tasked with finding you, but as to telling you—it was complicated. I was told to say nothing until what I referred to as the final piece of the puzzle was resolved, but it wasn't only that. There was so much I knew of your heritage that was likely to come as a huge shock to you, and from the first time we spoke, I felt...'

'Don't!' She jumped to her feet and hurried over to the window, throwing it open. 'Please don't, Rory. We—I— whatever you are feeling, I don't want to know.' She turned back around, but kept her distance, her hands clasped at her breast, her eyes pleading. 'You were right, what you said when we—after we—you were right. It was a mistake.'

'I didn't say that.'

'You said you were sorry.'

'I was, but not...'

'Please! We have been foolish and irresponsible, and it is as much my fault as yours. It was I who insisted that I was meant to help you. I who inflicted my company on you.'

'Inflicted! I clutched at any excuse to spend time with you.'

'Even though you knew me for an escaped lunatic.'

I opened my mouth to chastise her again, then I closed it. Her eyes were bright with tears, but her mouth was trembling in an attempt at a smile. 'Your sense of humour is part of your charm,' I said. 'One of the many reasons I was drawn to you.'

'Oh, Rory.'

She turned her back on me again, but not before I caught a glimpse of my own feelings reflected in her face. Or thought I did. And I tried to tell myself it didn't matter, but it did. It did my heart good, even if it changed nothing. Then she turned around, and it was clear that she had herself back in check, and that brought me back down to earth.

'You could have told me before now.' Her tone was businesslike. 'As I recall there were several occasions when you were on the brink of telling me the truth, but you changed your mind. Why?'

'I didn't have the full story and I was told to wait until I had it.' The facts, but not the truth. I couldn't leave it at that. 'I was to keep an eye on you, make sure you didn't come to any harm, and I was very happy to do that, because it was what I wanted, to spend time with you.'

'So you lied?'

'I have never lied to you. I've not been completely honest with you, but I've never lied.'

'Did you think I needed protecting, Rory, was that it? Did you think that I wasn't strong enough to deal with what you had to tell me?'

'You're strong, all right, but that place still haunts you, and no wonder. Then there was the fact that you had built a new life for yourself...'

'One I'm perfectly happy with.'

'That too. And I can relate to that. So I decided to wait

until I was in possession of all the facts. After Glasgow though, I'd decided to tell you anyway. It just so happened that when I got back to my digs, I had a telegram telling me to go ahead.'

Marianne narrowed he eyes at me. 'What else do you have to tell me?'

For a wee tiny moment, I wanted to end it there. I'd already put us both through the wringer, but we weren't even halfway done. I fingered the telegram in my pocket.

Legal matters resolved. Inform my cousin of her good fortune. Then return immediately to London to address the matter of retribution regarding Eliot.

Twenty-three words, ten of them instructing me to turn Marianne's world upside down. And the other thirteen forcing me to part from her, even though I'd already decided I needed to do that. Twenty-three in total. I'd choose my own with care.

'Rory?'

First things first. 'Your father didn't raise you, Marianne, but he did make provision for you.'

'The allowance that was paid to my foster parents, and then to me.'

'It was much more than that.' I took a breath. 'He left you a fortune.'

'What do you mean, a fortune?'

Keep it simple, I reminded myself. Stick to the facts. I told her the sum that Lord Westville had given me. She had the same reaction that I'd had. Her jaw dropped.

'Exactly.' For the first time, I hesitated.

Needless to say, she pounced. 'What?'

'There were conditions attached.' I told her, sticking to the facts again. Marianne turned paler and paler before my eyes. 'Do you understand what I'm telling you?' I asked, when the silence became unbearable.

'The man you tell me is my father left me a fortune, but though he had never met me, he believed me incapable of administering it, or perhaps he thought I'd fritter it away over the next hundred years, which is what it would take, given the huge sums involved. For whatever reason, he decided that I needed a sensible male to look after it for me. A husband, in other words. Do I have that right?'

'You do. And until you married, a trustee.'

'When did he die, Rory? The man you tell me is my father?'

'About seven years ago.'

I hadn't thought she could turn any paler, but she looked like a ghost now. There was something wrong. Something I didn't understand.

'And the name of my trustee?' Her voice wasn't much more than a whisper.

A horrible premonition took hold of me. 'Francis Eliot.'

I leapt to my feet, thinking she was about to fall off her chair, but she shrank from me. 'Don't touch me!'

It was a kick in the teeth, that look, those words, but I bit back everything I was feeling, and made myself sit back down, let her be, trying desperately to keep a rein on myself.

'Francis Eliot was the man who had me committed. I presume you knew that, Rory?'

I nodded, afraid to speak. I felt almost as sick as she looked.

'But what you didn't know—ah, but I can see you have

now put two and two together. Francis Eliot was the man that I...' She broke off, pushed her chair back but changed her mind about getting up. 'Francis Eliot was the man who wanted to marry me. So you were right all along, Rory. It really was all about the money.'

The last vestiges of colour drained from her face. I was on my feet as she began to topple sideways.

Chapter Twenty-Seven

Marianne

Edinburgh—
Wednesday 15th August 1877

I woke up on the floor, cradled in Rory's arms. For a blessed, wonderful, magical moment I lay there, drinking in the tender expression on his face, bathed in the warmth of the love that emanated from him, soothed by the gentle touch of his hand stroking my brow, and his embrace keeping me safe. Rory loved me. I loved him.

'No!' I yanked myself free and struggled to my feet. A wave of nausea hit me, but I pushed him away, clutching at the chair instead. It all came flooding back to me then. I sank on to the chair, waving Rory away. 'Sit down. Keep away from me.'

He did as I bid him, though he looked as sick as I felt. I poured the dregs of the coffee, aiming for my cup and only managing to get some of it in. It was cold and much stronger than I'd have made. I gulped it down. The harshness of it in my throat, hitting my stomach, steadied me.

Across from me, Rory's hands were shaking. He clasped

them together on the table. His frown was so deep it drew his brows together. 'So that's how Eliot gathered the evidence that was used against you...'

'He used my own words against me. Like an idiot I trusted him.'

'Oh, Marianne...'

I shrank back, though he'd made no move to reach for me. 'Did you suspect him from the first? Or was it when you saw his name on my papers in the asylum?'

He cursed under his breath. His father's language, but he made the soft Gaelic sound vicious. Then he gave himself a shake and began to speak in a tone I recognised, drained of emotion, reined in tight. 'Lord Westville and I—we've been very careful to make sure Eliot knows nothing of our suspicions, but, yes, we did suspect him from the first. He was the obvious candidate.

'It's a great deal of money and he was left solely in charge and unsupervised, so it was easy for him to take advantage. Eliot's family have served the Westville family for many years. Lord Westville—your father—left him a token sum in his will, and a hell of a lot of responsibility. I reckon he resented the fact that you, who'd never even been acknowledged by his employer, had been given what he could have put to better use. So when the next Lord Westville, my client's father, showed no interest in you or the money, Eliot decided to appropriate it.'

'By appropriating me.'

Rory winced, then nodded.

'And when I refused to be appropriated...'

'He came up with an alternative.' He turned green. Pushing back his chair, he strode for the scullery. There was silence, then a clattering. When he returned, his face was damp. 'I'm sorry.'

'Not as sorry as I am.' A cold rage had seized me. 'I gave him the evidence of my own free will.'

'And he contorted it and turned it against you. It's not your fault, Marianne. Men like that are utterly selfish. Once he got his hands on the capital, he thought of it as his own, to do with as he pleased.'

'And provided I remained safely out of the way, and your client's father remained indifferent to my fate, he did just that. Did he attempt to find me after I escaped?'

'I don't know. I doubt it.'

'No, your right. I was even less of a threat to him, as an escaped lunatic, wasn't I?'

Rory flinched. 'He knew you wouldn't want to be found.'

'And by escaping, I'd saved him the expense of keeping me in the institution,' I said bitterly. 'How unfortunate for him, that your Lord Westville's father died prematurely. I'm afraid he has still managed to spend some of the money or rather lose some of it, in poor investments. He's greedy, but he's not canny.'

'I don't care! I'm not interested in the money. Why the devil would you think I'd want it after all the pain and suffering it has caused me?'

'But this is about more than the money. I told you, I distinctly remember telling you that day in Greyfriars, that it was about putting things to rights. Giving you answers to the questions that you've been asking yourself for years. And making Eliot pay, Marianne. You want that, don't you?'

Eliot. Francis Eliot.

The name made me sick to my stomach. I stared at Rory, my head reeling. What I wanted, what I desperately wanted, was to be in his arms again. To wrap my body around him. To forget all of this, all that he'd told me, everything. To see that look on his face. Tenderness. Love.

No, it couldn't be love. Right from the very start Rory had been lying to me. More importantly, I had been lying to myself, telling myself we were meant to be together, finding reasons to justify my desire, fooling myself into thinking that he wanted it too. It was all a lie. I hadn't learned from my catastrophic mistake, and this time it hurt so much more. This time, even though I knew Rory must have been pretending, just as Francis must have been pretending, this time my own feelings persisted.

I had fallen in love with Rory. Too late, I saw it so clearly. Rory wasn't Francis. I had recovered from what I felt—from what I thought I felt—for Francis in an instant. As I looked at Rory across the table what I felt, to my horror, was a conviction that I would never get over him.

It's why I told him then, all of it. The sad story of a poor nobody who had been so easily wooed by a vile, twisted, money-grabbing lawyer. As soon as I began to speak, the dam burst and it all came flooding out. How flattered I had been to have such a personable, charming man pay attention to me. How naive I had been, imagining that Francis saw something no one else had in me. How clever he had been to see that I had never been loved. How manipulative I knew now he had been to endear himself to me.

'I was convinced that he loved me. I sensed his desperate need of me from the first,' I said, forcing the words out, lacerating myself with them, and Rory too, set upon teaching us both a lesson we would not forget. 'The clues were all there, but for once I failed to make a picture of them. "I couldn't believe it when I discovered you were not already married", he said to me. "You have no idea how much I need you. No idea how much I want you." Looking back, I can't recall that he ever told me he loved me. I thought he did.'

Rory listened, frozen in his chair, saying not a word.

'I let him make love to me.' I continued, though the memory made me want to retch. 'I *wanted* him to make love to me.' Had I? It had been nothing like the wanting I'd felt for Rory. And it had been disappointing, though I had not dared say so, even to myself. I had had nothing to compare it with. Now I did. Now I knew. Rory.

Oh, Rory.

Francis! I made myself recall his face. Francis, my betrayer. 'I trusted him.' Here, I was on horribly solid ground. 'I told him about my insights, I told him some of the pictures my mind made for me. He was so interested. Fascinated. I'd never told anyone before. Then when I declared I could not marry him, he took what I'd told him and he made his own version of it all. "If I can't have you, I'm going to make sure no one else can." Those were the words he threw at me that night. I had no idea what he meant. I had no notion. None! All the time I was locked up, when the doctors were telling me that I was mad, when I was trying to tell them, to explain, the one thing that almost drove me mad was not knowing why. What had I done to make him hate me so much. And now I know.'

I hadn't meant to cry, but when the tears came they flooded my eyes and streamed down my face. I scrubbed at them, but more came and with the tears the memories I thought long lost. '"I won't let you ruin me," Francis told me. And he said that I was ruined for any other decent man. He said that no other man would have me now. As if I cared. As if I would be so stupid as to ever want another man.'

Except I had indeed been so stupid and the evidence was sitting opposite me, looking at me as if his heart was breaking.

No! If anyone's heart was breaking, it was mine. My tears dried. I dabbed my face with my sodden handkerchief. 'I would like you to leave now,' I said, my voice hoarse with crying.

'I can't leave you like this, Marianne.'

Rory looked wretched. Well, and so he should! 'There's no point in you remaining. You may return to your client and tell him that you've done what he paid you to do.'

'It's not as simple as that. There's your inheritance to be considered. Think of all the good you could do with that money. You could open as many schools as you wish. You could give so many wee lassies an opportunity they'd never get otherwise. If you wanted to, you could even help Flora escape her sordid life.'

I hated that he understood me so well. I had allowed that. I had let him into my mind and my thoughts. And my heart. 'Her name is Katy, not Flora,' I said.

He chose not to engage with this petty line of conversation. I wanted him to argue with me. I wanted him to get angry. I wanted him to be unreasonable. I wanted him to behave as Francis had, lobbing accusations and insults. Rory remained in his seat. He was hurt and he was angry, but not with me. 'What made you change your mind about marrying him?' he asked. 'It must have been something more than you waking up one morning and realising you didn't love him.'

'Does it matter?'

'Only to me, and you've made it pretty clear that I don't count.'

I should have been pleased to hear him say so. I didn't have to tell him, but I did. 'After the first time. The only time we—he—I felt there was something wrong.' I closed my eyes, not wanting to recall, but my mind produced a vivid memory. 'He was—he was jubilant.' And I had been— deflated? No, disappointed.

'So you sensed, though you didn't know you knew, that he was leading you on?'

'I wanted to believe that someone loved me. I had never been loved so I was ripe for the plucking.'

'Ach, don't say that, Marianne.' He pushed his chair back, made to move towards me, but I warded him off. 'Don't take the blame for what that man did to you, do you hear me?'

'It was my fault! I knew, you've just pointed out that I must have known, and I didn't listen to the warning bells until afterwards. And then—and then I knew he would be the death of me.'

'You thought he'd kill you?'

I shook my head. All those times I'd tried to explain, and no one had listened. What was the point of explaining again? Still, I wanted Rory to understand. Even though it didn't matter. 'I thought that if I married him, it would kill me—inside.'

'Your spirit? That he'd crush your spirit?'

Tears welled up again. I wished fervently now that I had not told him, that he had not understood. It didn't matter because he didn't love me, and even if he did, it didn't change anything. 'I thought I'd saved myself,' I said, the words uttered of their own accord. 'By refusing him. But I didn't.'

'You did, though. You survived three years of incarceration. You escaped. And now look at you. You're a wonderful woman, Marianne.'

I wouldn't listen. I wouldn't believe him. I shook my head fiercely.

'You knew,' Rory insisted. 'Your instincts weren't wrong. You knew he was desperate to marry you. You knew that he needed you. Both of those were true. What you got wrong were his reasons. And now you're thinking that I'm like Eliot, aren't you, history repeating itself? I turned up out of the blue, and I pretended to be taken with you. Not because I was, but for my own reasons. You're thinking that I pretended that I wanted you, because it suited me to get to know you, to make sure that you were who I thought you were.'

'You're a detective on a case!'

'And what I was feeling for you—as a detective on a case—was morally wrong. I've known that. I've fought it. But I kept giving in to it, even though I knew I shouldn't.'

'So that's why you were so sorry in Glasgow. Because you broke your own rule book.'

'I wasn't sorry for what we did. I'll never forget what we shared together. I was only sorry that it could come to nothing.'

'Because you'd eventually have to admit you'd been lying to me.'

'I wasn't lying! Whatever you want to tell yourself, what happened between us it's something special. But we've no future together, I've known that from the first. You made it clear that you're not interested in marriage...'

'As did you!'

'I've never been interested in marrying anyone until...'

'Until you met an heiress! Ah no, that was unworthy of me.'

'It makes no difference,' Rory said, after a moment. 'You don't believe a word I say now, and I completely understand why. As far as you're concerned I've been lying to you, and after what you've told me about Eliot...'

'You're not Francis.' I hadn't meant to say so, but I couldn't help it.

However, he shook his head. 'It makes no difference. You don't trust me, and why should you. Fact is, what I've just told you puts us poles apart. I'm a detective...'

'And I am an escaped lunatic.'

'You're a survivor, is what you are! You are...'

He broke off, shaking his head again. When he spoke next, the emotion was stripped from his voice. He sounded intensely weary. 'You're a peeress in your own right. You've a title, a family, and a fortune. You don't have to have anything to do with Lord Westville if you don't want to. He's your kin, and he's sorry for how you've been treated, and he wants to make amends, but he's not the type to force his company on anyone. He's a cold fish, but he's a decent man. But whatever you do, Marianne, take the money. Not for yourself, but for what you can do for others.'

He picked up his hat, looking at it as if he had no idea what it was. 'Where are you going?' I asked, panicking, speaking without thinking again. I wanted him to go, didn't I?

'London. Lord Westville wants Eliot dealt with before he becomes suspicious. We want to make sure he doesn't make a bolt for it.'

'Will he go to prison?'

Rory set down his hat again. 'You want him to pay, don't you?'

'You've asked me that already. I never thought it possible until today.' I thought of it then however, and my hands curled into fists. I imagined Francis locked up in a cell, as I had been. I imagined him, unkempt, dirty, dressed in rough clothes, doing menial work. 'I don't want him to hang.'

'Nor do I,' Rory agreed grimly. 'It would be over too quickly.'

'Will I have to speak against him in court?'

'Possibly. If you want to.' More pieces slotted together to show me another picture. The way he had spoken of his own experience, his name dragged through the mud in the press. The shame and humiliation. Each time, it had been there—empathy. Understanding. Sympathy. No wonder he had wanted to protect me.

By lying. I hardened my heart. 'I want to think about it. All of it.'

'Of course you do. It's a lot to take in. There's no need to be making any decisions right now. I'm thinking,' Rory said, picking up his hat again, 'that I'd best go.'

'You're going to London now? Today? Do you intend to come back?'

'I reckon Lord Westville will want to take it from here. I forgot, he said to tell you he would write.'

So this was goodbye. It was what I wanted, wasn't it? Rory had lied to me. He had betrayed me. He had *made* me fall in love with him. He'd made me believe that he had fallen in love with me. And he hadn't, he really hadn't, even though the way he was looking at me now, with such yearning, and even though I could sense it, he'd never said, I love you. Not aloud.

He was on his feet. I pushed past my chair and threw myself into his arms. It may all be a lie, but I loved him all the same. He pulled me so close, achingly close, and when

he realised his mistake, when he would have released me,
I put my arms around his neck and pressed myself tighter.

Hold me, hold me, hold me.

His arms went gently around me again. He burrowed
his face in my hair.

I love you.

He didn't say the words.

I love you.

I didn't say the words. I turned my face up towards his.
His lips met mine. Our kiss spoke. Longing. Such longing.
Our lips clung. Then gently, he eased himself free of me.

'If you ever need holding again,' he said, giving me a
business card. 'Just holding. Any time. Always. You only
have to ask and I'll be there.'

I needed holding now.

'Goodbye, Marianne. Take good care of yourself.'

The door closed behind him. I heard his footsteps on the
stairs. I ran to the window and leaned out, watching him
cross the Grassmarket in the direction of Victoria Street. I
watched until he was just a speck, but he didn't once look
back.

I had made a huge mistake. No, I had done the best and
only thing possible. I collapsed on to the floor then. I didn't
cry. I sat there, my back against the wall, my legs stretched
out in front of me like a lifeless rag doll, like a wrongly incarcerated woman in her cell.

I didn't move until night fell. Then I crawled into my bed
and lay wide awake, staring at the ceiling. I would reclaim
my life. I would carry on as before. I'd been perfectly content before. I hadn't been unhappy. I loved Rory but it didn't

matter if I did because no matter what I thought I felt, he couldn't possibly love me. If he did, he wouldn't have left.

My twisted logic was giving me a headache. I wanted to run. I had done it before. I could do it again. No, I would remain in Edinburgh. I'd remain in the city where he wasn't welcome. Not even by me.

I got up as the grey dawn gave way to a watery sun, weighted down by the knowledge that whether I wanted it to or not, my life would never be the same again. There were decisions to be made, life-changing decisions that didn't only affect me. This was the first day of my second new life. I had never been so miserable.

Chapter Twenty-Eight

Marianne

Glasgow—
February 1878, six months later

'You really do have a magnificent view from here. The city spread out for your delectation and delight, Cousin.' Lord Westville turned away from my drawing room window, smiling his thin smile. 'You will be able to oversee progress on your good works from here.'

'I don't consider my plans to be charitable,' I said to him. 'I see them more as efforts to redress imbalances.'

'Now that your inheritance is yours, you can redress a great many.'

'I must thank you, Lord Westville...'

'You must not,' he said, looking pained. 'Call it my contribution to redressing an imbalance regarding you. You have been treated most unjustly by our family. If my father had shown an ounce of interest in you, that villain would never have had the opportunity to exploit...'

'You are not responsible for what Eliot did to me. He is paying for it now.'

'And will do, for the rest of his life thanks to Mr Sutherland's testimony. And yours, of course.'

As always, the mere mention of Rory's name made my heart flutter, and as always, I ignored it. I had written my testimony for him, and he had given it in court on my behalf, anonymously, but the judge had been more interested in the money.

'My dear Marianne—may I call you that?' Lord Westville had taken a seat next to mine. 'It seems wrong, I know, that so little weight was attached to the crime of having you wrongly incarcerated, and so much to the misappropriation of funds, but the end result is that Eliot will never be free again. The law is not always just, I am afraid.

'Mr Sutherland himself was most—really, he was quite beside himself on the subject. And I—he has told me sufficient of what you suffered, Cousin, to stir me into action. As a peer of the realm, I have the right to put forward changes to the law. I don't know if I will succeed, but I intend to try to make it more difficult for anyone to be committed as you were, with no right to review.'

'Would you be able to make a stronger case using me as an example?'

Lord Westville raised a brow. Just one. I wondered if it was a family trait. Rory found my brow alluring. I mustn't think of Rory.

'Mr Sutherland was at great pains to keep your name out of the case,' the Marquess said. 'If you chose to help me I could not guarantee your anonymity.'

'I hope that Mr Sutherland knows how much I appreciate his efforts,' I said, choosing my words with care. 'You will tell him, Lord Westville, won't you, how much I appreciate it? But I also feel—I'm stronger now, and if I can use my experiences to help others—unless you would rather not associate…'

'I beg you to believe, that I give not a fig for what people will say. I am honoured to claim you for my kin.'

'You are very good to say so.'

'I never say what I don't mean.' Lord Westville studied me for a moment, his pale blue eyes intent on mine. 'Mr Sutherland assured me that you were an astute judge of character. I consider myself one such too. You have a strength and a fortitude, a singleness of mind that I very much admire. Your experiences could have made you bitter. They could have broken you. I believe, however, that they have made you into a very remarkable woman.'

I felt myself blushing. Though his expression remained cool, his eyes detached, I sensed that he meant what he said, and detected a glimmer of humour in his icy eyes. 'You like to confound expectations,' I said.

'That's better! I do, very much. I shall take pleasure in owning you, if only you will permit it. You would wield a great deal more influence if you claimed your rightful title, you know.'

'If I had continued to reside in Edinburgh, perhaps. Here in Glasgow, they consider the aristocracy sleekit.' I smiled, seeing his confusion. 'Sly. You see, I'm learning the lingo. I shall earn more respect as plain Mrs Crawford.'

'You couldn't bring yourself to claim Miss Westville? No, I should not have asked.' Lord Westville got to his feet. 'I must go, I have an express train to catch, but if you are serious about assisting me…'

'I am, very serious. If we can prevent one person enduring what I did then it will be worth it.' I got up and held out my hand. 'Thank you again, for all that you have done.'

To my surprise, he retained my hand. 'Mr Sutherland gave me strict instructions not to try to interfere with how you spend your inheritance. "Trust her, she knows her own mind"—to use his own words—"she'll do a power of good." I shan't interfere, but if I can be of help at all I trust that you do know you can count on me, Marianne?'

His hands were as cold as his eyes, but I sensed a genuine warmth emanating from him that brought a lump to my throat. 'Rory—Mr Sutherland—will you tell him that I am taking my cue from Octavia Hill? He'll understand.'

'I shall tell him if I see him, but now that your case is closed, our paths are unlikely to cross.'

'Oh. I see.' I couldn't keep the disappointment from my voice.

'You could tell him yourself. Write to him, let him know your plans, I am sure he would be interested, and I believe you have his business address?'

I snatched my hand away. 'You will miss your train if you don't hurry.'

'Indeed.'

I escorted him out to the hallway, where he took his time with his hat and gloves. 'I have been inept,' he said, pursing his thin lips. 'If I gave you the impression that Mr Sutherland urged me to tell you to write, that is. I asked him, you know, if he had a message for you, but he was quite adamant. "What I said to her still stands," he said. "I've nothing to add." Ah. Yes. I can see you do understand. If you will permit?'

Lord Westville saluted me chastely on the cheek. 'It has been a pleasure, Marianne. One I hope we will repeat soon. Until then, au revoir.'

I watched from the bay window as his carriage made its

way down Park Circus, but I wasn't thinking of my cousin. My thoughts were only of Rory.

What I said to her still stands. I've nothing to add.

I pressed my head against the window pane, gazing out beyond the park that spread before me, to the misty curve of the River Clyde and the hazy cranes of the shipyards. Rory's Glasgow. I felt closer to him here, but that wasn't the only reason I had moved from Edinburgh. I felt at home here. Here in the city, for less than a day, I'd been truly myself, with Rory. I loved him so much.

Did he truly love me? Six months ago, I had been so confused. Terrified by my previous experience of what I thought was love, I had clutched at every possible reason to reject Rory. I'd always known that Rory wasn't like Francis, that my feelings for Rory were different, but I hadn't understood that his feelings were different too.

Rory always put me first. Even though he had not been honest with me, it was because he put me first. He knew the worst of me from the outset, and he saw it as the best of me. He saw me for who I was, and he never once tried to change me. He trusted me, before I could trust myself. He believed in me, before I believed in myself. I knew those things now. I'd had six months to learn them.

Was that what defined love? He'd been right about my insights too. I did sense Francis's true feelings, but I misunderstood his motives. Francis *would* have been the death of me, one way or another.

I had saved myself though, and now I had the power to save countless other women and children—or to provide them with the opportunity to save themselves. I had not forgotten my experiences in the asylum, but my dreams these days were of Rory, not of that vile place. Or not often. I was looking forward now, not looking back. I was often happy. But not always. Always, I missed Rory.

Did he miss me? He hadn't said the words I love you aloud, but he had made love to me. He had shown me he loved me by leaving me to be me. And that last time, that last kiss. *I love you.* I heard it, though he had not spoken it.

I missed him so much. The ever-present ache became an intense longing. I didn't need him in order to survive, I didn't need him to make the most of my life now, to make decisions for me or to guide me. I didn't need him, but I wanted him. Did he want me?

I'd never felt safe in anyone else's arms. Rory had given me my freedom. I was free to share it with him, if I had the courage. Because I believed him. Because I trusted him. I always had. It had been trusting myself that was the problem. It seemed so simple, all of a sudden, but it had taken me six months to see that. Six months, and Rory had not once tried to get in touch. Not for the lack of love. Because he loved me. Because he understood me.

If you ever need holding again. Just holding. Any time. Always. You only have to ask and I'll be there.

I didn't want to wait another day, never mind another six months. I raced to my bedroom and grabbed a hat and cloak, then ran all the way to the nearest telegram office. I needed holding. It was time to ask him to keep his promise.

Chapter Twenty-Nine

Rory

Glasgow—
February 1878

I was glad that the Caledonian Railway took me direct to Glasgow rather than Edinburgh. That city had no appeal for me now that Marianne wasn't there. With every passing mile, after we steamed over the border, I felt as if the pistons of the engine were singing I'm coming home, I'm coming home, I'm coming home. Home! I'd never thought of my house in the London suburbs as home. It was a decent house in a good neighbourhood. My ma would have thought it a palace. I'd been content enough there before I met Marianne. Since Marianne—oh, since Marianne my world had changed.

For a start, I'd put the case of Ada Soutar well and truly to bed. I had my suspicions about who had been behind her death, who had been behind blackening my name, but I'd given up any notion of doing anything about it. Giving the Soutars answers, even though they weren't really answers, had proved to be enough for me. I was done with looking over my shoulder. Marianne had taught me that. I was done with the past. I was done with being feart of going back to Edinburgh too. What benefit would there be for whoever had it in for me, to finish me off now? They'd risk being collared for a second crime. I had the Capital back, if I wanted it. Point was, I didn't want it. Marianne wasn't there.

I tried to get on with my own life. No, I *got on* with my own life. New cases. Some good ones, thanks to the Marquess, but work wasn't the be all and end all it had been for me before. I missed her. Not consciously all the time, but there was a gap beside me, and I was constantly aware of it. A place where I felt she should be. I missed her like hell. I loved that woman. By the sun and the stars, I truly believed that I loved her more with every passing day. Every day that we were apart I missed her.

I tried not to think too far forward, for the notion of missing her for the rest of my life would have scuppered me. I missed her, and of course I wondered if she was missing me, but what I wanted more than anything was for her to be happy. I wanted her to learn to enjoy her freedom. I wanted her to make something of herself. I knew she would. She simply needed time, and that's the one thing I could give her. As long as she wanted. For ever if she needed it.

That was what I told myself, but when the telegram arrived, I knew before I opened it what it would say, and I knew then that I'd been right not to give up hope.

I need holding.

Three words.

I was packed and on the express train north first thing the next morning.

The train was pulling into the station. My heart was hammering harder than the pistons of the engine now. There was so much we'd need to talk about, but what I knew for certain was that we'd finally talk about the most important subject of all. I loved her. She loved me. We'd not spoken those words but they were suspended there, in the three-word message in the telegram that I was clutching inside my coat pocket like a talisman.

I'd already arranged to have my bags sent on to the Queen's Hotel. I didn't know if Marianne would be waiting for me. She knew I was coming though, so I hoped. I threw open the door of the First-Class carriage and was caught up in the belching black smoke of the still-slowing engine. She didn't need me, Marianne, but she wanted me, so I hoped she'd be there.

I pelted down the platform, first out of the train, first to the waiting huddle of people looking anxiously for their friends and family. I saw her before she saw me. She was wearing a new cloak in emerald-green, with the hood pulled up over her hair. She was standing stock still, eyes wide, emanating anxiety. And then she saw me, and I slowed down to walk, because I wanted to remember this moment for always. I wanted to remember every step.

The hiss of the steam coming from the trains. The smell of the smoke. The soot settling on my face. The shouts of the porters. The other people waving, calling out greetings. And her face. Her smile dawning so slowly, creeping up to light up her eyes. The half-step she took towards me. My name on her lips. And as I got closer I felt it. Saw it light up all of her. Felt it light up me too. Perfect, perfect love.

I took her outstretched hands in mine. Her gloves were new, dark leather, neatly fitted. Her fingers curled around mine. But we didn't say it then. We'd waited so long, but we didn't dare say it yet. 'I know a place,' I said, and she nodded, as if she knew what I was on about, though how— but maybe she did.

There was a hackney carriage waiting outside. It had been snowing, fresh snow, so fresh that George Square was carpeted in white. It wouldn't last, but for now it looked almost perfect, only one set of footprints streaking across it. Our carriage made fresh tracks. The streets we passed through were hushed, or so it seemed to me, though they couldn't have been, there must have been the usual bustle of the East End.

Maybe I didn't notice because all I could see, all I could think about, was Marianne sitting silently beside me, her hand in mine. The journey must have taken a good while, but I didn't notice that. There was the Cathedral, soot-black and stark against the snow. The Royal Infirmary beside it. And then the gates of the Necropolis, where we got down and I paid the driver off.

I led her up the steep paths. 'Top of the world,' I said to her, indicating the view spread out before us. The skies had cleared—of course they had! 'Our world, any road.'

'Ours?' She sounded breathless. The first words she'd spoken, and it was a question. It shouldn't have been, she must have known why I was there, but it was.

We were at the highest point of Glasgow's biggest grave-yard, surrounded by memorials to the great and the good. The sun peaked through the clouds, and far away you could see the River Clyde. Closer to hand were the factories and works of Glasgow's industrial engine. The houses for the people who worked there. The city itself, where the money was. 'Our world,' I said, getting down on one knee and taking her hand in mine. 'I love you,' I said, putting all my heart into it. 'I love you with everything I am. I love you for all that you are, just exactly as you are. I can get by without you, Marianne, but I don't want to. Whatever we do, however we do it, I want us to be together. Will you marry me?'

She dropped on to her knees beside me and threw her arms around me. 'Will you hold me, Rory, like you promised?'

I put my arms around her. I pulled her close, careful still, but she wriggled even closer. 'I love you,' she said. 'You know that, don't you?'

I had a lump in my throat, so I nodded.

'I didn't know,' she said to me. 'I thought I was in love before, but I was so wrong. And I was frightened to trust myself. Frightened of what you made me feel. You mattered so much, and in such a different way, but I didn't trust myself.'

'You do now, though?'

'Oh, yes. It took me a while,' she said, pushing my hat off and running her fingers through my hair. 'But you gave me the time I didn't even know I needed. I love you, Rory Sutherland.'

'I love you, Marianne—it's just struck me. I don't know—is it Little, Crawford or Westville?'

'What about Marianne Sutherland?' she said, with a smile that went straight to my groin. 'The answer is yes, Rory. I will marry you, with great pleasure.'

I couldn't wait any more, and nor could she. Our mouths met in a kiss that was desperate and without finesse. We kissed, kneeling in the snow in a graveyard, with the sun weakly shining on us. We kissed frantically, our tongues clashing, our hands fevered, hampered by cloaks and gloves and hats and the cold. Then our kisses slowed, became tender, and I told her with my heart and my lips, how much I loved her, and she told me too, how much she loved me, in the same way. And nothing, nothing had ever felt so perfectly right.

Chapter Thirty

Marianne

Glasgow—
March 1878, six weeks later

We had the simplest of ceremonies, in the simplest of churches in Govan, where Rory's parents lay buried in the churchyard outside. We made no announcements, though we sent a telegram to Lord Westville and received three words in return.

At Last. Congratulations.

'We are married,' I said to Rory as we stood together at the window of our flat in Park Circus, looking out at the driving rain. 'I can't quite believe it.'

'Nor I. These last few weeks have seemed like an eternity.'

'I know.' It had been Rory who insisted we wait. Rory who asked me at least once a day, whether I was certain this was what I wanted. Rory who assured me each day that he could wait as long as was necessary. I told him that with every passing day I was more sure, and less inclined to wait. But now the moment was here, now the gold band on my finger proclaimed me his wife, now that we were alone in this place that would become our home, I was besieged by nerves.

'Don't fret,' he said, taking my hands in his.

'What if I don't...?'

He kissed the rest of my words away. A gentle, tender kiss, the same kind of kiss he had bestowed on me every day for the last six weeks. Reassuring. Pledging his love. 'You are everything to me,' he said. 'My only worry is that after all this time, I'll be the one who won't—who will lose control too early.'

His words gave me confidence. My nerves turned into anticipation. 'I want you to lose control.'

He inhaled sharply. He gave me one last, assessing look. Then he pulled me into his arms, and our mouths locked. Heat seared through me. At last, our kisses were without restraint. Deep kisses that lit flames inside me, made me molten, made me raw with desire. Kisses that had no trace of gentleness, but that roused and demanded a response, that made every bit of my body throb with wanting more.

It was the middle of the afternoon, but we were in our own flat, on our own. We neither of us made any attempt to reach a bedroom. Rory let me go only to pull the long, elegant curtains over the windows before he returned to my waiting arms, to my eager body. His fingers shook as he undid the fastenings of my gown. My own shook as I undid the buttons of his waistcoat.

We shed clothes equally this time, not like the last time, shared kisses equally, hands smoothing, caressing each newly exposed piece of skin. My petticoats. His shirt. My boots, then his. My stockings, then his. I kissed the scar on his abdomen. He teased my nipples into aching, hard peaks. And all the time we communed.

Rory.

Marianne.

I love you.

I love you.

I want...

This?

Yes.

This?

Yes. Oh, yes.

And this?

Yes!

I thought I would melt with desire. His breathing was ragged. So too was mine. He undid the string of my drawers. I was naked before him. He gazed at me for a moment and I relished his gaze, the hunger in him reflecting my own, the colour slashing his cheeks. The pinpoints of his pupils.

So lovely.

He dipped his head to take one of my nipples into his mouth. I groaned aloud, arching backwards. His hand slid between my legs, slid inside me, and I clenched around him. Melting. Desire building and building as I clutched desperately to maintain an element of self-control.

Let go.

Not yet. Not yet.

I tugged at the waistband of his trousers. He released me to finish undressing himself. When he made to pull me back into his arms, I shook my head. I drank my fill of him as he had me. His hard-muscled body. The smattering of hair on his chest leading my eyes down, past the scar, past the dip of his belly, to his aroused member. I wanted to touch him. I had never before—so I wanted to touch him. He took my hand, wrapped my fingers around him. I felt him throb at my touch. Heard him moan at my touch. My name, a soft exhalation of desire. I stroked him, relishing his moaning response, but then his hand stayed me.

'No more.' He spoke as if through gritted teeth. 'Can't wait.'

'Don't.'

Kisses again, as we sank on to our knees. More kisses as we fell on to the floor. His member was pressing into my belly. His fingers easing inside me. I was losing control. Wave after wave of desire gripping me as he kissed me and stroked me, but still I clung on, wanting, wanting, wanting, restless with wanting, until he pulled me astride him, and I let go of all control as he entered me, his own hoarse cry echoing mine as he bucked under me, going deeper.

Wave after wave engulfed me. I heard myself crying out my pleasure, felt him inside me, barely moving, saw his desperate attempt to control himself etched on his face, and then he thrust, thrust again, and I moved with him, taking him inside deeper, faster, until he too lost control, and I toppled on to him, clinging for dear life, sweat-slicked, sated, floating.

'I love you.'

A slow, delicious, sweet kiss.

'I love you.'

He held me close. And later, after we made love in our bed, he held me close again. And when I woke to my first morning as his wife, he was still holding me and I knew not only where I was, but that it was exactly where I needed to be.

Epilogue

Rory

Glasgow—
July 1878, four months later

The day began as it always did. I woke slowly, and the first thing I was aware of was Marianne. Usually she was nestled against me, her hair tickling my nose. Sometimes her head was still resting on my shoulder, just as it had been when we'd fallen asleep, one of her legs between mine, her hand resting on my chest. On the morning of our fourth month as husband and wife, she was curled into my back, her mouth on the nape of my neck, and her hand—she was stroking me. Not asleep, then, my wife.

I gave myself over to the pleasure of her gentle, sure touch until she whispered my name, and I turned, and she pulled me on top of her and I slid inside her. I can't get used to that. I never want to get used to it. The sheer delight of being inside her, of her legs wrapping themselves around me, of her urging me on with her mouth and her hands. The way she tightens around me. The soft moan she lets out. The way she says my name. It tips me over every time. Every sweet, wonderful time.

We had breakfast together, as we do every morning, even when I've an early start. Coffee and bread and butter, eggs sometimes, sitting in our fancy wee dining room in our dressing robes, staring at each other across the table as if we can't believe our luck. Which I can't.

We don't keep a servant, but we have a couple of women who come in later to clean and to cook dinner. Women Marianne knows from Partick. Women who worship the ground Marianne walks on. As do I. At breakfast, we plan our respective days, but that morning it was all arranged, so we put on our best clothes—nothing too good mind, Marianne doesn't have a taste for the fancy and I've always been a plain dresser.

It was a lovely morning, considering it was July in Glasgow and Fair Friday to boot, which I don't recall ever being dry when I was growing up here. Marianne tucked her hand into my arm as we made our way out, smiling up at me in a way that made me want to take her right back inside and make love to her again.

'Happy fourth month of marriage,' she said to me.

'I couldn't be happier, you know that?'

She laughed. 'You say that every day, and then the next day you say it again.'

I did kiss her then, just a quick kiss, but I couldn't resist her. 'I'm planning on saying it every day for the rest of our lives. I love you.'

'And I love you.' She tugged me forward into the West End Park. 'But if we're going to walk all the way to Partick, we'd better get a shifty on.'

I burst out laughing.

'Don't I have that right? Get a shifty on?'

'You've got it right, but it sounds so funny in your accent. We'll make a Weegie of you one day, but not yet.'

'Thank you for taking the time away from your case, I really wanted you to be with me today.'

'I wouldn't miss it for the world, and Gordon Munro is more than happy with what needs to be done in the office today.' I had been delighted to employ my father's old colleague into my business. As the man himself had suggested, there was plenty of work in the city, so much that we were actually considering taking his son on too. And unlike the police in the capital, my name here was neither poison nor mud.

It wasn't even eleven, but there were already plenty of people in the park taking the air, and plenty of them on nodding and greeting terms with Marianne. She smiled sunnily at mill workers on their break, and stopped several times to exchange banter with weans. 'It's as well we don't have to be there until noon,' I said to her.

'I'm thinking Rory, that it might be a good idea to speak to some of the mill owners along the Kelvin. The school they have for the little ones isn't nearly big enough, and if there was a nursery, then it would mean that some of the women could go back to work if they wished, earlier. Do you think I'd be standing on too many toes doing that?'

'Has it ever bothered you, standing on toes?'

'Well, no, but it is much easier to make progress if one doesn't.'

'I think it's a wonderful idea, but I was hoping you'd take a couple of weeks off before launching yourself into another project. It's the Fair. I thought we'd take a bit of a holiday ourselves. What do you think?'

'Shall we go—what is it?—doon the watter?'

'I was thinking somewhere a bit further north. With golden beaches and…'

'Harris!' She gave a leap of excitement. 'Rory, are we going to Harris?'

'I'd like to introduce you to my family, at long last. We leave tomorrow.'

Her eyes were sparkling as we walked the rest of the way, out of the park over the Snow Bridge and along to Partick. The new block of tenements was on Anderson Street, a couple of blocks from my own childhood home. Blond sandstone, it had its own bathhouse out in the back courts, and above the entrance to the freshly tiled close, a plaque.

Marianne was immediately lost to me in the crowd of women waiting to receive her. I watched from a distance, my heart bursting with pride. There was Katy, formerly Flora, in her smart new outfit, the housekeeper in charge of this experiment. There were Mr and Mrs Soutar and Oscar, pointing up at the plaque, surrounding by what must be their friends and family from the South Side. And Mrs Oliphant, standing nervously to one side with an outsize pair of scissors to cut the ribbon. A stamping of feet, a few whistles, and my wife stepped out in front of the crowd.

'Ladies—and of course gentlemen,' she said, with a bow at the few men there and a smile for me, 'I won't bore you with speeches. I just want to say a huge thank you to everyone for all the help and support you've given me in making this project happen. I will now ask Mrs Oliphant, to whom I owe a great debt for drawing my attention to the work of Octavia Hill, to perform the opening ceremony.'

Mrs Oliphant, looking so nervous I thought she might faint, stepped up to the ribbon and with some difficulty sawed it in two. 'I now declare the Ada Soutar Residential Rooms for Women open.'

There was tea and cake for everyone, and lemonade for the weans. I don't know how many times I assured someone or other that I was very proud of Marianne—indeed, I'd never tire of telling the world that.

'Are you happy?' I asked her, when I finally got a moment alone with her.

'I couldn't be happier,' she said, handing my own words back to me, and meaning them too.

I kissed her then, a chaste wee peck on the lips, but it still got us a cheer. 'There's only one thing missing, to make the day perfect,' I said.

She took one look at me. She smiled, a slow smile that did sinful things to me, and that I'd come to know very well these last four months. 'I think that can be arranged,' she said. 'Give me ten minutes and we'll head home.'

'Make it five,' I said, grinning.

* * * * *

*If you enjoyed this story,
be sure to read Marguerite Kaye's
previous Historical romances*

His Runaway Marchioness Returns
The Lady's Yuletide Wish
Lady Armstrong's Scandalous Awakening
A Most Scandalous Christmas
The Earl Who Sees Her Beauty

Historical Note

First of all, a huge thank-you to Early Police historian Dr Elaine Saunders—@hertfordshirehistory—for all her advice and guidance on the police service in Rory's time. I've only used a fraction of the answers she gave me to my many questions, but she gave me an invaluable insight into the kinds of crimes Rory would have been tackling in Edinburgh, and the kinds of prejudice that his father would have encountered at the time, when Highlanders really were seen as coming to Glasgow and joining the police simply to 'put boots on their feet'.

Clive Elmsley's excellent book *The Great British Bobby* gave me an insight to the life of a police detective. Rory's 'fist, feet and teeth' quotation is taken directly from one of those real detectives quoted in Elmsley's book. Private detectives like Rory really did exist at the time, and they were often used to investigate crimes which the great and the good wished to keep out of the press.

Marianne's main place of incarceration was inspired by a tour led by Mostly Ghostly of the Crichton in Dumfries, which I took with my sister Johanna. I am afraid I've used and abused the Crichton in this book, for it was in fact very much a forward-thinking institution for its time, though there were locked wards such as the ones in which I placed poor Marianne. The coffin cart which Marianne sees as she escapes is real, and on display in the crypt at the Crichton.

The story of Angus Mackay's escape is one that I also heard on the Mostly Ghostly tour. It happened in 1859, a few years too early for Marianne's escape, but it was too good a story not to use. Sadly, Sarah Wise's book *Inconvenient People, Lunacy, Liberty and the Mad-Doctors in Victorian England* documents cases very similar to Marianne's.

I have borrowed a story from another tour I took recently, of Glasgow Central Station, with my sister Fiona—I have very tolerant sisters…they're always happy to come along while I play the geek, provided lunch is involved. It was here that I heard the story of pickpockets hanging about the platforms waiting for the moment of darkness caused by steam enclosed under a station roof to take the opportunity to pinch both the purses and the bottoms of the female passengers.

As you'll know, if you're read some of my other books, I have a deep and abiding love of both Edinburgh and Glasgow. This time I wanted to showcase the 'hidden gems' in the cities, and some of my own favourite places to wander.

The obstetrician and pioneer of chloroform James Young Simpson really did reside at Number Fifty-Two Queen Street, and the gardens—if you have a key!—are a lovely spot to have a picnic. Dean Village, which is now a heritage site, was very, very different in Marianne and Rory's day, and I'm not actually sure if you could have walked along the Water of Leith back then—though you can now. The Dean Orphanage is now part of the National Galleries of Modern Art. Dean Cemetery is a wonderful place to wander, full of fascinating graves and memorials—including one for one of my own favourite artists, John Bellany.

And finally I should say a word about Rory's language, which is very much *not* Victorian, but fairly colloquial Weegie and Scots. I chose to do this partly to make his speech quite distinct from Marianne's, but also, to be honest, because some of the words he uses are my favourites. Thank you to my family WhatsApp group for the many suggestions, including all those that didn't make the cut—sorry, Mum, but 'oxter' was just a step too far.

As ever, I've done a ton of reading and research for this book, and shared most of it on social media. And, as ever, all mistakes and inaccuracies are entirely my own.